THE INNOCENT

A Ryan Lock Novel

SEAN BLACK

The Innocent

ABOUT THE BOOK

When college basketball coach Malik Shaw goes missing after a family tragedy, it looks like just another retired athlete gone off the rails. But Malik's childhood friend, private security specialist Ty Johnson, quickly begins to suspect that there is more to it.

Chasing the truth, Ty and his business partner, Ryan Lock, begin to uncover a sinister conspiracy of silence in a sleepy Minnesota college town.

It's not the crime that kills you — it's the cover-up.

For Pat, mother-in-law extraordinaire

ONE

Long Beach, California
July 1999

A S A UNITED STATES MARINE, Ty Johnson had one advantage. He already knew what it was like to face down someone who wanted to kill you. Growing up in Long Beach in the nineties had taken care of that.

To Ty as a child, and then a teenager, violence had been commonplace. He'd seen people shot, stabbed and beaten to death. Sometimes they just happened to be in the wrong place at the wrong time. Others, someone had come looking for them. Not that it mattered much to the family gathered around the casket.

This time had been one of those wrong-time-wrong-place deals – a basketball court in early summer, playing a little one-on-one with his friend Malik Shaw. Ty had been standing with his back to the hoop: 'Let me see what you got, Mr All Star.'

In front of him, Malik gave that easy smile of his. Ty spread his arms wide and bounced on the heels of box-fresh white sneakers that were already acquiring a dirty tideline from the hot asphalt of the playground.

'What I got? Got you in my pocket for a start,' said Malik.

'That so?' said Ty, flipping his left hand out to try to steal the ball.

1

With a flick of his right wrist, Malik spun it away from him. He took a step back. He feinted hard left, and then he was on the move, zipping past Ty, like he was a mirage, and moving toward the basket. Caught off balance by the feint, Ty tried to sort out his feet, almost falling over.

Malik must have pulled the same move a thousand times with him, but even though Ty knew it was coming, he could never stop him. He feinted left, and sometimes it wasn't a feint. Other times it was. There was nothing in Malik's expression to give Ty a clue. He just grinned at you, and then he was gone, springing up toward the hoop and slamming the ball through it. Meanwhile Ty would still be turning round in a futile attempt to stop him, but Malik would already have picked up the ball and thrown it back to him.

That usually irritated Ty, which would crack Malik up, so much so that sometimes Ty scored the next basket because Malik was doubled over, laughing.

'Oh, man, don't feel bad. I'm sure you must be good at something, Tyrone. I mean, girls like you. That's got to be worth something, brother?'

Ty glared at him. Looking at the two sixteen-year-olds side by side without watching them play, a stranger might have figured Ty as the ball player. He was already six feet even, with huge feet and hands, like a German Shepherd puppy with oversized paws that hinted at further growth to come. By contrast Malik was only five ten, wide and broad-shouldered: a lot of players his age were skin and bones – they tended to fill out in college when they were pushed into a rigorous diet and training regime. At this age, though, it was all about raw talent, which Malik had to the extent that when their high school team played away the kids supporting their opponents would fall silent. Afterwards their coaches would crowd round him. In their high school, Malik was a rock star.

'Just messing with you, man,' Malik said. 'You're good at shit. Anyway, you got the Marines, right? You'll be cold chillin'. Ain't nobody be fighting no more. Hell, that probably make you smarter than my ass. Parade round in a uniform, pick up a pay check from Uncle Sam.' Malik stopped, aware that his friend's attention was elsewhere. 'Hey? Ty?'

Ty was looking across the playground to a low-slung Pontiac that had just pulled up with four young black men sitting inside, all wearing red. Members of the bloods gang. Or, to be more precise, 18th Street Bloods.

Malik had seen them now. Ty saw the easy smile fall away from his friend's face. Instinctively, Ty stepped to the right so that he was standing directly in front of Malik, shielding him from the barrel of the pump-action shotgun that the front nearside passenger was pointing at them.

Hard eyes peered out from the car. Ty could smell dope smoke in the air. The thump of the bass line from a rap song sound-tracked the scene. Neither Ty nor Malik was involved with a gang but that didn't matter. Their neighborhood was blue, Crips territory. Their neighbors, their relatives, the kids and young men from their block were all Crips. And, as far as the gang-bangers in the Pontiac were concerned, that made Ty and Malik guilty by association.

Red and blue. Those were the two tribes in Long Beach. You were one or the other, even if you wanted no part of either. The fact that Malik wanted to wear the blue and white uniform of the LA Lakers, and the only blues Ty wanted to be seen in were US Marine Corps dress blues counted for nothing to the four young men staring at them.

Here, lives ended this way. A car pulling up. A window gliding down. The ratchet of a fresh round in the chamber. Then a burst of gunfire.

Ty met the gunman's eyes. He turned his lower arms so that they were facing out and opened his fists, which had been clenched with fear and adrenalin, to reveal that they were empty. He didn't stare but neither did he look away. As was the way with this place, the message didn't require words.

Do what you gotta do.

The barrel was raised and, for a split second, Ty thought the moment had passed, that they were going to take off. Then he saw the gang-banger's right hand slip to the grip and heard the ratchet. He swallowed hard as the barrel was lowered back into position and he saw a finger fall to the trigger.

'Get the fuck out of here, Malik,' he said, not daring to glance back.

'No, man. I'm staying.'

'Do what I said. Take off. I mean it. How your momma gonna ever forgive me if I let you get shot?'

Malik didn't move. Ty could feel him still standing behind him. The sour smell of fear was coming off him, the same as it was off himself.

All Ty could see now was the pad of flesh straining against the metal trigger of the shotgun. He closed his eyes, preparing for the blast, making his peace with God.

Whoop.

The sound of a siren snapped his eyes open. The barrel disappeared inside the car. The window went up. There was a squeal of tires and the roar of an engine as the car took off.

On the opposite side of the street a Long Beach Police Department black-and-white pulled a U-turn and stopped where the Pontiac had been only a few seconds previously.

Two patrol officers got out They walked toward the two boys, the black sergeant's thumbs hooked into his utility belt, like some pastiche of a gunslinger.

Walker. Everyone in the neighborhood knew Sergeant Walker. And everyone hated him – mommas, crackheads, grandmas, gang-bangers, churchgoers, people who didn't break the law, people who did, even little kids. He was ten times worse than any of the white cops, even the old racist ones. Walker hated black people more than they ever could and even now, at his young age, Ty knew it was because Walker hated himself. But Sergeant Walker had one soft spot. He loved basketball.

Sergeant Walker looked past Ty, like he didn't exist, hitched his belt over his gut and nodded from the road to Malik. 'They have a beef with you?'

Ty and Malik gave identical shrugs. They knew better than to say anything to the cops.

'How's that jump shot, Malik?' Walker asked, acting like Ty wasn't even there or that car full of armed gang-bangers hadn't been about to shoot both of them dead.

Malik studied the ground. 'Okay, I guess.'

'Okay?' Walker repeated, turning to his partner. 'You should see this kid. He's gonna go all the way.' He turned his attention back to Malik. 'What college you thinking about?' he asked. 'UCLA, right?'

Malik shrugged. 'I don't really know.'

Walker leaned over and slapped his shoulder. 'Y'know, I played a little ball. I was pretty good too.'

His partner chuckled, and Ty saw Walker get pissed at his laughter. Ty wondered if that was what had made Walker like he was. Always being belittled. Always second class. Knowing he'd never be good enough, when being good enough in the LBPD still meant being white.

Walker straightened up. 'Anyway, you take care now,' he said to Malik.

Ty stood with his friend and watched the two cops leave. 'You got yourself a fan,' he said.

Malik spat on the ground. 'I don't need no fans like him.'

Ty smiled. Malik had always had an idealistic streak. If there was a kid being picked on at school, he would be the first to step in. But Malik couldn't fight for shit, apart from on a court, so Ty would have to straighten out whoever Malik had a problem with. Even the toughest kids, the kids on their way to juvenile detention, the ones with big brothers already in the pen or who'd done time themselves in juvie didn't mess with Ty. They didn't mess with Ty because he was that much tougher. They didn't mess with him because they knew he could hold a grudge. You might think he'd forgotten about you, but he never had. He'd bide his time, and when the moment was right, he'd mess you up in a way that meant you stayed messed up long enough not to tangle with him again.

Malik looked at him. 'You'd really take a bullet for me?'

Ty hadn't thought about it. He'd acted out of instinct. You protected those you cared about. That was Ty's first rule. The second rule was you didn't talk about it.

PART ONE

TWO

Fourteen years later
Harrisburg, Minnesota

MALIK SHAW CLIMBED INTO THE front cab of the Dodge Ram pick-up he'd bought to deal with the harsh Minnesota winter that lay ahead. He patted his lap, and the family dog, a six-year-old golden retriever called Flint, launched himself into the cab. The dog clambered over Malik's lap and settled himself in the middle of the truck's bench seat. As Malik started the engine, the dog nudged his elbow, as if to say, 'Let's get going already.'

Malik glanced down at the text message that had woken him less than fifteen minutes ago – *Prob at the stad*. The number had been withheld, but the message had been signed *Mike*. Mike was one of his assistant coaches.

It had taken Malik just a moment, as he rubbed the sleep from his eyes, to decode the truncated message: 'Problem at the stadium'. He had slipped out of bed, careful not to wake his wife, and called Mike. He went straight to voicemail. There had been nothing else for it but to get dressed and go check it out.

Taking his time, Malik backed slowly out of the driveway and turned the nose of the truck toward the end of the cul-de-sac, Flint beside him. He pulled out onto Buffalo Drive, skirting the University of Minnesota campus, with its red-brick buildings.

A lone campus-security patrol car slowed as it passed him in the opposite direction. Malik stopped, and pressed the button to lower his window. The officer, a doughy white kid who looked barely old enough to be driving, never mind in uniform, leaned out of his window, greeting him with a grin. 'Hey, Coach! Tell me we're going to win tomorrow.'

'Bet on it,' said Malik. 'Hey, you get a call about something happening at the stadium?'

'Nope. Everything's quiet. Hey, you want me to come with you?' the young cop asked.

'No,' Malik said quickly. 'You're good. It's probably nothing.' If it was a prank, the last thing Malik wanted as coach was the head of campus security, an officious overweight asshole called Tromso, getting involved and making a mountain out of a molehill.

'Okay. Well, holler if you need us,' said the cop, his window gliding back up as he took off.

Malik watched him go, taking a second or two to wonder at the power of sport. A lone black man driving around a Minnesota college town late at night could usually expect an encounter with law enforcement to play out a little differently. But make that black man the coach of the college basketball team and it was a whole different story. Not that Malik minded his celebrity status: he didn't. It was just that he'd seen enough to know that it wasn't about him. The real star was sport. He was just a lucky guy who got to bathe in its reflected glory.

He came to the intersection with Main Street. He drove straight ahead, past the administration building, and hung a left onto Wolf Road.

There was a Wolf Road in every town across America. It went by different names but the destination was always the same. It could be a small, open high school football field burning bright under Friday-night lights, or an indoor cavern of a basketball court, surrounded by ghetto-murder streets, or a college stadium vast enough to shame a pro team.

The names changed, the physical form of the battlefield varied, but the destination remained the same. At the end of the road lay a temple of hopes, dreams, failures and fight-backs. No towns worshiped more devoutly than those who had not much else to shout about. In these places, places like the one to which Malik had brought his family, defeat tasted bitterer than it did elsewhere, and victory sweeter.

It was part of the reason he had taken the job in the first place. He could have gone to Florida as an assistant coach for twice the salary they could offer the head coach here. He could have gone to a similar-sized college in New Hampshire that, courtesy of some seriously wealthy alumni, had an annual endowment ten times what they had at Harrisburg. Hell, he could easily have secured a post somewhere that didn't require snow chains for three months of the year. But he hadn't.

Malik had come to Harrisburg because he knew he could make a difference to people's lives. And that was all he had wanted to do. God had granted him a gift, and he wanted to go where that gift could do the most good. It sounded cheesy, but it was the truth. When it came time to meet his maker, Malik knew that what mattered more than money, acclaim or any of the other superficial, materialistic nonsense the country obsessed about, was the difference he had made to the lives of others.

Malik pulled up his Dodge at the small side entrance used on game days by the coaching staff and players. That was when he noticed the dark grey sedan tucked in next to the entrance. It stood out because, apart from his truck, the rest of the stadium parking lot was empty.

He turned off his engine and got out, leaving the dog in the cab. He walked over to the sedan and peered through the windshield. There was no driver, and no one in the passenger seat.

Malik walked round the car. There was no one in the back seats either. The car had a Minnesota license plate. There were two bumper stickers. One announced that the owner was a college alumnus, and the other read 'Go Wolves.' Malik racked his brain: had he seen the car before? Alumni who hung out around the stadium were hardly a rarity, though they tended to show up for practice or pep rallies, rather than at midnight the night before a game.

He dug his cell phone from his pocket and snapped a picture of the car. There was likely a perfectly reasonable explanation as to why it was there, but in case there wasn't . . . He put his cell back in his pocket, and let the dog out of the truck. Flint immediately ran over to the sedan and cocked a leg against the rear wheel.

Choking back a laugh, Malik unlocked the side door of the building and stepped into the narrow hallway that led toward the locker rooms. The dog at his side, he stopped to take a deep breath. He loved the smell of these places. That mix of sweat and floor polish did it for him every time. It was the scent of hard work and challenges faced.

He walked past the locker rooms, heading for the caretaker's office. The office was unlocked. The alarm system inside was unarmed. Usually it would have blinked red if the alarm was on, but tonight it was flashing green: disarmed. Malik glanced to the side entrance door. That had definitely been locked. The two things didn't square, unless the caretaker had forgotten to activate the alarm.

He kept walking. He pushed open a set of double doors that opened straight onto the court and walked to the center. He looked at his watch. It was a minute to midnight.

As the seconds fell toward twelve, he closed his eyes. That was when he heard it. At five seconds to midnight.

THREE

FOR THE FIRST FEW SECONDS Malik thought it was the dog whimpering. But Flint was right there, tucked in next to him in the middle of the court. He must have heard it too, because first he cocked his head, and then he stood up, front legs spread out, lips peeled back from his teeth, a ridge of hair standing up all the way down his back.

'Hey!' Malik yelled. 'Who's in here?'

He waited as the echo of his own voice died away to silence.

'I said, who's in here?'

He scanned the empty bleachers. He looked down at Flint. When Malik used to play hide-and-go-seek with the kids, he'd sometimes use the dog to flush them out. Flint loved the game even more than the kids did. He'd chase furiously around the house until he tracked them down, showering them with slobbery kisses when he found them.

'Go on!' Malik said to the dog. 'Go find them.'

Flint took off. Malik followed, breaking into a run as the dog headed straight for the locker area.

Malik pushed through the double doors, Flint squeezing ahead of him, almost knocking him over as he shouldered past his legs. 'I know you're in here,' said Malik.

The dog hung a left into the locker room reserved for the visiting team. Malik followed.

Before he made it into the room, he heard a car engine start outside, quickly followed by the squeal of rubber as the vehicle took off at speed. Malik changed direction, hurtling down the corridor, his long, lean, basketball-player legs eating up the distance to the side entrance door. He pushed it open just in time to see the lights of the grey sedan sweep past his truck, heading for the exit.

Turning back, he heard Flint barking from the locker room, a yelping sound, the kind he made when he'd cornered a squirrel up a tree and the terrified creature wouldn't come down to resume the chase.

All of a sudden the realization of what was happening came to him. It was so obvious he felt like an idiot. He even laughed at his own stupidity. The car might have belonged to an alumnus, but Malik was pretty certain it was being driven by a couple of kids. Maybe the janitor had been in on the prank, hence the alarm being switched off, or maybe the kids had just gotten lucky or had found someone who knew the code to switch it off.

It was obvious now what was going on. The tip-off was the visitors' locker room. Someone had probably snuck something in there to unsettle tomorrow's opposition. A skunk, or a couple of rats stolen from one of the college labs, something like that.

Malik called the dog back to his side. Whatever was in there, he didn't need the dog in the mix. He walked outside and put Flint back in the pick-up. Then he went back.

Bracing himself, he pushed open the door into the visitors' locker room. He'd been partly right. Something was huddled in the far corner. Only it wasn't a prank.

The small naked white figure of a young boy, aged no more than twelve, looked up at Malik, a long brown fringe masking tear-filled brown eyes.

FOUR

O NCE HE HAD CHECKED THAT the boy wasn't injured, or not in any life-threatening way, Malik stepped out into the corridor and called the campus police, wishing now that he'd taken up the young security officer on his earlier offer. 'This is Coach Shaw. I'm down at the stadium, and . . .'

And what? He didn't know how to describe what he'd found, or what had just gone on while he was yards away. Worse, he didn't want to think about what might have happened if he hadn't been there.

'Listen, get someone down here. Now. We have a situation. I found . . . Just get someone down here, okay?'

He finished the call, and walked back into the locker room. The boy visibly flinched as Malik knelt down next to him.

'It's okay,' Malik said. 'You're safe. The cops are on their way.'

There it was again. That tensing of the boy's body, the squeezing shut of his eyes as he heard the word 'cops'.

'I'm Coach Shaw,' said Malik, starting over, trying to find some point of contact. It was only now that he realized the kid was wet, and so were his clothes. He was small for his age, and skinny, the kind of kid you'd expect to see bullied in the schoolyard. Putting all that together just made it worse, as far as Malik was concerned. He got up and went to the shower stalls.

One of the heads was still dripping from recent use. *Lord help me*, he said to himself, grateful for the first time that whoever had been with the boy had fled because he would have beaten them to death right there.

'What's your name, son?' Malik asked. He couldn't bring himself to ask what he really wanted to know. It wasn't that he couldn't form the words. It was more that he wasn't sure he could live with hearing the answers.

The boy shook his head, eyes closed.

Malik tried another tack. 'Who was here with you? I mean, I know someone was here. I saw their car.'

The boy's eyes screwed up tighter until they were little more than two lines above his nose. He didn't answer. Instead he shook his head. Some of the water from his hair splashed onto Malik's polo shirt.

Malik let it go. He wasn't a cop. There was a vending machine out in the hallway.

'You want a Coke?' he asked the boy.

A nod. Malik walked out into the hallway. He wanted to call Kim, his wife, but he didn't like to wake her and the kids. He dug some change out of his pockets and got a Coke. He took it back into the locker room, and gave it to the boy.

The boy took a sip. 'Am I in trouble?' he asked Malik.

'No, of course not.'

Malik glanced at his watch. Where the hell was security? Maybe he should have called the state police, after all. Just then he heard someone calling from the area of the side entrance.

'In here,' Malik shouted, relieved not to be alone with the boy any longer.

The cop who showed up was the same kid he had seen earlier. Malik gave him the basic facts. He'd come to visit the stadium while it was quiet. He told him about the grey sedan, and about hearing a noise, then seeing someone flee and finding the boy in the locker room, all wet. The cop seemed even more freaked out by it than Malik had been.

As he talked to the boy, Malik stepped outside, and called Mike, one of his assistant coaches. It was a while before he answered. When he did, he sounded groggy.

'Hey, Mike, it's Malik. Did you text me earlier?'

'Huh,' said Mike. 'Yeah, about the line-up. I thought we should maybe keep Darius on the bench for the first quarter.'

'No,' said Malik. 'This was just before midnight. You texted me about a problem at the stadium.'

'Not me, Coach,' said Mike. 'Why? What's happened? You want me to come down there?'

'No, it's fine,' said Malik. 'Go back to sleep.' He ended the call, and walked back inside the stadium to check on the boy.

Five minutes later, further reinforcements arrived in the shape of the five-foot-six-inches-tall, 250-pound head of campus police, Captain Keith Tromso. Malik had met him a couple of times, once to discuss a frat party attended by some of his senior players that had gotten a little rowdy, and again when a freshman had been pulled over for a DUI. The partygoers had been let off with warning, but the DUI had led Malik to end the freshman's time at the college. Tromso hadn't impressed him on either occasion.

The head of campus police seemed to have a chip on his shoulder the size of a boulder. Maybe it was his height, or that he was head of a campus police force rather than state or federal, but he seemed to regard even the most insignificant discussion as some kind of pissing contest. When Malik had suggested that he talk to the players who had been at the party, Tromso had shot him down, making a big deal of how he was the law, not Malik. The guy was a grade-A asshole.

But all that said, Malik was still glad to see him, and he was impressed by Tromso's reaction to the incident. For a start, he seemed to grasp the potential gravity of what Malik had found.

'You said you got a picture of the car?' Tromso asked, as the younger cop waited with the kid while a female officer was summoned.

Malik nodded and pulled out his cell phone. Tromso took it from him and studied the grainy image.

'Outstanding, Coach! You got the plate and everything. Y'know, most people wouldn't think to take a picture.'

'You have any idea whose car it is?' Malik asked.

'No, but we'll find them,' said Tromso.

As he'd handed over his cell phone, Malik had caught sight of the time. It was after one in the morning. Kim would be worried if she had woken up and found him gone.

'Listen, Chief, if you don't mind, I have a game tomorrow.'

'Right, of course. Go Wolves,' said Tromso, in a way that undid whatever improved feelings Malik had for him. Tromso held up the cell. 'I'm going to need to copy this. Do you mind if I keep a hold of it?'

Malik grimaced. 'I kind of need it for work.'

'I'll drop it back first thing. You're on Beech Avenue, right? I'll be able to bring you up to speed on what we've found out too,' Tromso said, with a nod to the locker room.

'Sure,' said Malik. 'I guess that's okay.'

'Appreciate it,' said Tromso, slapping Malik on the back. 'Now, I know I probably don't even need to mention this to a man like yourself, but don't go talking to anyone about it. Y'know, live investigation and everything.'

From his brief time as a pro ball player, Malik had come to trust cops as much as reporters. 'Don't worry,' he said.

Tromso smiled. 'Knew I could count on you.'

FIVE

MALIK DIDN'T GET TO SLEEP until sometime after four, and even then, he kept waking up. He was thinking about the boy he'd found in the visitors' locker room, after midnight, soaking wet from the shower. More than anything he couldn't shift from his mind the look on the boy's face when he'd found him. A mixture of sadness, shame and fear.

He tried to tell himself that, while there might not be a completely innocent explanation for what he'd discovered, it wasn't necessarily what he thought it was. But what else could it have been? If it had been innocent, why had whoever was with the boy, the person in the grey sedan, hightailed it out of there? If someone had been showing the kid around the stadium, or sneaking in to shoot some hoops, why had they fled? Running away was hardly the action of someone who had nothing to hide.

But, then, what if they had stuck around? Malik didn't want to contemplate what might have happened. If someone had been messing with the kid, he already knew what he would have done. Right now, he wouldn't be back home, lying in bed next to his wife. He'd be cooling his heels in a cell, waiting to see if he could make bail on a homicide charge.

Worse, he thought, what if he hadn't walked in? What if he hadn't gotten that text? What if he hadn't seen it until the morning? And, while he was at it, who was to say that he'd just happened to stumble in on something that wasn't a one-off? What if someone was using the locker rooms as— Well, he didn't want to think about what they might have been using them for, but what if this was part of a pattern?

He tried to comfort himself with the fact that it had to be pretty easy for the cops to work out who had been there. He had given them a picture of the car, complete with the plate. There had been no sign of forced entry, so it had to have been someone who had access to the stadium after hours. That had to be a pretty short list.

It would all be fixed, he told himself. The cops would find whoever had been there with the boy and the system would swing into action. And maybe, just maybe, there was a reasonable explanation.

At six thirty, with less than ninety minutes' sleep under his belt, Malik admitted defeat, threw back the sheets on his side of the bed and padded into the bathroom to take a leak. He closed the door so he wouldn't wake Kim. Malik could get by on very little sleep, his wife not so much. She needed a solid eight hours – minimum.

He washed his hands and went into the hallway. Flint was lying next to the stairs, ostensibly on sentry duty, but in reality dead to the world. Malik crossed to the kids' bedrooms and, ignoring the various signs warning parents and other adults to keep out, took a peek inside. Landon, the older of the two, was stretched out on his bed, his calves and legs hanging over the end. Like Malik, he was tall, and likely to end up taller than his dad. He played basketball for his local high school and was already drawing some serious college interest. He could empty a refrigerator in seconds flat, had a smart mouth, and didn't much like being told what to do. Those were qualities Malik recognized in himself.

Malik closed Landon's door, and went to check on Katy. In contrast to the bombsite that passed for Landon's room, Katy's was immaculate. She lay on her side in bed, wide awake and reading: the Kindle they had got her last Christmas was propped up on a pillow next to her. Boy, could that kid read. He and Kim weren't wild about kids staring at screens all day, but the local library couldn't keep up with Katy's voracious habits so they had broken down and got the Kindle.

She looked up at him and yawned. He walked in and sat down on the edge of her bed. 'You're up early. You have a nightmare?' he asked her.

'Nope. Just wanted to finish this book. It's *so* good.'

She put down the Kindle and sat up. 'Big game tonight. We going to win?'

'Hell, yeah. Why you even ask me a question like that, girl?'

She seemed to study him. 'You look tired.'

'Didn't sleep too good. Big game. You know how it is. You go finish your book. I'm gonna let Flint out.'

'Okay, Daddy,' she said, rolling over onto her other side, Kindle in hand.

He walked back out onto the landing. He should have felt comforted by the kids, safe, warm and happy in the home he and Kim had made for them. But he wasn't. It made him think about the boy he'd found last night. How had that happened? How could someone not know their child was out at that time of night?

He stopped himself right there. He knew the answer. He'd grown up in a place where lots of parents had no control over their children, and for the ones who did, keeping control was a constant battle. He guessed he hadn't expected it to happen in small-town white Minnesota.

The dog studied him with one eye, slowly got to his feet, and padded after him down the stairs. Malik walked into the kitchen, and opened the door that led into the backyard. Damn, it was cold. Right now, back in California, it would still be in the low sixties, even with the time difference. The cold in Minnesota was the one thing he'd never get used to. It bordered on painful. You'd step out into it and the wind would be knocked from you.

Out front he heard a car drive down the street and stop. *Weird*. There was almost never any kind of traffic on the street before seven. He closed the back door and walked through to the front of the house.

He saw a college-security patrol car pull up right out front of the house. The driver's door opened and Tromso levered his fat ass out. He waddled toward the front door.

Malik didn't want the whole house woken. Not to mention the questions he'd have to answer about why the cops were there first thing in the morning. He opened the front door and, still in his boxer shorts and T-shirt, braved the cold in his bare feet, meeting Tromso halfway up the path.

Tromso greeted him affably enough. 'Hey, Coach.'

Malik nodded toward the upstairs bedrooms at the front of the house, the drapes still closed. 'Family are sleeping.'

Tromso lowered his voice. 'Sorry. I just figured you'd need this.' He dug into various pockets before coming up with Malik's cell phone. He handed it to him.

Malik took it. 'Thanks.'

Tromso about-turned and started back toward the cruiser. Malik called after him, forgetting that most of his family were still asleep,

'Hey, wait up.'

He caught up to Tromso at the sidewalk.

'You figure out what was going on last night?'

Tromso turned with a smile, and a gee-shucks shrug. 'Crazy story. One of the trustees was showing his nephew around. Lost sight of the kid entirely. Freaked out when he couldn't find him, went searching all over the place. Turned out the kid had been hiding where you found him.'

Ordinarily when someone was spinning a yarn, Malik would have greeted it with 'Uh-huh,' or 'That so?' But this was such an obvious bunch of lies that, before he'd even thought about what he was saying or who he was saying it to, never mind why they might be saying it, the first word out of his mouth was 'Bullshit!'

Tromso's smile fell away. 'Excuse me?'

Malik didn't know why the hell Tromso was feeding him this line, but he was insulted. 'Come on, man. That's the guy's story and you believe him? You have to be kidding me, right? That kid wasn't hiding. He was crying. Brother, you saw him.'

'He was upset that he'd been caught. He thought he was in trouble when you showed up.'

Malik stared at Tromso. He was half expecting some cheesy-ass TV presenter to step out from behind a bush with a camera crew and tell him he'd been punked, only this was so far from funny that he couldn't imagine even the TV dirtbags trying to squeeze a laugh out of it.

'That's not what was going on there last night, and you know it.'

Tromso was pissed. His little piggy eyes were boring into Malik and his lips had all but disappeared. 'So, what *was* going on, Coach?' It wasn't so much a question as a challenge.

'Well, it sure as shit wasn't hide-and-go-seek between some uncle and his nephew.'

He and Tromso were almost nose to nose now. Malik glanced down to see the chief's left hand resting on his pepper spray. If he even thought of threatening to use it, Malik would kick his ass all over town, all day long, cop or no cop. Malik had never liked cops, and now he was remembering why.

'So who was this trustee?' Malik said, his voice calm. 'You get a name?'

The question seemed to throw Tromso off. He backed up a little. 'Take it easy, Coach. I looked into it. I can see how you might have got the wrong idea. Hell, I was thinking what you were when I arrived. But there's no mystery. It was a misunderstanding.'

He was around the other side of the patrol car now.

'I'm going to follow up on this,' Malik told him.

'Do yourself a favor, Coach. Just win that game for us tonight,' said Tromso, clambering into the car, starting the engine and taking off before Malik could react.

Malik turned back to his house. His wife was at the bedroom window. She looked worried. He wondered how much she'd heard. Their elderly next-door neighbor was peering out too. Likely most of the street had woken up by now.

Malik headed back inside, his cell phone in his right hand.

SIX

WHAT WAS THAT ABOUT? ONE of your players in trouble?' Kim asked, as he walked into the kitchen for a refill of coffee from the pot on the counter.

He put his arms around her, swept aside her long black hair, and kissed the back of her neck. Katy looked up from the library book she was reading at the kitchen table. 'Gross, you guys.'

'No,' said Malik. 'Something else. I'll tell you about it later.'

It was natural for Kim to assume that a visit from the cops was connected to the team. Over the years the kids he'd coached had had numerous run-ins with the law. Although there were exceptions, sports, especially basketball, tended to attract the ones who saw it as a way of escaping bad circumstances. That had certainly been the case for Malik.

Landon came loping into the kitchen, heading straight for the refrigerator. Malik was amazed at the boy's capacity to eat and not put on so much as a pound. 'What were the cops here for, Dad?'

'Just something at the stadium last night.'

Kim studied him. 'That's where you were? Someone break in?'

Malik really didn't want to have this conversation with Landon and Katy present. He did his best to shield them from the sickness in the world.

He took a sip of coffee. 'Yeah, a break-in. Someone goofing around. Nothing was taken. That was the head of security checking in.'

Kim stood there, hands on hips. He couldn't get anything past her. 'So how come he had your cell phone?'

'I'll tell you later, okay?' Malik said softly, hoping his tone would convey that he didn't want to discuss it in front of the children.

'Uh-huh,' said Kim. 'Well, I'm going to shower.' She turned to her son, who was still busy looting the refrigerator. 'Leave some food for the rest of us, Landon.'

With Kim out of the way, Malik dug out his cell phone and scrolled to the picture folder on the display. He tapped it open. He was going to email that photo to himself so he'd have a copy. He couldn't. The picture he'd taken last night of the grey sedan had been deleted.

SEVEN

MALIK BLEW STRAIGHT PAST THE line of people waiting patiently in the anteroom of Allan Laird's office. Laird was the chancellor. He had headed the committee that had appointed Malik to the job. Malik liked Laird well enough, in as much as there wasn't anything actively to dislike about the man. He was a glass-of-milk kind of guy, the type who ended up in jobs like chancellor because they'd never held an opinion strongly enough to piss anyone else off. Laird's secretary got up from behind her desk, attempting to block him.

'Coach Shaw, the chancellor is in the middle of—'

But her 120 pounds was no match for Malik in full flow. She was used to blocking access, but Malik had spent years in the NBA getting the ball to the basket past ghetto-determined men who were a lot bigger than he was. He dodged round her with a polite 'Don't worry, Suzanne. He's expecting me.'

He turned the handle and walked into Laird's office. Laird was on the phone. He looked vaguely startled by Malik's appearance, but waved him into the chair opposite. He covered the mouthpiece with his hand. 'Be right with you, Coach.'

Many men in Laird's position would have resented the intrusion, and reacted accordingly. Not Laird. He didn't do ruffled, or not that Malik had seen. It was a power thing. When you held the whole deck, you deployed power differently. Power was an absence of reaction. Malik knew because he had seen the same trick from the head coaches of pro teams. There were only so many times you could lose your temper before it lost its impact. It was more effective to leave players and staff to fill in what you were thinking for themselves. As a management style, it worked.

Laird was playing another trick that Malik knew all about. Giving someone who was clearly agitated time to cool off. Laird was likely done with the call but he kept the other person on the line, asking about the man's family and kids.

Malik used the time to study Laird's office. There was something in particular he was looking for. He found it easily enough. Then he waited for Laird to finish the call.

Laird hung up, and smiled benevolently across the desk. 'Coach, always a pleasure. You ready to win this for us tonight? Eleven and two. Pretty incredible.'

Malik got to the point. 'Captain Tromso speak to you about what happened last night?'

Laird's smile vanished. He stretched his arms into the air. His hands settled behind his head, a hostage to fortune. 'I know what you're thinking, Malik.'

Malik had never heard Laird use his first name before. It unsettled him. It was the language of someone who badly wanted him on-side. 'That so?' he said.

'You think I'm going to ignore this but, believe me, I'm not. Whatever went on last night, innocent or not, was wholly unacceptable to me and this institution. I'm going to deal with it.'

Malik locked eyes with Laird. 'How?'

'Firmly,' said Laird. 'The individual in question has been asked to tender his resignation from the board of trustees. Furthermore, he is going to be told that he is no longer welcome anywhere on campus. His relationship with this university is over.'

Malik didn't say anything. The rage he had felt when he'd arrived was nothing to what he felt now. He wanted to stand up, grab Laird by his fancy tie, drag him over the desk, and explain to him what 'firmly' meant where he came from. Malik counted to ten. Slowly. It didn't help. Finally, he said, 'That's it?'

Laird leaned forward, steepling his fingers under his chin. 'What more would you like me to do?'

Suddenly the room felt hot. Malik reached up and loosened the tie he was wearing. 'You're serious? What do I think you should do? I caught a kid in the shower with one of our trustees and you're asking *me* what I think *you* should do?'

Laird appeared taken aback and, for a second, Malik took it at face value.

'That wasn't what I was told, Coach. Captain Tromso said that . . .' he flicked through some notes on his desk '. . . shortly after midnight, this morning, campus dispatch received an agitated call from you that you had a found a young man in the shower area.' He kept reading from the report. 'And that, furthermore, you had seen someone flee the stadium. No one told me that you had caught both parties actually *in* the shower together.'

Malik knew what Laird was doing. 'You're playing with words, Chancellor. Okay maybe I didn't actually see them together, but you don't have to be a genius to know what was going on. What was a grown man doing with a child – not a young man, a child – alone in the middle of the night?'

It was obviously time for Laird to up the ante. He got up, walked round his desk and perched on the corner. Malik had a feeling that this was a conversation the chancellor might have had before and that he'd used exactly the same approach to deflect it. Deny, deflect and, finally, downplay.

'Coach, when matters like this arise I have a duty of care. Let's assume you're right. That something untoward was going on before you interrupted. It's not enough to suspect. There has to be proof. Think of the damage that could be done to a man and his family. What if we, you, were wrong? The legal implications don't bear thinking about.'

'And what about that kid? Has anyone spoken to him?'

Laird shot Malik a benevolent smile that came off patronizing. 'The boy is denying that anything out of place happened. Now do you see why I'm reluctant to go in all guns blazing?'

Malik looked past Laird to the trump card he had scoped out earlier. A series of silver-framed pictures of Laird's wife and three kids, two boys and a girl, stood on a credenza behind his desk.

'And if it had been your son, Chancellor, would you be so ready to accept that nothing happened? I know I sure as hell wouldn't. And while we're at it, who is this trustee? He have a name?'

Laird glared at Malik, which gave him some satisfaction. It meant he had touched a nerve. If you thought the whole thing was innocent, a misunderstanding, you didn't react in the way Laird just had.

The glare was folded up and put away, replaced by the patronizing smile, which meant that a guy like Malik, a jock from the ghetto, could never understand the complex moral and ethical issues at play, not to mention the sensitivity of such a matter. Only Malik didn't need to understand any of that. All he needed to appreciate was that there was right and there was wrong, and what he'd seen was all kinds of wrong.

Laird got up and walked toward the door, a clear gesture that the unscheduled meeting was over. 'I'll take on board what you've said, Coach, but I think it might be best for everyone if you left this with me. You have a game to win.'

The last thing Malik cared about right now was the game. Twenty-four hours ago that would have seemed unthinkable, but a lot could change in twenty-four hours.

The two men's eyes locked. 'Thanks for your time, Chancellor Laird,' Malik he id.

Laird raised a bunched hand, as if he were about to give Malik an attaboy punch to the shoulder. Malik threw him a look to suggest that he might not have a hand if he tried it. He settled for an open-palmed pat. 'You're doing great work, Coach. Great work.'

EIGHT

MALIK SAT IN HIS PICK-UP. He was angrier than when he'd arrived. He hadn't thought that was possible. He was angry at Tromso for covering the whole thing up. He was angry at Laird for treating him as if he was making a mountain out of a molehill. But most of all he was angry at himself.

The trustees were all men with either money or serious political connections. No doubt the guy had cooked up some bullshit story about what he'd been doing. Laird had probably bought it, but he was chancellor because he was an operator. Getting the perpetrator to stand aside was probably as good as it got, especially if the kid was too scared or embarrassed to file charges, or even to admit anything had happened. And who was going to take the word of a black coach versus some buttoned-down white trustee?

Malik had been wasting his time going to see Laird. And Laird was right: he did have a job to do, a game to win. But that didn't mean this was the last they'd heard of it. If for no other reason than that Malik had to be able to look at himself in the mirror every morning when he was shaving, he was going to figure out exactly what had happened.

He'd get some answers, and if they made him unpopular, so be it. Like the rest of the country, he had watched what had gone down at Penn State, and how Joe Paterno's legacy had been tarnished by the sin of omission. Malik wasn't going to let himself suffer the same fate. There was no way someone was going to turn to him one day and ask why he'd left things alone instead of satisfying himself that he'd done everything he could.

If Tromso or Laird didn't like it, well, that was too damn bad. Malik was his own man, and he wasn't planning on changing now.

Malik walked into the kitchen. The kids were at school and Kim was unloading the dishwasher. He grabbed some plates from the bottom rack and began to put them away. He and Kim had always shared domestic chores, much to the amusement of male buddies and teammates, who'd arrive to catch him sweeping the hallway or vacuuming the carpets. But it was that kind of marriage. A partnership. Malik was pretty sure that was one of the reasons they had lasted where so many others had failed. They'd kept it real.

'You going to tell me what's going on?' she asked him, lining up some glasses in a cabinet.

He sighed. 'That obvious?'

'Who are you talking to?' she said, smiling.

She sat down at the kitchen table. He sat next to her. He explained as best he could what had happened – what he had seen, then how Tromso and now the chancellor were making out like it was none of his business. She listened quietly.

As he finished, he said, 'Before you say anything, I know what I saw, Kim. I've been over it in my mind a dozen times since last night.'

Last night? Was it really that short a time ago? Sitting here with his wife, unburdening himself, with the watery spring Minnesota light filtering in through the window, it felt like a week had passed already.

Kim looked at him. 'I believe you, and I trust you.' She reached out and wrapped her hands around his.

It was what he had needed to hear. 'So what do I do?' he asked her. 'I mean, I can't just pretend it never happened.'

'No, you can't.'

Neither of them said anything for a moment. Then Malik said, 'I kept thinking, what if it had been Landon in there with some weird guy? Or Katy? How would I feel if someone saw that happening to one of our kids, and turned their back?'

'But you didn't, did you?' Kim said.

'And look where it's got me. I have a feeling that, even if I win this game tonight, Laird's got me down as a troublemaker.'

Kim's brow furrowed. 'Why doesn't he want to take it any further? So they kick the guy off the board. Big deal. He's still out there, doing whatever he was doing before.'

Malik had a feeling they both knew the answer already. The college didn't want to get involved. This way they could say they had acted decisively. But they hadn't dealt with the problem: they'd just stopped it being their problem.

'I know,' said Malik. 'Someone has to stop him.'

As soon as he said it, he realized he didn't even know the name of the person they were talking about. He didn't have a face either. Laird knew, so did Tromso, but there was no way they were going to volunteer that information.

'You could call the state police, couldn't you? Or the FBI?' Kim suggested.

Malik had already thought about it. Sitting in his car after he'd seen Laird, he'd almost made the call then and there. But something had stopped him, and it wasn't just that he didn't have much to give them. As ashamed as he was to admit it, he didn't want to do anything until after the game this evening.

Despite his lingering anger and resentment, he couldn't help but get caught up in the excitement of the final game of the Wolves' season. He might have played in bigger games, but for the kids on his team this was the pinnacle of their college career. For them it would be their high point of playing basketball, a memory to be cherished, something to tell their own kids about. They wouldn't be going on to the NBA. This was it for them, the top of the mountain. Malik couldn't afford to let what he'd stumbled upon ruin that. He wanted them to be able to remember finishing as winners. He owed them that. The rest would wait, and there was something to be said for allowing himself to make his next move, whatever it might be, with a clear mind.

'Malik?'

His wife was looking at him, waiting for a response.

'They don't have state police here, but I'll follow it up tomorrow. See if I can't speak to some more people, find out if they know what's been going on.'

Kim squeezed his hand. 'I know you'll do what's right.'

NINE

MALIK WENT UPSTAIRS, SHOWERED, PUT on slacks and a polo shirt, then headed back to college. There was less than six hours until the game started and a lot left to do. He got into his car, and drove to his office in the athletic department. He met with his assistant coaches, including Mike, whom he questioned again about the late-night text, getting the same answer he had before ('I swear, I was home asleep the whole time, Coach'), and went over final preparations.

The game plan for the evening was already decided. Malik didn't believe in setting out to frustrate the other team. His approach had always been simple: play fast, be aggressive, everyone to know what their job was ahead of time.

He watched some tapes of potential freshmen recruits. There was a kid from Gainesville he was desperate to have on the team, but he was pretty sure that a bigger college would land him. Despite all the noises that were made in public, all kinds of under-the-table deals were still being struck. Malik wouldn't play that game, and if it meant he lost out, then too bad. He had seen, up close and personal, how money had tainted college sports. He always told his kids to worry about the game first, and the money would take care of itself. It was an increasingly tough pitch to make in a country where the only thing that seemed to matter, these days, was the mighty dollar.

He arrived at the stadium with ninety minutes to go before tip-off. Unlike last night, the parking lots were full, with students, alumni and locals partying. He lowered his window, and waved to people as he drove through. The smiles and whoops he got as he inched the car forward couldn't help but make him feel good.

This was what sport was about, he thought. A way of bringing people together.

He parked and ducked in through the side door as he had last night. The corridor was crowded with people. He couldn't help but glance at the visitors' locker room as he opened the opposite door and headed into the home-team area.

His boys were already there, some with headphones pumping rap and rock into their ears, others standing about chatting to each other or to the assistants. He worked the room, shaking hands, patting backs, offering words of encouragement to the nervous, and trying to keep a lid on one or two players who had let the mood outside carry them away. They had reached the final, and that was great, but they still had a ways to go, and while they were favorites, there was no such thing as far as Malik was concerned. You treated the opposition with respect or you paid the price.

The players went out to warm up. He could hear the crowd rise to them. As they filtered back in and sat down, Malik kept his final words brief.

Enjoy it.

Leave your game out there on the floor.

Make sure you won't have any regrets later.

He repeated the last part, which was more for himself, a testament of faith, than for the young men huddled around him.

They were three down at the half, some sloppy defense having cost them. They huddled up one more time. Malik dug a little deeper, got a little more serious, reprimanding a few of his players.

He sensed the determination in them. By the time they went out to start the third quarter, he would have bet his home that they would win.

He was right. By the end of the third they were in the lead by five points. He kept at them, losing himself in the game as he stood at the side of the court. All thoughts of the previous evening were gone now. There was only the present. Only the here and now.

Malik, the crowd and the team were one, playing every pass, jumping for every rebound, holding their collective breath in the seconds between the ball leaving a player's hands and whooshing through the net, or rattling off the back board.

Forty seconds to go. Up by nine. All they had to do was stay cool. It was their game to lose. He called a final time-out. He wanted to kill the pace. They needed to nag and niggle and frustrate.

He looked over their heads into the stands for Kim but caught the eye of Tromso. The short, burly cop, his face flushed with beer, raised his hands and gave him a double thumbs-up. It was as much as Malik could do not to wade into the stand, pull Tromso out and kick his ass right then and there.

As the players headed back out on to the court, whatever rush Malik had going on evaporated. Not even the final buzzer could bring him back. As the crowd erupted, and one of his assistant coaches hugged him, Malik stood, impassive.

He plastered on a smile. Shook hands and exchanged hugs. He feigned anger as a cooler was dumped over him by the players, ruining the suit he'd put on and leaving him soaked. As he stood there, water running down the back of his neck, he thought of the boy.

As the celebrations continued, Malik Shaw pushed his way through the crowds, headed down the corridor, got into his car and drove off into the night.

TEN

H E DROVE FOR MILES, HEADING south for no particular reason and with no destination in mind. Driving helped clear his mind. It always had. He craved empty roads, big spaces and his own company. He would think of everything and nothing. But not tonight. Tonight he could only think of how hollow the victory had made him feel.

A hundred miles out from home, he felt his mood begin to clear. He pulled over and checked his cell. The cell with the missing picture. The cell that had been wiped clean by Tromso, as if that would erase what had happened.

He had a dozen missed calls, and several voicemail messages. He sat beside the highway and listened to them. The first was from his assistant coach, Mike, who was concerned that he was missing out on the fun. The second was from a worried Kim, wondering where he was and asking him to call her straight away. The third was the real surprise. It was from Laird. The chancellor was offering his congratulations and asking to see him in the morning, telling him not to worry, it was good news.

Malik called Kim back, reassured her that he was fine: he had just needed to clear his head and would see her soon. He got back on the highway, got off at the next exit, then back on, this time heading north toward Harrisburg.

The party was still in full swing when he arrived back. It had spilled out from the stadium onto the usually deserted streets. It seemed like everyone in the whole town was there. Young, old, middle-aged, students, faculty, locals.

Malik told himself he could let the dark stuff go for one night. In any case, Chancellor Laird had known what he thought, and presumably, now he'd had time to think about the seriousness of what had happened and reflect on the consequences, he had come round. Malik would no doubt walk into the man's office tomorrow to find a prosecutor waiting to speak to him, and real action being taken.

That was the lie Malik told himself as he hugged his wife and kids, convinced that with victory would come justice.

ELEVEN

THE NEXT MORNING MALIK WAS ushered into the chancellor's inner sanctum without delay. A silver coffee pot and china cups had been laid out on a small table. Laird made a big show of serving Malik. The message was as subtle as a Patrick Ewing charge to the basket.

'Didn't see you at the celebrations last night, Coach?'

Here it came, thought Malik. Laird was testing the ground, seeing where his head was at, if he'd calmed down, the win having distracted him.

'I needed some time to clear my head.'

'And?' said Laird, offering cream from a tiny silver jug.

Malik wasn't enjoying this as much as Laird had probably assumed he would. He liked people who were direct. 'And what?'

'Well,' said Laird, 'did it work?'

Malik watched as Laird, his serving duties done, retreated behind the safety of his desk.

'I guess it did,' said Malik.

'Good,' said Laird. 'I wanted to see you to discuss your contract.'

Here it comes, thought Malik. He'd signed up for an initial period of two years. The package they'd offered had been surprisingly good. At the time Malik had guessed that they'd already lost out on a few people. A lot of coaches didn't want to move to a division-two college, and if they did, they usually wanted to go somewhere with better weather, such as Florida or California.

Of course, there were other factors in play. A successful sports team on campus could be a powerful revenue generator. But to achieve that you needed quality players, and one way of doing that was to hire a coach whose name they'd at least recognize. That was what they'd paid for when they'd hired him, the use of his name. There had even been a clause in the first draft of the contract about image rights.

Laird shot Malik that shark smile of his, all teeth and gums. 'As you know, we've been without an athletic director for the past couple of months.'

When Malik had been hired the director had been a guy called Bob Lovitz, who had been around a long time. He was a decent man, keen to hire Malik, and had pretty much left him alone to run the basketball program. He'd also had a drinking problem. When he'd left at short notice the rumor was that his drinking had become an issue.

Laird opened a manila file, pulled out a sheaf of papers, and handed them to him. 'How'd you like to step up?' Malik took them but didn't glance at them. He didn't say anything.

'I told you it was good news, Coach.' Laird smiled.

'Chancellor, I'm a basketball coach. That would be a big step up, different set of skills.'

'I think you're being overly modest, Coach. Plus we've been looking at candidates since Bob left, and we've yet to find one who would be a good fit. You already have a feel for the place.'

Malik started to leaf through the new contract. The new headline salary surprised even him. The college must have been in better financial shape than he'd suspected.

'We're keen to have this resolved as soon as possible,' said Laird. 'I'm sure after last night there will be more schools taking a look at you, and we don't want to lose out now that we have you here.'

Malik said, 'I'll need to have an attorney check it over.'

'Of course.'

There was an awkward silence. Laird drummed his fingers on the desk, as if to signal that the meeting was over. 'So, you'll get back to me?' he said.

Malik figured now was as good a time as any to acknowledge the elephant in the room. 'I actually thought you wanted to talk to me about what we discussed yesterday.'

Laird's face showed a flicker of irritation, but he moved fast to cover it. 'I'm glad you brought that up, actually.'

Malik looked at him, playing the chancellor at his own game, using silence to force a response. Laird might have been used to running the play in his office, but Malik knew more about steering things than most people. It was at the center of being a coach, the ability to push buttons and provoke a required response.

'I was a little tetchy,' said Laird. 'And the last impression I wanted to give you was that we as an institution wouldn't take seriously an incident such as the one you described. In fact, my next meeting this morning is with Captain Tromso.'

'So,' said Malik, 'what you gonna do?'

'Coach, I hope you'll understand when I say that before the meeting it would be premature of me to discuss that with you. But I promise I'll keep you fully informed of any developments. As long as you understand how sensitive this matter is.'

Malik could feel anger rising, like bile, at the back of his mouth, but he did his best to tamp it down. Losing his temper would achieve nothing.

The meeting hadn't been a complete waste of time. At least he knew now that they were playing a game, trying to soften him up with a new contract, offering him a bigger job. Making all the right noises about doing something but stopping short of actually committing to what that something might be. Malik was being played. And when you're being played the best strategy is often to play dumb.

'Oh, I do,' said Malik. He rolled up the contract, got up from his chair, and placed his china coffee cup back on the table. 'You can count on me,' he said to Laird.

'I never doubted it for a moment,' said Laird, the smile back.

Malik walked out. As he opened the door, Tromso practically launched himself from the chair where he'd been waiting for his turn with the chancellor. He bounded over to Malik, offering a beefy hand.

'Great result, Coach. Just great.'

Malik shook his hand, playing along with the forced bonhomie, but thankful he had some hand sanitizer in his car. 'Thanks.'

'Well, keep up the good work,' Tromso said, blundering past Laird's secretary and into the office.

Malik watched as the door shut. Fuck you, guys, he said to himself.

TWELVE

ALIK'S OFFICE WAS QUIET. HE had given the rest of his coaching staff the day off. There was a victory rally later and, no doubt, more raucous celebrations that evening. Right now he was guessing that most of the team would be nursing hangovers. The short walk from his car to his office had been filled with people wanting to talk to him about the game or shake his hand. There was a buzz in the air.

He wished he could have enjoyed it with everyone else. He sat down at his desk, piled high with papers and DVDs of potential recruits for next year. He unrolled the contract offering him the new job and flattened it on his desk. He began to read it. It was a slow process: like most contracts it had been drawn up to be about as clear as mud.

After a few moments, he checked the page count:–nineteen, including the definition of terms. He got up, went to his filing cabinet, and scrabbled around for the original contract he'd signed. He checked the page count: seventeen. He doubted the difference could have been accounted for by the number of zeroes added to his salary, which they'd raised by about a half, a ridiculously generous amount, even allowing for the win and what might lie ahead.

So where had the two extra pages come from? He laid both contracts side by side, and worked through them page by page, matching sections, clauses and paragraphs. About half a page could be accounted for by changes to the structure of his bonus payments, which, like the salary, seemed over-generous.

He found the bulk of the changes around page fifteen. The section was headlined: 'Non-disclosure Agreement'. Even allowing for the legal jargon, Malik could figure out what it meant. Signing it would mean he could not discuss any aspect of his job without prior approval. There was a specific clause pertaining to 'revelations that may be detrimental to the image and standing of the college'.

The clause was retrospective. They were giving him a big chunk of extra cash to keep his mouth shut. The contract was their way of bribing him without it being completely obvious.

Malik grabbed the new contract, threw it into the metal wastepaper bin next to his desk, grabbed a box of matches from a drawer and sparked one. Cupping his hands around the flame, he lowered it toward the edge of the contract. He watched as it caught the edge of the paper and slowly took hold.

As the contract burned, grey-black smoke curled upwards. A few moments later, the fire alarm began to shriek. Malik grabbed a bottle of water from his desk and doused the flames. He grabbed his jacket from the back of his chair, and headed out of his office.

THIRTEEN

MALIK MARCHED ACROSS CAMPUS. HE was so consumed with anger that he almost didn't recognize him. He stopped dead.

He stared at the boy's floppy fringe and large brown eyes. Then he noticed the woman with him, a regular suburban mom with a blonde bob, wearing a long skirt and a white blouse.

The boy held out a program from the game and a pen. As Malik took it, he had a moment of doubt. Maybe he just looked like the same kid. Yeah, that had to be it. Lots of white kids had the same floppy Justin Bieber-style haircut.

But it wasn't. The boy's features had been burned onto Malik's consciousness. It was a face that would haunt him. A face he would see for years.

This time the boy wasn't crying. But there was something in the way he looked at Malik that hadn't changed since the first time they'd met. His eyes held a plea that Malik shouldn't say anything, a plea born of shame.

Malik turned to the boy's mother. She smiled at him, her eyes crinkling. She was a good-looking woman. Nothing in her manner suggested that she was anything other than a mom out with her son. She sure as hell didn't look like a woman who knew what her son was mixed up in. Her normality freaked Malik out. It would have been easier if she'd seemed beaten down or anxious. Maybe then he'd have been able to find the words to tell her what he knew.

The pair were both looking at him now. 'Could you sign it "to Jack"?' she asked.

Malik uncapped the pen, and signed the program. 'You have a second name, Jack?'

The boy's eyes made the same plea.

'Barnes. Jack Barnes,' said the mom. 'And I'm Eve Barnes.'

Malik managed, 'Nice to meet you.' He wanted to talk to the boy. To be able to reassure him that there was one adult who wasn't about to abandon him. But he didn't want to say anything to the mom. Not in public, anyway.

'Hey,' said Malik, 'I've an idea. If you like I could get the team to sign it, then mail it back to you. How does that sound?'

Jack seemed to sense where this was going and didn't like it. 'It's okay,' he murmured, so softly that Malik had to strain to hear him.

'That would be wonderful, Coach Shaw,' said Eve. She rifled in her handbag and came up with a slip of paper. She scribbled an address on it and handed it to Malik.

Malik waved the game program. 'I'll get the guys to sign this and mail it back to you soon as I can. Okay?'

Jack gave the barest nod as his mom beamed at Malik. Her smile broke his heart. There was no way he was walking away from this, and no way he was signing any goddamn non-disclosure agreement.

'That's so good of you,' said Eve Barnes. 'What do you say, Jack?'

'Thank you,' said the boy, as he studied the sidewalk.

'Well,' said Eve, 'let's not keep Coach.'

He watched as they walked away. A couple more people passed Malik as he stood there. One of them high-fived him. Malik looked around. The campus had taken on a surreal edge. Everywhere he looked, people were smiling, walking around with extra pep in their step. If only they knew, he thought.

He turned to walk away, and as he did so, he heard the boy calling after him, 'Coach!'

He swung round to see Jack Barnes running toward him. He held out the pen. As he gave it to Malik, he whispered, 'Please don't say anything.' There were tears in his eyes. He swiped them away with the back of his sleeve. 'If they find out I've told, they'll kill me.'

Then he turned and ran after his mom, as Malik thought, *They*. He didn't say *he*, he said *they*. He walked back toward his office, pulling out his cell phone as he went.

FOURTEEN

Fifth Avenue and 47th Street,
New York City, NY

BULLET-SIZED DROPS OF RAIN ricocheted from the hood of the black Lincoln Town Car as it pulled up outside the apartment building. A doorman stepped forward with a golf umbrella as the passenger door opened and Ty Johnson stepped out.

'Thanks,' he said, taking the umbrella and using it to shield his principal, a nine-year-old girl with long, curly blonde hair as she scrambled out, laden with shopping bags from the FAO Schwarz toy store on Fifth Avenue.

'You want me to carry those for you?' Ty asked her.

'No, thank you, Mr Johnson. I'm perfectly capable,' came the reply.

Ty bit back a smile as Ryan Lock, his business partner and friend, walked round from the front passenger side to join them on the sidewalk. The doorman had retreated under the building's green canopy, already soaked by the downpour, his grey hair matted to his skull.

Together the two men escorted Kristina Makarova into the building. When they hit the door, Ty stepped aside as Lock escorted the child toward the elevator and up to her parents' apartment – an eight-room, 4000-

46

square-feet piece of Manhattan real estate that was worth a cool twenty million dollars.

Ty sheltered under the canopy and scanned the street. He was watching for a loiterer across the street, a vehicle parked with someone inside, anything that suggested surveillance. In truth, the security risk to the family was low but they were wealthy, which made Kristina a potential kidnap-for-ransom target. The chances were that no one was looking at the family but neither Ty nor Lock liked to phone things in. No matter the job, no matter the principal, they liked to do things right and maintain standards. Switching off was not an option they entertained.

Satisfied, Ty walked past the soaking doorman and into the lobby. Lock was waiting at the elevator with Kristina, who was investigating her purchases. She pulled out a fairy costume, complete with wings, and held it up for Ty's inspection.

'What do you think?' she asked the six-foot-four, 230-pound African American.

'Don't think it's my color,' he replied, deadpan.

'No, it's for me, silly.'

Ty made a show of taking a closer look. 'It's real nice.'

'Thanks,' said Kristina, jamming it back into the bag.

Ty had grown attached to the little girl, who sounded more twenty-nine than nine. He and Lock both had. She was capable, like most kids, of being bratty, and there was no question she was spoiled, but she wngaged with and was interested in others. The way Ty looked at it, she'd had no more say in her circumstances than some kid from the projects.

The elevator doors opened and they got in, Ty first, to hold the door, then Kristina and Lock. It was always the same drill. The principal never went first into an elevator, vehicle or building – too easy for a door to be closed and secured, separating them from their close-protection detail.

They rode three floors in silence. The doors opened and Ty stepped out. There were only two apartments on this floor. The other was owned by a Wall Street trader, who was currently skiing in Europe. He and Lock knew about all the neighbors – how many lived in each apartment in the building, whether they owned or rented, what they did and, most importantly, what they looked like. They had also built a profile of their regular visitors and anyone who made deliveries. It all came down to being observant, and looking for two things: the absence of the normal and the presence of the abnormal.

Ty opened the door to the main apartment and they walked inside. Kristina's father was at work. Her mother was in the kitchen, supervising a small army of caterers who were preparing for a dinner party. Kristina disappeared to her room with her spoils.

Lock had some business to attend to while Ty stayed at the apartment, providing some light residential protection before he, too, headed home until the morning. As Ty stood by the window, scanning the street below, Lock came over and stood next to him.

'I'm going to head out. You good?' Lock asked.

Ty turned. 'Yeah, enjoy your evening.'

'Just don't let them catch you trying on that fairy costume.'

The retired marine smiled. 'I'm all over that shit. Nothing I like better than strapping on a pair of sparkly wings and going for a fly round the living room.'

Ty's cell phone chirped. He dug it out of his pocket. 'Yo, Malik!'

Lock shot him a look. Ty's 'Yo!' greeting was one of the reasons Lock handled most of their business calls.

Ty waved him off. 'I got this. Go do your thing.' He turned his attention back to the call. He'd planned on calling Malik later to congratulate his old friend on his team's victory, which had even made the press in New York, albeit a one-line mention in a round-up of college basketball.

As soon as Malik spoke, Ty knew this wasn't an old pal calling to shoot the breeze.

'Ty, I need your advice on something.'

Ty stepped off into a far corner of the room. 'You okay? Has something happened to the family?'

'It's kind of difficult. I don't even know where to start.'

'Take a breath, and start at the beginning,' said Ty.

FIFTEEN

I F YOU WORKED IN HIGH-end private security, as Ty did, you got used to panicky phone calls from people driven into unimaginable places, often for no other reason than bad luck. Like cops, Ty, with his partner Ryan Lock, encountered people who were at what was often the lowest, or most challenging, part of their lives. Kidnapping, stalking, extortion, terrorism, child abduction, blackmail, people like Kristina's parents being targeted for their wealth, these were the horrors they had to deal with. When the police or other civil authorities couldn't be called upon, they steered people through these events as best they could and, sometimes, meted out a form of justice to the perpetrators.

But this call was different. Ty had known Malik since third grade. They didn't see much of each other, and hadn't for years, but there was still a bond between them, deep and abiding. Childhood bonds could be strong. Stronger still when you'd grown up in the kind of place that didn't offer much besides family and friendship. Ty had been best man when Malik had married Kim. He had got to know their two kids. Malik had a life that part of Ty craved, especially as he had moved into his thirties – stable, three-dimensional, filled with small challenges and satisfying milestones.

All of this made what Malik was telling him even more unreal. Not to mention worrying. It wasn't what Malik had likely walked in on that shocked Ty. He had seen enough to know that while child predators were hardly commonplace (despite what the media would have us believe) they were out there. And, like lions prowling next to a water-hole in the middle of the savannah, they went where the prey was, which included anywhere that involved sport. What worried Ty about Malik's story was the reaction to it of the authorities where he was teaching. It worried him because Ty knew you could tell a lot from someone's first response to an incident like that. A regular person's reaction would have been horror, followed fast by anger and outrage.

The clincher, the thing that had freaked Ty out in the same way it had Malik, was the kid saying *they*, suggesting at least two people had been involved in the abuse, or one person involved and another facilitating it.

'Tell me again exactly what this Laird cat said to you?' Ty asked Malik, who seemed to have calmed down since the start of the phone call. 'His exact words.' He listened as Malik went through what had happened when he'd confronted the chancellor. He glanced across the room: Kristina had appeared, dressed up in her fairy outfit.

'How do I look?' she asked, with a twirl.

Ty put his hand over his cell. 'Like a princess.'

She feigned annoyance. 'I'm a fairy.'

'Like a fairy princess,' Ty said, extricating himself.

He heard Kristina's mom call to her from the kitchen: 'Kristina, leave Mr Johnson alone.'

'Okay, Mama.' She darted off.

At the other end of the line, Malik said, 'Oh, yeah, the cop, Tromso – when he gave my cell back, he'd deleted the picture I'd taken of the car. Ty, I don't know what to do, man.'

'You need me up there, brother?' Ty asked. 'I don't finish this gig for another week, but I can ask Ryan to duck out early.'

'No, you're good. I appreciate it. And it'd be good to see you. Landon's always asking about you.'

Ty smiled. He loved Landon like he was his own. He was a great kid. They both were. Smart, talented and, like their mom and dad, they had good values.

'Soon as I'm done here, I'll come up. Spend a few days. How about that?' Ty said.

'Sounds like just what I need. And in the meantime?' Malik asked.

'Well, that depends,' said Ty.

'On what?'

'How much do you like your job?'

Ty had known the answer before he asked the question.

'I don't like any job enough to cover up something like this,' said Malik.

'I hear you,' said Ty. 'So, for one, don't sign that new deal. See if they follow up. Then, if you don't get anywhere with the college, I'd go to the state police. That's where the campus police should have gone in any case. One more thing. Don't go playing detective, Malik. Leave this to the people who get paid to do it. You don't know who might be mixed up in something like this.'

There was silence at the end of the line. Ty said, 'I mean it. Let the cops do their job.'

'I hear you,' said Malik. Ty wasn't convinced he meant it, which worried him.

SIXTEEN

MALIK ENDED THE CALL. HE already felt better. Ty had always been able to calm him. Part of it was his sheer physical presence, but there was hardness too. If Ty told you it was Tuesday then it was Tuesday, even if you could see people heading to church. There was a problem this time, though. Malik knew that Ty was right when he'd said leave it to the cops, but he'd tried that already and it hadn't worked.

He pulled the piece of paper with the boy's address from his pocket, and studied it. He knew the area. It was a lower-middle-class part of town. Not poor, but not wealthy either. There wasn't a lot of money in Harrisburg. Apart from the local Walmart, and a nearby online retail warehouse, the biggest single employer was probably the college. Most of the bars, restaurants and smaller stores were dependent on the college kids too. He could see why the likes of Tromso and Laird wanted to keep everything quiet. In economic terms, the college was the town.

He slipped the piece of paper inside the program, and headed back toward the office. It was usually a brisk ten-minute walk across campus, but with well-wishers and others wanting to talk about the game, it took him forty. When he got there, he passed the program-signing job to one of his earnest young assistants, headed to his office and closed the door.

He pulled up the college website on his computer and clicked on a link that took him to a list of trustees. He was counting on it not already being updated. There were twelve trustees in total. He studied their faces, as if somehow that would be enough. He jotted down names on a pad and started Googling them one by one. He recognized quite a few: he'd had to glad-hand them, along with some of the richer alumni, after games.

After a half-hour, he was ready to give up. No one stood out. Nothing suggested anything untoward about any of the ten. But what had he expected? A trustee wasn't going to walk around with 'child molester' tattooed on his forehead.

Of course, he could wait for the website to be updated, and the man to drop off the list. Work out his identity by a process of elimination. But that could take months, and likely would if Laird didn't want to draw attention to the man's resignation or removal from the board.

Tromso wasn't going to tell him who he was. Neither was Laird. And asking would only alert them that Malik wasn't prepared to go along to get along.

The phone on his desk rang, startling him. The display told him it was an internal call. He picked up the receiver.

'Coach Shaw, this is Suzanne in the chancellor's office. Do you have a moment to speak to the chancellor?'

'Sure,' said Malik, reaching over and closing the web browser with its pictures of the trustees, one of whom he was all but certain had been preying upon young Jack Barnes.

'Hey, Coach,' said Laird, full of bullshit bonhomie. 'Have you had a chance to look at the contract?'

Two can play dumb, thought Malik. 'I have, Chancellor, but it's not really my area. My eyes kind of glaze over with contracts so I've passed it on to my old sports attorney. Hope that's okay?' Malik couldn't have cared less whether it was okay with Laird or not, but he figured his best tactic was to play along. He needed to stall, and what better way than to have Laird think he had an attorney looking over the deal?

'Well,' said Laird, 'that makes sense. But you're happy with what we've offered?'

'It's an incredibly generous package,' Malik said. 'And I'm sure any issues that do crop up will be a formality. Was there anything else, Chancellor?'

'Just wanted to make sure you're happy, Coach.'

Sure you did, thought Malik. Happy enough to keep my mouth shut.

SEVENTEEN

THE VICTORY CELEBRATIONS ALL BUT passed Malik by. He was there, but not present. He smiled, shook hands and applauded his team while his mind was elsewhere. A gnawing feeling in his stomach told him the college wasn't going to make a move without being prompted. He would have to go talk to the cops in St Paul or the FBI.

He was already dreading the conversation and the questions it would bring. Why had he waited until now to report it to them? He was pretty sure it would be near the top of the list. He didn't doubt that he could provide an answer that might satisfy them. He could explain that he'd felt duty-bound to contact the campus authorities first. The problem was that he wasn't sure the answer satisfied him. From early on Malik had decided that you had to have your own standards, your own code of ethics. It was fine taking your lead from other people if their morals were solid. But what if they weren't? What then?

It was all too easy, with the way the world was, to let things slide. To look the other way. To allow money to cloud your judgement. That was what Laird was counting on. He was about to be disappointed.

Malik grabbed the signed game program from his desk, got up and headed for the parking lot.

In less than fifteen minutes, Malik drew up outside the address he had for Jack Barnes. It was a small, single-story ranch house. The homes lining the quiet street were all but identical. For the most part, they were neatly kept, but showing signs of age.

As Malik got out, he noticed an elderly woman with hair pinned up in a bun watching him from behind her curtains. When she saw him looking at her, she stepped back.

Malik walked up three steps onto a small covered porch. The doorbell hung from the frame on a wire. He knocked instead.

A few moments later, the door opened. Eve Barnes stood there. She was wearing jeans and a grey marl Harrisburg Wolves sweatshirt. Her eyes widened. Malik held up the program but made a point of not handing it to her.

'Coach Shaw! I wasn't expecting you to drop it over yourself. I thought you'd mail it like you said.'

Malik smiled. 'Didn't want to risk it getting lost. Plus I'm on my way home, so . . .'

'Well, that is so kind of you. Jack will be thrilled.'

She called to her son. 'Jack! Coach Shaw's here.'

There was a mumbled response from somewhere inside the house. Malik didn't catch the words but the meaning was clear. Jack wanted to stay wherever he was.

Eve Barnes rolled her eyes. 'Sorry. He just got this new games console yesterday. Can't get him away from the damn thing.'

Malik had the same problem with Landon, who was video-game crazy. In the end, he and Kim had had to ration him to two hours at weekends, on condition that his grades were good and he did all his chores.

'Got the same problem with my son. The new Sony that just came out?'

'That's the one,' said Eve.

Malik knew how much they cost. Looking at the house, he imagined Eve would have had to save to buy it. 'Birthday present?' he asked, aware that the question might be seen as prying. One of the things he'd picked up on when they'd first moved here was how guarded people could seem. In California people shared all kinds of information with relative strangers.

'Present from a friend,' she said casually.

The alarm that had been going off in Malik's head as soon as she had mentioned the expensive games console went up a notch in volume. Malik was by no means an expert, but he knew that predators, like the man he'd almost caught Jack with, often used gifts to bribe their victims into silence. The fact that it may have been a recent gift was even more alarming. Now Malik was wondering just what that meant. Was someone trying to buy the kid's silence in the same way that the college was trying to buy his?

'Pretty generous friend,' said Malik, still holding the program.

Eve Barnes finally took the hint. 'Where are my manners? Why don't you come in, Coach Shaw?'

'Please, call me Malik,' he said, walking through into the hallway.

'Can I get you something to drink? Coffee? Water?' She turned. 'Beer? I'm sure I have some somewhere.'

"Water's fine," said Malik.

He followed her through into the living room. The curtains were closed. The TV was on. Jack was sitting on the floor with a games controller in his hand, his eyes glued to the screen as he played GTA V. Landon played it with his friends. Kim was dead set against the violence, but Malik, having lived through the real-world version growing up in Long Beach, took a more relaxed approach. Landon had a pretty level head on those broad shoulders. He was a good kid who'd been taught the difference between right and wrong, and Malik doubted a video game would knock him off course.

'Hey, Jack,' said Malik. 'I got your program signed.'

'I'll get you that water. Jack, will you please switch that thing off?'

Jack hit the pause button, the screen freezing on a car careening down a street full of pedestrians. Avoiding eye contact, he took the program from Malik. Malik knew that he had just a few seconds before Eve came back from the kitchen with his water.

'Jack?'

The boy looked up at Malik, eyes narrowed. He was scared, but the fear was expressing itself as anger. It came off him in waves. Malik was so used to dealing with young men and usually read them better than their own parents could. When one of his team came in to practice, he could tell almost straight off the bat where his head was.

'You said if someone found out they'd kill you. Who are *they*, Jack?'

The boy picked up the program and threw it to the floor. 'I don't want it. I don't even like basketball. It's stupid.'

'I can help you, Jack,' Malik whispered. 'I can make sure no one hurts you.'

The boy resumed the game, and pushed forward on the black hand controller. On screen, the car mounted the sidewalk and rolled over a woman pushing an infant in a buggy. 'I don't know what you're talking about,' the boy said, just as his mom appeared with the glass of water.

'Jack,' she scolded. 'Will you please turn that off while we have company!'

'It's fine,' said Malik. 'I really need to get home anyway.' He waved away the glass of water.

'Are you sure?' said Eve.

'If you need anything else,' said Malik, digging into his wallet, 'here's my card.' He scrawled his cell number on the back, handed it to her and made to leave.

Flustered, Eve turned back to her son. 'Can you at least thank the coach for bringing over the program for you?'

'Thanks,' muttered Jack.

Eve chased after Malik as he headed for the door. He needed to get some fresh air. If he'd had any doubt about what he'd stumbled over in that locker room, it was gone now. The boy was scared. Sacred of *them*, whoever *they* were.

At the door, Eve Barnes grabbed his elbow. 'I'm sorry, Coach. He can be very . . .' She trailed off. 'It's been tough since his dad left.'

Malik sensed an opening. 'Can be tough if a young man doesn't have some kind of male presence. A teacher, family friend.'

He waited for her to offer a name, but she simply nodded. 'Thanks for coming over, and getting that signed for Jack.'

'No problem.'

The door closed on him. He stood there for a second, then walked back down the path. As he stepped onto the sidewalk, he heard a squeal as a car parked directly behind his, pulled out at speed and roared off down the street. It was a sedan, dark blue or grey – hard to tell in the fading light of late afternoon. The windows were tinted so he hadn't been able to see the driver.

The only thing he was sure about was that whoever had been sitting inside the car had been watching him.

EIGHTEEN

MALIK KEPT CHECKING HIS REAR-view mirror as he drove home. He was pretty sure that the car that had been parked outside the Barneses' place wasn't the same as the grey car that had been at the stadium. Pretty sure, but not certain.

He jumped as his cell phone rang. It was Kim. He hit the button to answer it, trying to keep his voice light.

'Hey,' she said. 'You coming home for dinner?'

It was one of the fundamental sacraments of their marriage that, wherever possible, he ateat dwith the family in the evening. 'Sorry, got caught up with stuff.'

She must have sensed something from his voice because she asked him, 'You okay?'

He reached up and rubbed his temple. 'Just tired. All this excitement.'

'Tyrone called.'

'Oh, yeah?' said Malik.

'He sounded worried. Said he planned on coming up here next week to see us.' There was a pause. Malik knew what was coming next. You couldn't be married to someone for as long as he had, and sure as hell not a woman as smart as Kim, without her figuring out when something was off.

'Are you going to tell me what's going on?'

Malik sighed. 'Yes. Tonight.' There was silence at the other end of the line. 'Kim?'

'Yes?'

'I love you. You know that, right?'

'Okay, now you're starting to worry me.' He could hear the kids arguing in the background, Landon teasing his little sister about some boy in her class.

Malik's eyes flicked to the rear-view mirror and the empty road behind him. He thought of his own kids, and what he would do if someone was messing with them in the way someone was with Jack Barnes.

He'd see it, he told himself. But what if he didn't? What if he and Kim had split up and he wasn't around them? Or he was totally wrapped up in work to the exclusion of all else? What then? He doubted Kim would let it happen. But what about Eve Barnes? She hadn't seemed like a bad mom. She loved her son – that was obvious.

More questions tumbled around in his mind. He'd read that most abuse went on in families. It was relatives or friends who hurt kids, not strangers skulking around play parks. Most people remained oblivious, either because the perpetrator covered their tracks, or maybe because something in their subconscious shut it out.

What if someone else knew Malik's son or daughter was being preyed on? He'd expect them to tell him. He'd be angry if they said nothing. Above all else, he would want to *know*, however painful or gut-wrenching it was.

In that moment, he knew he was going about this the wrong way. He had been all along. It was obvious what he had to do now. It was staring him right in the face.

'Sweetie,' he said to his wife, 'you go ahead and eat without me. I'll be a little longer. There's something I forgot to do earlier.'

What had been apprehension in his wife's voice was replaced by irritation. 'What did we talk about when you took this job? It was so we could spend more time together as a family.'

'I know, baby. I know. But this is important.'

NINETEEN

E VE BARNES OPENED THE DOOR, a glass of red wine in her hand, her glazed eyes suggesting that, even though he'd left only a half-hour before, this wasn't her first of the evening. 'Coach Shaw?' she said, startled.

'There's something I need to talk to you about. In private.'

Malik followed her into the living room again. 'Jack, could you go tidy your room? I need to talk to your mom,' he said.

The boy's eyes pleaded with him. It was the look Malik had seen in them on the night they had first met. A toxic mix of shame and guilt. It was time to put an end to it, or at least to begin the process. Malik saw it now for what it was: a festering wound that would only grow worse without air and light. Of course Jack didn't want Malik to tell his mom what he'd seen. But Malik knew he had no alternative. To stay silent. To say nothing. To allow whatever was going on to continue. None of those were options.

Eve Barnes wasn't smiling now. She looked worried. She knew something was wrong. Very wrong. And she knew it related to her son.

The boy threw down the games controller, and ran off to his room. There was a loud bang as he slammed the door.

Malik closed his eyes for a moment. When he opened them, Eve was sitting on the couch, the wine glass drained.

The only way to do this, he'd decided, was to start at the beginning. He told her about how he'd driven out to the stadium and how he'd found her son in the showers. By the time he'd got to that part she was sobbing loudly, her body folded in on itself. She had aged by a decade, and Malik knew that the change would stay with her.

As a player, then as a coach, he had realized long ago the power of words to inspire. This was the first time he had seen, really seen, their ability to crush.

She looked up at him. 'I'm glad you told me. It's like, it's . . .' Her words fell away. She swallowed, collecting herself. 'Things make sense now. How he's been acting around me.'

Malik nodded. 'The man he was with? You know who it was, right?'

She swiped at the mascara running down her cheeks with the back of her sleeve. 'I can't believe he would do something like that. He's been like a father to Jack.'

One fucked-up father figure, thought Malik. 'Who has, Eve? Who was there with him?'

'You don't know?' It was only then he realized that he'd told her the man had fled before he'd caught up with him, not that he hadn't seen him.

Malik shook his head. 'I never got a good look at him.'

There was a loud crash, like a window breaking. Eve got up and rushed from the living room. Malik followed her to the back of the house. The door, with its stickers and prominently displayed red and white 'Private! Keep Out!' sign, was closed. Eve tried to open it, but it wouldn't budge. She pounded on it.

'Here,' said Malik, putting a hand on her back.

Eve stood aside as he threw a shoulder against it. The lock flew off, and Malik's momentum carried him into the room. Through the layers of tween detritus, Malik's gaze snapped to the broken window.

Jack Barnes was gone.

He walked across to look at the jagged hole where the glass had been punched out. It crunched under his feet. It had been broken from the outside.

TWENTY

A BREEZE PICKED UP, WHIPPING the drapes into Malik's face. He reached up, pushing them away and stared through the broken window, only to be met by darkness.

'It's not the first time he's run away,' Eve Barnes said. 'That's why I had to put the lock on the window.'

She seemed not to have noticed the floor, or if she had, she hadn't realized what it meant. Malik moved past her, almost tripping on a pile of dirty clothes. 'He didn't run,' he said.

He moved through the house, breaking into a jog, covering the ground fast. Eve was chasing after him. 'What do you mean?'

He didn't have time to stop and explain. He reached the front door, threw it open and ran out onto the porch. For the second time in less than a week, he caught the red tail-lights of a car as it roared down the street. Eve caught up to him. He turned to face her. 'You know where this guy lives?'

She didn't say anything. She still looked to be in shock. Malik grabbed her by the shoulder, trying to snap her out of it.

'He wouldn't have . . . I don't believe that . . .' she stuttered. 'I mean, I've met his wife.'

Lord help me, thought Malik. Had no one ever explained to this woman that being married didn't mean anything when it came to stuff like this? Marriage was just a cover for people, all the better to make sure that kids and their parents lowered their guard.

'Where does he live? You been to his house?'

She nodded.

'Good. You show me,' he said, grabbing her and heading for his car.

He bundled her into the passenger seat, and they took off. He got Eve to dial 911 and hold his cell phone up to his mouth as he drove. She was still far from coherent, in no state to talk to the dispatcher. He had to ask her for details, though.

He glanced at her 'What's the guy's name?'

'Aubrey Becker,' she said.

He was taking a corner as she said it. The wheel slipped through his hands and he almost lost control of the car. He corrected the steering just in time. An oncoming vehicle blared in fury at the narrowly avoided collision.

He lowered his voice. 'Aubrey Becker?' he asked.

'Yes.'

'Yeah, the man's name is Aubrey Becker. B-E-C-K-E-R. No, we didn't see him, but we're fairly sure that's who Jack's with.'

The dispatcher asked for an address. Eve gave it to him, and he passed it on. 'And can you put out a call to all your units to keep an eye out for his car?'

The dispatcher did her best to tell him that he should take Eve Barnes back to her home and wait for a patrol car to arrive. Malik agreed, killed the call and kept driving.

Now he finally understood why everyone had been so cagey. Aubrey Becker wasn't just a respected pillar of the community. He wasn't just wealthy, and one of the biggest donors to the university: he pretty much owned this corner of the state. And he just happened to be the brother of the governor, Tom Becker, who was hotly tipped to be making a run in the next presidential election, with the opinion-poll ratings and the cold, hard cash to stand a good chance of making it all the way to the White House.

TWENTY-ONE

MALIK FOLLOWED EVE'S DIRECTIONS DOWN a narrow country road, with switchbacks and sharp bends that loomed out of the darkness. As he drove, she managed to fill him in on a little of the history. He got the feeling that she was still overwhelmed by the whole thing.

On the one hand, in her gut, she knew that Malik was right. But part of her wanted to be protected from the horror of it. And the best way of protecting herself was to come up with reasons why it couldn't be true. From his own experience, Malik knew that the truth can be a lot harder to take than what you want to believe, but sometimes you can't avoid it. This time the truth had to be faced. No matter how painful.

They pulled up to a set of black gates set into a seven-foot-tall stone wall that ran as far as Malik could see in either direction. A police cruiser was already parked outside, its roll bar sending a red wash splashing across the entrance. A lone state trooper pushed off the side of the cruiser as Malik stopped his car. He seemed casual for a cop who'd just turned up to the scene of a possible child abduction.

Malik tried not to let the paranoia he'd begun to develop get the better of him. Maybe the trooper was relaxed because Jack had already been found.

Malik hit the button to lower his window. 'This is Jack Barnes's mother. We called in that her son was missing.'

'Uh-huh.'

It wasn't a promising start. What the hell was 'uh-huh' supposed to mean? Malik wondered.

'Can we go up to the house?'

The trooper took off his hat. 'And you are?'

'Malik Shaw. I work at the university in Harrisburg.'

Eve leaned over Malik. 'Is my son here or not?'

The trooper ignored her. But his features did soften. 'The NBA player Malik Shaw? Guy that coaches the Wolves?'

Malik tried not to roll his eyes. 'That's me. Now, can we go up? You have people there, right?'

'Yeah, the captain's up there now. Hasn't found the boy, though.'

'I need to find my son,' said Eve. She was bordering on hysterical.

Malik didn't blame her. If it had been Landon, he would already have driven through, whether the gates were open or not.

'Your captain's going to want to talk to Mrs Barnes here in any case.'

That piece of logic seemed to work. 'Yeah, okay.' The trooper turned and waved at a man in a dark blue private-security-guard uniform. The man was about six feet even, 240 pounds, with fair hair that ran to his collar and a three-day beard. He didn't look to Malik like your standard-issue mall-cop type.

The man shrugged, and said something into a walkie-talkie that Malik didn't catch. A few seconds later, the gates began slowly to open.

Driving through them, he had an uneasy feeling. Here they were, looking for a boy presumably abducted by a pedophile, and they were being treated with suspicion. He hadn't liked the look of the guard either, and now he wished he'd asked for a name, or at least that of the company he was working for.

The driveway was long. They drove slowly. On either side open land sloped upward. After a full thirty seconds they breached the top and saw the house. It looked as if a typhoon had picked up an estate from the Hamptons and dumped it there.

Three cars were parked at the front of the sprawling house. Malik pulled up next to them and got out with Eve.

The cops here must have known they were coming because an older guy in a grey suit headed them off as two uniforms spoke to a distressed blonde woman, whom Malik assumed was Becker's wife. She was in her late forties, with perfect hair and makeup, and was clutching to her chest the kind of small, yappy designer dog that Flint, his retriever, hated.

The guy in the grey suit introduced himself as Detective Johanssen from the state's Bureau of Criminal Apprehension. Once the pleasantries were out of the way, he said, 'So, tell me what happened.'

Malik took him through both of his visits with the Barnes family, all the way up to Jack's disappearance.

Johanssen listened patiently. 'I'll need to get all that in a statement from you. Including what you saw at the stadium.'

'No problem,' said Malik, relieved that someone finally seemed to be taking him seriously.

Johanssen took Eve Barnes by the arm. 'We're doing everything we can to find your son. We've issued an amber alert statewide, and if we don't locate him soon we'll widen it.'

'I just want him home,' she said.

Over her shoulder, Malik could see the blonde woman with the dog growing more agitated. She kept glancing at them, and the two cops with her were trying to distract her. 'Is that her?' the blonde lady shouted. 'We're going to sue you. And your son.'

Eve Barnes couldn't help but hear. Anyone within a half-mile radius would have heard. Malik moved in front of Eve. 'Ignore her . . . That his wife?' he asked Johanssen.

'Gretchen Becker,' said the detective, with a nod.

'I mean it,' shouted Gretchen Becker. 'I know what this is. We have money, and you think that if you make up some outrageous story about Aubrey we'll pay you to keep quiet. Well, think again.'

Eve pushed Malik, and began marching toward her. Malik and Johanssen had to race to catch her before the two women went toe to toe.

Behind them a car horn sounded. Everyone stopped and turned, as a grey Volkswagen sedan rolled slowly down the driveway toward them.

Malik froze. His hands bunched into fists. Even without looking at the bumper stickers on the rear, he was almost certain it was the car that had fled the stadium. Next to him, Eve was frozen too.

Johanssen stepped in front of them. 'Let's just stay cool, okay?' He waved over one of the state troopers.

The car rolled to a stop. Malik noted the smoky tint of the windows. The passenger door opened. No one moved. Jack Barnes got out, a hoodie obscuring his face. His right hand was swathed in a thick white bandage.

Letting him get out first was a smart move on the part of whoever was driving. Eve rushed to her son. He stayed motionless and she threw her arms around him, sobbing with relief.

The driver's door opened. As it did so, an SUV raced up behind the sedan, skidding to a halt. The fair-haired security guard leaped out and ran toward Aubrey Becker as he emerged from the grey sedan. As he reached Becker, Malik saw his jacket ride up to reveal a gun holstered on his right hip.

Aubrey Becker looked around at all the assembled people, the cops, his wife, Malik and Eve. He didn't look like a guilty man. He stared at everyone in turn. If anything, he looked pissed. He stood up straight, shoulders back, chest out, chin tilted upward. 'Would someone like to explain to me what the hell is going on?'

No one moved. No one spoke. Malik had expected the cops to rush him and slap on the cuffs, private security guard or not. But they didn't. They just stood there and stared at the man who had just shown up with a twelve-year-old boy in his car.

Malik was the first to move. He nudged Detective Johanssen with his hand. 'What are you standing there for? Aren't you going to arrest this guy?'

Johanssen had the look of a man to whom the idea hadn't yet occurred. 'Coach Shaw, I wouldn't dream of telling you how to do your job. I'd appreciate the same courtesy.'

Malik looked at him. The two state troopers were busy studying the ground, like it held some sort of ancient secret. 'You're kidding me. This is the guy who was with Jack at the stadium.'

'You told me you didn't actually see the person,' Johanssen said.

'It's the same car,' said Malik, pointing at the grey sedan. 'His mom told me he's been "mentoring" the boy as part of some school program.' He lowered his voice to spare Eve the details. 'The kid was butt naked. At midnight. You need me to draw you a picture?' He stopped himself adding 'asshole', but only just.

'We will certainly be talking to everyone involved,' said Johanssen.

'Talking? You should be slapping the cuffs on that goddamn freak.'

Becker wouldn't meet his stare. He tilted his chin to avoid making eye contact with Malik. But the security guard's hand fell to the butt of his handgun. That was enough to make Malik take a step. 'Oh, yeah? You want a piece of me?'

Johanssen got between them. 'Cool it,' he told Malik.

From behind them, Gretchen Becker said, 'Aubrey, would you please tell me what this is about?'

'Yeah, Aubrey,' said Malik. 'Let's hear it.'

Aubrey Becker finally deigned to speak. 'Jack called me. He was in some distress. I found him wandering near his home. He was bleeding. I took him to have his hand attended to. You can speak to the doctor at the Harrisburg emergency room if you don't believe me. Now, I don't know what anyone else thinks happened but that's the truth.'

'And what about the night before the game when you were with him in the goddamn shower?' Malik shouted.

Becker looked at him. 'I have no idea what you're talking about.'

Malik turned to Johanssen. 'What else is he gonna say?' He glanced back at Gretchen Becker. 'Why don't you ask your husband what he's been doing hanging out with a twelve-year-old boy?'

There was a flicker in her eyes. Malik caught it, even if no one else did. Then the calm, Botoxed WASPy mask went back on.

'Am I going to have to call my attorney?' said Becker to Johanssen. It was more challenge than plea.

It was clear to Malik that Aubrey Becker had already decided to butch it out. And who knew what he had said to Jack Barnes while they'd been alone together, or what threats he'd made? And without Jack telling the cops what had happened, where could it go?

The whole thing was playing out right before Malik's eyes, and there wasn't a goddamn thing he could do about it. Johanssen must have been thinking the same thing because the next thing he said was 'Jack? Do you feel able to talk to me?'

TWENTY-TWO

ECKER AND HIS WIFE WERE left at home. Eve Barnes and her son were put into a black-and-white. Johanssen wanted to speak to them further. Malik was left hanging, an uninvited guest. He followed the state troopers back to the station. On the way, he called Kim. He didn't have it in him to tell her on the phone what had happened. Instead he made up a story about one of his young players being in trouble with the cops after some overly exuberant celebrating.

He parked outside the station, walked in and waited. He didn't see Eve Barnes or Jack. After about an hour Johanssen appeared and led him into a room where he ran through what he had seen. He left Laird and the contract out of it. He mentioned Tromso and the missing picture.

When he was done, Johanssen thanked him for his time. 'You did the right thing, Coach Shaw. Absolutely. This is a serious matter.'

'So you're going to arrest him?'

Johanssen looked at him, across the half-empty plastic coffee cups, with bloodhound eyes. 'There hasn't been a complaint.'

Malik sat up straight. 'The kid's terrified. Becker must have threatened him. Or someone else did. I told you he said "they", right?'

Johanssen nodded. 'I'm not going to let this go. I will look into it more, I promise you.'

Malik was going to get nowhere. Yeah, Johanssen and the state police would talk to Becker and his wife, but good luck with that, he thought. There was no way Becker was going to come clean, and even if the wife suspected something had been going on, he doubted she'd risk admitting she was living with a man who preyed on kids.

And Malik hadn't actually seen Becker touching Jack.

He looked at the detective and knew he had lost.

TWENTY-THREE

WHAT ARE YOU TELLING ME, Malik? That you quit? That we move?' said Kim, blowing the heat from her coffee.

Malik sighed. 'Have you been listening to anything I've said? I can't sign that deal. Not now. It would make me as bad as the rest of them.'

It was close to five in the morning. Malik hadn't been to bed. Kim had been up since he'd arrived home in the early hours of the morning. They were in the kitchen. The kids were asleep upstairs. Or maybe not asleep after the way Malik had shouted.

He and Kim rarely fought. Sure there was tension in their marriage. There was tension in any marriage. But never anything like this.

It had been Malik who had pushed to take the job here. There were lots of reasons, some selfish. But one of the big ones had been that, in this slightly more rural part of the country, he'd figured the kids would be a little more isolated from all the crap that passed for American culture. Protecting his kids! The irony wasn't lost on him now.

Kim smoothed her hands over the kitchen table. 'And what if you're wrong?' He started to protest. She cut him off. 'Things like this need proof. That's all the detective was saying. And he was right. You can't ruin someone's life over what you think is going on.'

'The kid's terrified, Kim. That's why he's not saying anything.'

'And how is that our problem?'

He looked at her. It had been amicable up until now. Not anymore. He couldn't believe she'd said that. 'And what if it had been Landon? What if someone found him in a shower with a fully grown man in a deserted locker room at dead of night? Would you just shrug your shoulders like you're doing now? Would it be no big deal?'

She jabbed a finger at him. 'Don't put words in my mouth. I'm not saying that.'

'You might as well be. Ignore it. Forget it happened? What kind of a man would I be if I did that?'

He started to get up.

'Sit down.'

He stalked out. As he walked into the front hallway, their daughter was standing at the top of the stairs. 'Why is everyone shouting, Dad?'

'Ask your mother.'

He hauled open the front door and went to his car. He grabbed the driver's door handle before he clicked off the alarm. It began to squall loudly. He jabbed at the button, and finally managed to stop the damn thing. Kim was at the front door, still in her robe. 'Malik, where are you going?'

He ignored her, got in, slammed the door and reversed fast out of the driveway. As he put the car into drive and hit the gas, he saw the old lady who lived next door, Mrs Henshall, staring at him from a gap in her drapes.

'The hell with you too,' he muttered.

TWENTY-FOUR

MALIK TURNED THE DODGE PICK-UP onto Wolf Road and pulled into the stadium parking lot. It was still before six in the morning. There was a low mist on the ground, and a damp chill in the air. He was still wearing the clothes he'd put on yesterday morning, and he had yet to sleep. He was facing an impossible choice. He had to do something, but he wasn't sure what. He was hoping the court, a hoop and a basketball could give him an answer, as it had done before.

The janitor, an elderly guy who had worked the job forever, had just opened the place up. He greeted Malik with a grunt as he pushed through the side door, then went back to his coffee and newspaper. Malik thought of asking him about Becker, how often he'd seen him here, but decided against it.

He grabbed a couple of balls from a rack, and headed out onto the court. He stood at the free throw line and bounced the ball three times. He took his shot. It sailed in a perfect arc. He closed his eyes as it whooshed though the net. He retrieved the ball, and did it again, finding a rhythm, losing himself in the simple series of actions.

Slowly, his mind cleared. He tried to put some distance between himself and the events of the past few days. He did his best to imagine what advice he would give someone who came to him and told him what he had told Kim.

A door at the other end of the court creaked open. Malik didn't look around. He assumed it was the janitor doing his rounds. He heard footsteps. He took his next shot. It hit the back board and bounced off the rim. As he went to get the ball, he saw the fair-haired security guard from Becker's place, standing on the half court line.

Malik's eyes went to the gun holstered at the man's right side. The guy smiled at him. Fuck you, thought Malik, and turned away. Let him shoot me in the back if he wants, he thought. He'd always joked that he wanted to die on a basketball court.

He concentrated hard, lined up his throw. This time he made it. A perfect throw from three-point land. He picked up the ball and only then did he turn back to the guard.

Malik didn't use bad language. He fined players who cussed. But this situation took him back to his old life as a kid.

'What the hell you want?' he said, throwing the ball hard toward the guy.

He caught it. As long as he held it with both hands, he couldn't go for his gun. Malik advanced on him. 'I asked you a question.'

'I'm not here to give you a hard time, Coach Shaw,' he said.

'That so?' said Malik.

'The boy's not going to say anything,' he said, 'because there's nothing to say. You got the wrong idea. That's all.'

Malik was up close and in his face. 'Lots of people telling me that.'

'Then maybe they have a point. Look, Coach, you have a sweet deal here.' The guy looked around. 'Big fish in a small pond. Plenty of cash. Security. Nice place to raise a family. You got two kids, right?'

'Leave my family out of this.'

As soon as Malik said it, he knew he had made a mistake. Something registered on the other's face. He smirked, like he'd been probing for a chink in Malik's armor and had just located it.

'You keep pushing, and someone's going to get hurt, Coach. Take my advice. Forget about Jack Barnes and Mr Becker.'

Malik's hand shot up and grabbed the guy's throat. Malik had a strong grip and long fingers. He started to squeeze. 'Listen to me, motherfucker. This here, this court, this is my turf. You don't tell me what to do.'

The guard stared at him. He wasn't as certain as he'd been a few seconds before. Cutting off someone's oxygen would do that.

'You get me?' Malik said.

He relaxed his grip enough that the guy could speak. 'I get you.'

Malik let go. The man coughed and rubbed at his throat. He stepped back. 'Don't say you weren't warned, Coach.'

'I got my press conference in the morning. How about we let the good citizens decide if there's anything that should concern them about what I saw? How about that, huh?'

The guy's eyes widened a fraction.

'Oh, I got your attention now, do I?' said Malik.

'Don't say you weren't warned,' the security guard said. He turned and walked back to the doors.

TWENTY-FIVE

THE MAN BEHIND THE COUNTER greeted Malik with a grin. 'Hey, Coach, didn't know you were much of a hunting man.' Malik's gaze wandered around the firearms section of the sporting-goods store on Harrisburg's main street. He had already checked the appropriate laws. To buy a handgun, which was what he wanted, he'd need to apply for a permit. That would take a little time, and he'd have to go through the cops, which he didn't want. But there was nothing to stop him buying a shotgun and taking it home today.

Malik glanced back at the guy behind the counter. He'd always hated guns. He'd seen, up close, too many times what they could do to human beings. 'Figured I'd try to blend in around here.'

The guy chuckled. 'Good enough. So, what you looking for?'

'Something for home security,' said Malik. He caught the look in the guy's eyes. 'I was thinking maybe a shotgun. Pump-action.'

'Good choice. Nothing cools someone trying to break in like the sound of one of those. Here.' He grabbed a shotgun from the wall behind him. 'See how this feels.'

A little later Malik walked out of the store with the gun, and enough ammunition to hold a small siege. He placed it all in the trunk of his car. He'd thought that owning the gun would make him feel better. It didn't. If anything it left him more unsettled. *How the hell had he got from a man who hated guns to a guy who was loading up on ammo?*

On the drive home, his cell phone rang. It was Kim. When he answered, she didn't say anything. 'We should stay,' he said.

He heard something approaching a sigh of relief. 'Thank you,' she said.

'But I can't let this – this thing with the boy go. I just can't.'

'I don't understand.'

He told her what he planned to say at the press conference. 'At least then it'll be out in the open. I won't mention names. The media will do the rest.'

'That's as good as quitting.'

'They can fire me, but I won't quit.'

He heard his wife sigh again, a familiar sound to a man who'd been married as long as he had. 'It's the same thing,' she said.

'Maybe it is. But I have to do what's right.'

'You're tired. Listen, why don't you take some more time to think this through? If you want to do it, I'll stand by you. But this isn't something you should rush into, Malik.' There was a pause. 'And what are you even going to say?'

Malik could feel himself starting to get angry. 'Not you too, Kim. If there was nothing going on with that kid and Becker, why is everyone so desperate to shut me up? I even had some private security guy of his try to scare me off earlier.'

'Wait. What?'

'I went to shoot some hoops. He showed up and tried to warn me off.'

There was a worrying silence. 'What did he look like?'

'Why?' said Malik, pressing down on the gas pedal.

'Just tell me what he looked like.'

The way she said it really had him worried now. 'Kim?'

'Just tell me!' she snapped.

'Uh, about six feet even. White. Blue eyes. Fair hair. Collar-length, kinda scruffy. Now why are you asking?'

'Because there was someone who looked just like that here about a half-hour ago.'

A car pulled out in front of Malik. He braked and swerved hard as it blared its horn. He pressed down harder on the gas pedal, desperate to get home, the shotgun in the trunk feeling more like a good decision with every second that passed.

'What did he want?' he asked his wife.

'Just asked if you were home. He was real casual. Friendly. Asked about me and the kids. I assumed you knew him.'

'Never seen him until last night. Listen, I'm five minutes away. Don't answer the door. Not to anyone. He comes back, call nine-one-one.'

Six minutes later, Malik roared into the driveway. Kim's car was there. He got out, ignored the elderly neighbor's curtain twitching – let her look – and popped the trunk. He grabbed the shotgun, with a couple of boxes of shells, and headed to the front door. He unlocked it, and walked into the hallway.

Kim came out of the kitchen carrying a red mug. She froze and let out a shriek when she saw the gun, coffee sloshing over the side of the mug. She stopped, patting her chest with one hand. 'I'm sorry. I saw the gun before I realized it was you and . . .'

He'd expected her to go crazy at his having brought a firearm into their home. She hated them too – she hadn't even let Landon play with toy guns when he'd been small.

'Dad?'

Katy was standing at the top of the stairs. She was still in her pajamas, with a robe over them.

'She wasn't feeling well so I let her skip camp,' Kim told him.

'Why do you have a gun?' Katy asked.

Malik had been planning to have this talk at dinner, once he'd had a shower and a few hours' sleep. When his head was clear.

'We're gonna talk about that later, sweetie. Okay?'

Her frown said it was far from okay.

Kim was wearing the same expression as she said quietly, 'We should have talked about this first.'

Malik held up his hand. 'Not now, Kim.'

It was a stupid gesture to make under the circumstances. Kim did not respond well to being blown off, or being told what to do. She never had. She was a strong woman who didn't tolerate crap, which was partly why Malik had fallen for her.

Her hands went to her hips, as sure a sign of danger as a cobra rearing. 'Katy, go to your room.'

'But I—'

'Now!'

Katy retreated. The slam of her bedroom door registered her protest at her parents excluding her.

'I'm sorry. I didn't mean to cut you off like that,' Malik said.

'So why do you have a gun?' she asked.

'It's a precaution, Kim. That's all.'

'You know I won't have one in my house. What if Landon decides to start messing around with it?'

'He won't. I'll speak to them both. Get a gun safe, or a lock, or something.'

She took a step back. 'So you're going to go through with it? At the press conference.'

He felt despair fold over him. Of all people, he was hoping that Kim would understand. He couldn't pretend that none of this had happened. He just couldn't. It would go against everything he believed in, and would be a betrayal of everything he had taught his players and the young people he came into contact with every day.

Tell the truth. Stand up for what you believe in. Set an example to others by standing up for those who can't stand up for themselves. He had always told himself they weren't just words. But if he stayed silent, that was exactly what they would be.

'Yes,' he said to his wife. 'I'm going to go through with it.'

TWENTY-SIX

ELEANOR HENSHALL WAS WOKEN BY Flint scratching about on her front lawn. It was early, a little after six. Like a lot of retirees, she was cursed by early waking. She was usually alert by five thirty. She had just made coffee and wandered into her living room when she saw the dog through the window. She walked into her hallway, opened the front door and looked around for Mr Shaw or one of the kids. The Shaws never let the dog roam freely. Although it was a quiet street, there was still too much traffic and the dog had no road sense.

In her robe and slippers, Eleanor stepped out and called Flint to her. Like most golden retrievers it was usually very friendly. She had always thought of them as the canine equivalent of dolphins. This morning was the exception. The dog hunched its shoulders, lowered its head and let out a low growl.

Eleanor went inside, closed the door, grabbed her phone from the cradle and rang the Shaw home. It diverted to voicemail. She debated calling the local police but felt ridiculous. What was she going to tell them? That the neighbor's dog was outside, acting strangely?

She went into her bedroom, dressed quickly and went back outside. The dog was gone. She walked toward her neighbors' house. Surely there would be some rational explanation.

Eleanor had already been a fixture by the time Malik and his family had moved in. They had been good neighbors, kind, polite and helpful, without being over-friendly. Kim, the wife, always invited her over during the holidays, if she wasn't visiting her daughter in North Carolina, and Malik mowed her lawn, or sent his son, Landon, to do the job. The daughter, Katy, was a darling, always smiling, just the sweetest girl.

To Eleanor, they were the picture-perfect American family. That said, over the past few days she had noticed Malik was a little bit off. Where he would always give her a wave or offer her a ride if he passed her in his car, there had been a couple of occasions recently when he had driven straight past her without even a wave. She had also heard at least one loud argument between him and Kim. It had ended with Kim slamming out of the house, getting into the little sports car Malik had bought her for her last birthday, and speeding away. Eleanor had dismissed it all. Every family had its rough patches.

As she approached the front of the Shaws' house, nothing seemed out of place. She rang the bell and waited, starting to feel foolish. The dog had probably slipped out of the backyard and back in by now. She doubted they were even awake. She waited a full minute. No one came. She couldn't see if the family's cars were in the double garage because the doors were closed.

She rang the bell one more time. This time she held it for a few seconds longer. Still no one appeared. She stepped back onto the lawn and looked up. The blinds were still closed. She looked to her right. The side gate was open. That explained the dog's escape.

Eleanor went through the gate and walked down the side of the house into the backyard. Nothing seemed out of place here either.

'Hello?' she called.

No one answered. Normally she would never have dared walk into a house uninvited. But something was wrong. She just knew.

"Hello?" she called again taking a few more steps inside. That was when she noticed a spot of blood on the floor. It wasn't large, more of a smear than anything, but it reinforced her sense that things were not as they should be.

Eleanor patted her pockets for her cell phone. She usually carried it with her but she had left it at home. She had been going next door for just a few minutes.

That was when she heard the whir of the garage door. Without thinking, she did something that would leave her trembling at the thought of how stupid she'd been, even months after. She turned and moved back toward the front of the house to see who it was.

Thankfully, she wasn't as fast as she'd been before her hip surgery the previous year. As she made it to the side gate, Malik Shaw's pick-up was pulling out of the garage, a man alone in the driver's seat. He was wearing a red windcheater, just like Malik always wore and had a dark ball cap pulled down low. He must have seen her in the rear-view because he sped up. The Dodge pick-up took off with a squeal of rubber. Eleanor walked back round and went into the house, following her instincts. She found them upstairs.

Sixty seconds later, her stomach lurching, she was calling 911. Four minutes after that the first patrol officer had arrived. Many more followed, along with detectives, a criminalist, the medical examiner and three ambulances, one for each slain member of the perfect family next door. The only person they couldn't find was Malik.

PART TWO

TWENTY-SEVEN

T HE BLACK AUDI PULLED UP outside Joanna's Diner on the main
street in Harrisburg. The driver's door opened, and Ty Johnson
got out. He stood there for a moment, scoping out the main
street, bloodshot eyes that had shed some tears shielded by dark wrap-
around glasses. He was dressed for more than the cold: he was dressed for
war.

The pockets on the right side of his jacket were weighed down with
coins to conceal the SIG Sauer 229 holstered on his hip.

His first task was to find Malik before the cops did. Then he planned on
establishing the truth of what had happened here in Harrisburg, and hold
whoever was responsible to account for the death of Kimberley Shaw, and
the two children, Landon and Katy – by whatever means it took. And, to
make a tough gig even tougher, he knew that he had to make sure that a
young boy called Jack Barnes and his mother weren't added to the list of
casualties.

Passers-by skirted him as he stood, boots planted, on the sidewalk. Even
in a good mood, Ty had an intimidating presence that went far beyond his
size. Right now he was a long way from a good mood.

He pushed through the doors of the diner. The line of people waiting to
be seated was ten deep. A guy with a New York accent, most likely some

kind of media type, was busy haranguing an exhausted hostess. Looking at her, Ty figured she was doing the job to pay her way through college. She seemed close to tears as the guy continued his tirade.

'We have been waiting here for fifteen minutes.'

'I understand that, sir. You're on the list. As soon as we have a free table, I can seat you.'

'Fifteen minutes,' the guy said, flashing his fingers at her, as if she struggled with the concept of basic math.

Ty clamped a hand on the guy's shoulder, and squeezed hard enough for it to be uncomfortable. He turned his head. Ty pulled his shades down his nose and made eye contact. If there was one thing Ty hated it was self-entitled assholes, like this one, who treated people doing a job for a tenth of what they themselves made as second-class citizens. 'You're not on the Upper East Side anymore, Toto. Give those fingers of yours a break before I snap them off.'

The guy started to reply, then thought better of it. His mouth opened and closed. Behind them an attractive blonde woman did a bad job at hiding her smirk. The guy turned to the people he was with. 'This is bullshit. Let's go somewhere else.'

As they left, the blonde woman, falling in behind them, made eye contact with Ty. 'Who are you with? I mean, which organization?'

'I'm freelance,' he told her.

'Well, see you around,' she said, with a broad smile.

As she hustled back out, Ty looked around for the person he was due to meet. He spotted him sitting by himself at the counter, sipping a cup of coffee while tapping emails into a tablet computer. He was a barrel-chested Hispanic guy in his early fifties, a private detective out of Minneapolis called Luis Salas that Ty's partner, Ryan Lock, had hired to do some preliminary digging as soon as Ty had heard about the killings.

He saw Ty, slid ten bucks over the counter to cover his check, got up and walked over to him. 'Let's talk outside,' he said.

'Works for me,' said Ty, following him through the press of bodies to the door.

They hung a left, heading toward the main college campus. 'So, what you got?' Ty asked Salas, as he scanned the street to make sure they weren't being watched.

'Not much beyond what's been hitting the headlines. The cops only have the one suspect, and that's your boy.'

'What they going on?' said Ty.

'Gun used was a pump-action shotgun that he'd just purchased from a local sporting-goods store.'

'They have it?'

'Oh, yeah,' said Salas. 'His prints are all over it.'

That didn't mean much, thought Ty. Because of TV shows, people got all kinds of excited over forensics, but the truth was that there was a lot of room for interpretation. If Malik had bought the gun, his prints would have been all over it. Someone else had picked it up and used it because they'd wanted to make it look like Malik was responsible for the killings. They would have worn gloves. That meant only one set of prints.

'How'd it go down?' Ty asked, bracing himself for the answer.

Salas looked at him. 'You sure you're ready to hear this?'

Ty nodded.

'They were lined up and taken out one by one. Execution style, back of the head. Probably tied up first. They didn't stand a chance..'

Ty swallowed hard. 'Signs of a struggle?'

'Plenty,' said Salas. 'Lots of blood from her.'

'What else?'

'Clincher as far as the cops see it is a neighbor. A Mrs Henshall. Morning after the murders she saw the family dog roaming about. Went to check it out, found the bodies. Seconds later Malik roars out of the garage at top speed. She's pretty definite. Oh, and she said that she'd heard raised voices a couple of times in the days leading up to it. Him and his wife going at it. Reason she noted it was that they were such a quiet family. Never had a cross word before the past week or so.'

Ty chewed it over. It did sound textbook. Domestic tension, hubby goes out, buys a gun and does something crazy. It happened. Of course, they knew there was a lot more to it, which Lock had kept from Salas. He just wanted the PI to look at the bare bones.

'You speak to her?'

'Nope. This is all from the local police.'

'They say anything else? Were they aware of anything else going on with Malik? Threats to the family? Someone he might have had a run-in with?'

Salas stopped and looked at him. 'Didn't say anything like that. Why'd you ask?'

A patrol car rolled past them, the cop in the passenger seat taking a long look before it sped away. Ty noted the markings were those of the campus police department.

Ty traced the car down the street. 'What's the deal with the college police? Don't they have a town police department to cover off campus?'

'They're pretty much one and the same. College has ten or so bodies, plus support staff, the town has four. Plus the college cops here are sanctioned state wide.'

'Off-duty powers?' Ty asked. Often university cops who had the power of arrest could only exercise it when they were on duty.

'Same as regular officers. Twenty-four/seven.'

There was something that didn't fit, thought Ty. His knowledge of university and college law enforcement was fairly superficial, but one thing stood out. Presence of the abnormal, he thought. One of the two things Lock had taught him to seek out in any situation, along with the absence of the normal.

He chose not to ask Salas about it. 'Got you,' he said. 'Thanks for your help.'

Salas seemed to study him for a moment. 'Can I ask you something?'

'Sure,' said Ty.

'You think Shaw didn't do it. How come? Because he's your friend? I don't mean to pry, but people can do crazy things, including folks you think you know.'

Ty faced him. 'We'll see.'

TWENTY-EIGHT

WITH HER EYES ON TY, the young blonde woman stood on the sidewalk and hit the call button on her cell. 'Yes,' she said. 'It's definitely him. Yeah, Johnson, the marine.'

She waited for the person at the other end of the line to finish talking. Then she said, 'No, let's wait, and see what he does.'

TWENTY-NINE

A LOW GREY SKY HUNG above the campus buildings, the weather matching the leaden atmosphere of gloom. Students stood around in small groups or walked hurriedly between buildings, heads down. Looking around, Ty could already imagine how easy it would be to catch cabin fever up here. Malik, the ultimate big man on campus, must have been under the microscope the whole time.

A news crew had set up outside the chancellor's office, a female reporter delivering her commentary straight to camera. She fiddled with her earpiece, her expression sufficiently somber. Ty tuned in long enough to hear her spout the agreed line being fed by the authorities.

'That's correct, Joe,' she said. 'The authorities are not seeking anyone else in connection with this horrific crime. Former NBA player Malik Shaw is the man everyone here is looking for. He's believed to be armed and dangerous, and members of the public are warned not to approach him if they see him.'

Ty checked his campus map. The main college covered a lot of ground, almost seventy acres in total. He got his bearings and hung a right toward the building where Malik and the rest of the athletic-department staff had their offices. He pushed through the glass doors and into the lobby. Before he could reach the reception desk, a voice called to him,

'Hey, buddy, can I help you?'

Ty turned to find a doughy-looking security guard peering at him. From what he'd seen of the town so far, there was a lot of doughy to go around. Ty figured it must be the long winters – all people had to do was eat.

'Excuse me?' he said.

The guard waddled over to him. 'What's your business here, sir? We're not allowing anybody who isn't faculty, staff or student onto campus right now.'

Ty stared at him, a picture of innocence. It was a tough look for Ty to pull off, but he gave it his best shot. 'Why's that?'

The guard sighed. 'Are you a member of faculty or staff? Because you sure aren't here as a student.'

Ty glanced around. 'Brother, I don't know what your deal is, but your little college here is losing points with me fast. I get personally invited up here to take a tour for my son, and I have to deal with this bullshit. You know how many offers this kid has? Florida State. Texas Tech. Duke. Division-one schools. I only came up here as a courtesy to Coach Shaw. We have friends in common. Now, why don't you and your cracker ass go find him for me before I really lose my temper?'

The guard wilted. 'Coach Shaw?'

'That's what I said, motherfucker. You know who Coach Shaw is, right – Malik Shaw? What? You want me to show you a picture of the man?'

The security guard blinked. 'You don't know?'

'Know what? I know you're wasting my goddamn time, that's what I know. Now are you going to let the coach know that I'm here?'

'Sir, I'm afraid Coach Shaw isn't available. He's . . .'

Ty kept scowling as the guard struggled to find the words.

'Perhaps if you go speak to that lady over there,' he said eventually, indicating the receptionist. 'She'll be able to find someone from his staff.'

'Oh, okay. So it's fine that I'm here now?' Ty said. 'I'm not breaking any rules being on your precious campus?'

'No, sir. If you ask at Reception, I'm sure they'll be able to assist you.'

With a final growl in the guard's direction, Ty headed over to the desk. He decided to spare the lady behind the desk any embarrassment and asked her to see if one of the coaching staff was available to speak to him.

As she made the call, he continued to stare at the guard until it became too much for the guy and he decided to check the outside of the building for potential intruders. A minute later, a young guy dressed in tan pants and a blue polo shirt with the college crest appeared from a side door.

Ty went over to him quickly so they were out of earshot of anyone else hanging out in the foyer.

'Sandy said you're here to see Coach Shaw about your son.'

Ty clamped a giant hand on the assistant's shoulder, and started walking him out of the foyer toward the door he'd appeared through. 'What's your name?'

'Mike Browne.'

'Okay, Mike, here's the deal. I'm an old friend of Malik's. How long you work with him?'

'Since he started last year.'

'You think he did this?'

Ty watched the young man carefully. Any hesitation on his part would give him the true answer.

'No, sir, I don't. I didn't meet his family much, but I know he loved them.'

'Good. Me either. Now I need to find him, because if I don't he ain't going to make it to a cell, never mind trial. And if that happens this town is going to be in big trouble. So I'm going to need you to help me.'

They pushed through the door into a long corridor. 'Where's your office, Mike?'

'Uh, just here,' he said. He opened the door, and they walked in.

'Malik told me about you before all this stuff blew up,' said Ty, bullshitting furiously.

'Really?'

'Oh, yeah. He said you were his great hope on the coaching side. Now, listen, I want to find out what happened. If it turns out it was Malik, I'll turn him in myself. But I need to know if I can trust you to keep this between us.'

'I guess. I mean, I don't believe Coach could have done something like that. Although he did seem pretty stressed out, even after we won the championship.'

Ty took a chair, turned it around and sat down. 'He say why?'

Mike looked up at the ceiling, obviously trying to dredge his memory. 'No, he didn't.'

Ty considered telling him what he knew, but decided against it – at least for now. 'You know if he discussed any of his problems with anyone else here? Another coach, maybe?'

'Not that I know of. Mind if I ask you something?'

'Go ahead,' said Ty.

'If Coach Shaw didn't hurt his family, then who did?'

'That's what we need to find out. Before anyone else gets hurt.'

THIRTY

MALIK CREPT THROUGH THE WOODS at the rear of the house. He'd stayed away from the place. Even now he wasn't sure he was ready to go back inside. The bodies would be gone, but the images in his head were still there.

He clambered across the fence and dropped down into the yard. Katy's bike was still out there, propped against the back of the house, gently rusting in the rain, never to be ridden again. He choked at the sight of it. He'd bought it for her two Christmases ago, and for the first few months she had ridden it everywhere. Or everywhere he and Kim had allowed. She had wanted to ride it to school, but Malik had been worried about the traffic. It was the eternal parental dilemma. Knowing you had to let your kids learn how to function in the world, but not wanting to see them get hurt. He had relented in the end. But even then he had found himself following her in the car for the first week, albeit at a discreet distance.

And now this. Seeing her had been the worst of it. Katy had always been a daddy's girl, right from the get-go.

He dug into the pockets of his jeans and pulled out his keys. He walked to the back door and peered inside. The kitchen betrayed nothing of what had happened. Apart from a cereal bowl on the table next to a half-empty gallon container of milk, everything was neat and tidy, just as Kim had left it before she had gone to bed. Satisfied that the place was empty, he unlocked the door and stepped inside.

He suddenly remembered the alarm. He listen for its chirp, but was met by silence. The cops hadn't reset it. Why would they? There was no one left for the alarm to alert to danger.

He stood in the kitchen for a moment, then walked across to the refrigerator. Katy's last report card was still tacked up. He reached out to touch her name, and that was when he lost it.

Malik dropped to his knees. Why his family? Why not kill him and leave them? It was more than he could take, a burden too heavy for one man to bear. His body shuddered with the force of what he felt. He rubbed his eyes, the side of his hands chafing against a three-day-old beard.

Minutes passed. Finally, he grabbed the kitchen table, and hauled himself to his feet, no longer sure why he had come back. The only reason he could think of was that he had nowhere else to go. He wasn't going to turn himself in so that they could railroad him and end any search for who had done this. He knew that much.

He grabbed a clean glass from the dishwasher, filled it with water and drank it. He put the glass down and walked into the hallway. He took a moment to look at the family pictures arranged on a side table. It still seemed surreal to think that they were gone. His beautiful family, the people who mattered more to him than anything else. And for what? Because he had gone on some crusade for someone else's child.

No, he told himself. He couldn't afford to think like that. He had done the right thing.

He took the final few steps to the bottom of the staircase. He could see bloody footprints on the treads, barely dried. It took everything he had to climb them, stepping on his family's blood as he went.

THIRTY-ONE

T Y PARKED HIS CAR FIVE hundred yards from the Shaw house and got out. He didn't want to announce his arrival, or have any of the neighbors link him directly to the car. Plus he knew from years of experience that you saw more on foot than you did from a car.

The homes were detached, single-family dwellings, neatly kept, and well maintained with large front yards. Almost all had a double garage or a carport. The sidewalks were clean. He doubted that these streets had ever seen a single piece of graffiti, never mind a triple homicide. As he turned from Buffalo Drive into the Shaws' street, he stopped and listened.

All he could hear was the occasional chirp of a bird and the odd lone vehicle. There were no main roads within earshot, no industrial plants, no major commercial area to attract a lot of traffic. The only people coming through this part of town would be those who lived here.

He walked down the street, checking off the numbers. He reached the house of the lady who had made the original call to the cops. A dog barked as he walked up the path. He took off his shades and put them into his pocket. He heard a woman shushing the dog, then an internal door close. Finally, the front door opened.

'Mrs Henshall?'

She studied him through a gap in the door. He didn't blame her for being wary.

'My name is Tyrone Johnson. I'm looking into what happened at the Shaw family residence. I understand you were the first person to call it in.'

'Are you from the police department?' she asked him.

'No, ma'am,' he said. 'I'm working in a private capacity for a friend of the family.'

She seemed hesitant.

'It's just a few simple questions. I promise I won't take up too much of your time.'

'Time's not a problem. I'm retired. I have all the time in the world.' Behind her he could hear the dog barking. The door opened. 'Come in.'

'Thank you.' He walked into the neat-as-a-pin hallway. The dog's barking grew louder and more insistent.

'Their dog,' she said. 'I didn't want the pound to take him. In case, you know. It might be difficult to rehome him if people knew whom he'd belonged to.'

'That's very good of you.'

'He's a little on edge.'

'I'm fine with dogs,' said Ty.

She opened the door, and the retriever bounded out. He stopped when he saw Ty, launched himself toward him in an excited frenzy of tail wagging, then began to jump at him, licking his hand and whimpering with happiness.

'My,' said Eleanor Henshall, 'I've never seen him greet anyone like that.'

Ty shrugged. 'I have a way with dogs, I guess.'

'Well, it's nice to see him so happy. Poor thing. Poor all of them. Can I get you anything, Mr Johnson?'

'No, thank you.'

He followed her and the dog into the living room. The TV was on. Some kind of morning talk show. If Ty watched an hour of TV a day that was a lot. Eleanor clicked it off and they sat down. The dog sat next to him, shouldering against Ty's leg.

'Who did you say you were working for?' she asked him.

'A childhood friend of Mr Shaw's. He wants to locate him before anyone else comes to harm. And, of course, to establish what happened.'

Her eyes narrowed, and he thought he might have lost her. After all, Malik was the man responsible for slaughtering his family, according to everyone here.

'You don't think he did it?' she asked.

'Not from what I've been told about him, no, ma'am,' said Ty.

She took a deep breath. 'Thank goodness for that. Neither do I.'

That was not what Ty had expected to hear. 'You don't? But didn't you tell the police you saw him driving away from the house?'

She stiffened. 'I said I thought it was him. I couldn't be sure. It was definitely his car. Hundred per cent. And it probably was him . . .' She tailed off.

'I'm sensing a "but".'

She shook her head. 'It's just . . . he adored those kids. And his wife. I'd been hearing some arguments between them over the past week, so maybe they had problems, but kill them? I just can't believe it. I don't know. Maybe I'm just a naïve old woman.'

This was good. But he needed specifics. 'Did you hear what the arguments were about?'

'I thought maybe the kids. I don't know. I tried not to listen. I didn't want to be one of *those* neighbors.'

'And the night they were killed? What did you hear then?'

'I didn't hear anything. Are you sure I can't get you some coffee, Mr Johnson?'

'No, thank you, ma'am. You didn't hear anything? Nothing at all?'

She pointed at the dog, who had lain down at Ty's feet. 'First thing I heard was him barking.'

She was telling the truth, Ty was sure of it. 'Do you take anything to help you sleep, Mrs Henshall? Or wear earplugs? I mean, if there had been a noise, would you have heard it, or might you have slept straight through?'

'Oh, no. I'm a very light sleeper. When I sleep at all. Old age.'

Twenty minutes later, Eleanor Henshall walked him to the door. Ty thanked her for her time. Not that he'd had any doubt about Malik's innocence, but if he had, talking to Eleanor would have laid it to rest.

His conversation with her had left him with fresh questions, though. A shotgun made one hell of a noise. And Eleanor Henshall was a light sleeper.

That meant there was a more than even chance that the cops who had lied about everything else were also lying about how Kim Shaw and the two kids had been killed, as well as who had done it.

THIRTY-TWO

TY WAITED UNTIL ELEANOR HENSHALL had retreated into her house, then doubled back to the Shaw home. He walked to the rear of the property, stepped back and took a look. The upstairs blinds were still drawn, the windows closed. He walked to the back door, ready to force it. He turned the handle and met no resistance.

His hand fell to the butt of his SIG Sauer 226. He eased the door open, and slowly stepped inside. It wasn't unknown for crime scenes to be left unsecured, especially once forensics had been done. It was rare, but it happened. Something told him that this wasn't one of those times. Someone had either been here to take a look, or to pilfer from the dead.

Or they were still here.

He stood in the kitchen, staying close to the wall, and listened. His eye fell to the dishwasher. He crossed to it, weapon still in hand. The contents were clean and dry. Apart from a solitary water glass that was still wet.

He pushed off toward the door that led into the hallway, the SIG punched out in front of him. The hallway was empty. He kept moving. He checked the living room and the family room. Here, things looked undisturbed – as far as Ty could tell when there had been two kids in the house. He looked for open drawers, or upturned cushions, signs of someone searching for something. He came up empty.

Still, it was good to see it all for himself. Salas had given a good run-down of what the cops were saying, but he hadn't been able to access any of the paperwork. In any case, crime scenes were there to be absorbed. The subconscious worked on them as well as the conscious. You filed away details that you were barely aware of seeing. Things that seemed, to the conscious mind, to hold no significance. That was why, despite the wonders of modern science, there was still an art to deciphering what a crime scene revealed.

He moved back out into the hallway and started up the stairs. He was hyper-alert. You were rarely more vulnerable than when you were climbing a flight of open stairs. There were too many angles to cover. It wasn't a task for one man. If someone popped out, and they were armed, you just had to hope they couldn't shoot for shit.

He noted the bloody footprints as he skirted them. He made it to the top of the stairs. He checked the bedrooms, bracing himself for the horror that each might contain. The last bedroom he checked was the master, the one occupied by Malik and Kim Shaw.

This was the room that demanded the most attention. With each minute that passed he grew angrier. The rage built up until he couldn't take it anymore. He had to get out for some fresh air. There was no art needed here. No special discernment. It was all laid out in front of you, as straightforward as multiple homicides got, which was a tall claim given the lack of eyewitnesses.

He walked back through the rooms, and took some snaps with the camera of his cell phone. He started out wide, then moved in closer. He wanted evidence. They would need it, and a whole lot more. This house told a story, all right. It was a story that swooped right out of the front door, chased through the streets of Harrisburg, and whistled slam-bang into the police department.

As he placed his left foot on the second to last tread, he heard a noise from the kitchen. Ty jumped down into the hallway and ran. The SIG raised in a modified Weaver stance, he swung into the kitchen. Through the window that overlooked the yard, he saw a man's legs piston furiously in the air as he raced to the back of the property.

Bursting through the door, Ty took off after him. The legs disappeared over the fence, and they were off and running. Ty took the fence at speed, hands grasping the top. He hauled himself over. It was a hell of a lot harder than the person he was chasing was making it look. As he pulled himself up, he caught sight of the man booking it through the trees on the other side. He was fast, way faster than Ty.

His speed was no surprise to Ty. Even retired pro basketball players could outrun most folks. He stopped and shouted after Malik. But Malik either couldn't hear him, or was just too damn scared to register who he was.

After what Ty had seen back at the house, he didn't blame him. Who the hell knew the state of Malik's mind right now? If the roles had been reversed, and Ty was being pursued, he wouldn't have stopped running until he'd fallen down from exhaustion. At least he knew his friend was alive. He turned and started back toward the house.

THIRTY-THREE

TY STOOD IN THE MASTER bedroom and stared at the blood on the back wall. There were three main areas of spatter. All three patches were skeletonized – the blood drying to the point where it had begun to flake, leaving a ghost image of the outer circumference as the only clue to the original spread. The stippling was clear evidence of the use of a firearm.

The first two spatters were large, perhaps a foot or more in diameter. The third, the blood from the head shot that would have killed little Katy Shaw, was less than a foot in diameter. Smaller head, less blood. None of it was rocket science, which was what made the police line that had been fed to Salas all the stranger.

The height from the floor to the spatters were also different. The smaller spatter was lower, maybe three feet up the wall. The other two were four and a half to five from the floor. Three neat little circles marked where each round had passed through and into the wall. The blood patterns on the cream carpet were messier, less easy to read. Ty prodded at the first major area of blood with the toe of his boot.

The patterns didn't take a forensic expert to analyze. All three had been kneeling down, facing the wall. Going by the lack of handprints they had probably had their hands tied, likely in front of them, from the lack of the smear that would have been left if they had fallen forward, which they almost certainly had.

Ty stepped back into the doorway, and mimed the likely actions of the shooter.

The killer, or killers, must have lined them up one by one. He had already had them trussed by the time he'd got them here. He had made them kneel against the wall, then gone along the line, working fast so they were still absorbing the shock before it was their turn.

There hadn't been any shotgun involved. This had been up close and personal, with a handgun. And it wasn't a murder scene, domestic or otherwise. The bedroom had been a place of execution.

THIRTY-FOUR

TY SPENT SOME TIME CIRCLING the Shaw neighborhood, searching for Malik. But Malik had gone to ground. After a couple of hours he headed back into town and checked into his room at a small family-run motel a couple of short blocks from Joanna's Diner. The manager fussed over his late check-in, and how he could have sold his room three times over for double the price.

Upstairs, the place was bare bones, a little frayed at the edges. Ty guessed that most of the guests were parents dropping off or collecting kids from the college. It was another reminder of how central it was to the town. Apart from some agriculture, and a large e-commerce packing facility, it was a case of no college, no town. There were thousands of places like it around the country. Places dominated by one large institution or business.

He was given an actual key to his rooms rather than a plastic card, and headed up to the third floor in the tiny elevator. When he got inside his room, he followed standard operating procedures. He dumped his bag, checked for surveillance devices and placed small markers that would tell him if someone had visited while he was out.

A few minutes later, Ty rolled back out in the Audi. He drove with a map next to him on the passenger seat. Lock had drilled into him an instinctual distrust of satellite navigation systems, and now he avoided them when at all possible. As far as he was concerned, a well-used satellite navigation system was as good as having a tracking device attached to your car. Plus it was faster to pick up the layout of a new place if you weren't on auto-pilot. You saw more too. You had to look out for street signs, and generally be more alert.

Ty pulled up outside the Barnes family home and got out of the car. He walked across the street and knocked at the door.

There was no answer. He knocked again, this time more forcefully. Still no one came to the door. There wasn't a car in the driveway or parked directly outside. He walked back down the path and checked the mailbox. The mail hadn't been collected in at least a few days.

Ty walked to the back of the property. There were three windows. One had been boarded over. He pulled away the board, punched out the rest of the glass from the window with his elbow, and clambered inside.

He moved quickly through the house. In the mom's room, clothing tumbled from open drawers. The bed was unmade. He checked the bathroom. Toothbrushes were gone from the holder. The boy's room was also untidy, but that didn't signify much.

In the kitchen a heap of dishes had been left to molder in the sink. Ty opened the refrigerator. The milk was beginning to sour. In the crisper drawer there were two wrinkled peppers and a wilted lettuce.

Everywhere else in the house was clean and as tidy as life got with a young boy living there. Eve Barnes clearly took pride in her home. She had also left in one hell of a hurry. His day had just gotten a little better. If they had skipped town, there was a chance that Eve and her son were still alive.

THIRTY-FIVE

G RETCHEN BECKER'S FRIENDS CALLED HER Pollyanna. The nickname fitted her so well that she didn't even mind when they used it when she was in their company. She just laughed.

Gretchen was always optimistic, always cheerful. Nothing ever seemed to get her down. The past week had tested her sunny disposition, but she had done her best to maintain it. For a start she didn't believe a word of what was being said about Aubrey. It was simply preposterous. He was a good husband, kind, loving and considerate. And he most certainly wasn't a goddamn faggot, never mind a man with an interest in young boys. Oh, how Gretchen loathed fags – and to think she would have married one! The very idea made her want to vomit.

Having sent their housekeeper home for the evening, she had busied herself making dinner for the two of them. She called Aubrey into the dining room and asked him to select a bottle of wine to go with the lamb.

As he did that, she ferried the food from the kitchen, and began to serve. Aubrey looked exhausted. The poor man.

She started when the doorbell rang. They weren't expecting company.

'I'll get that,' offered Aubrey.

'Don't be silly,' she said, taking off her apron, and walking into the hallway. She skirted the sweeping staircase and made for the front door. She was slightly annoyed that the guard hadn't alerted them to their visitor. That was his job after all.

No matter, she told herself. She'd speak to him in the morning about it. Without a guard on duty, she would have asked who it was before opening the door. But with him out there, she assumed the person had already been spoken to. Most likely it was one of her friends. Aubrey's friends had disappeared from sight since word of the allegations had begun to circulate. Gretchen, however, had never been more popular. Or that was how she explained the continual offers to talk from friends she suspected were more interested in getting some salacious details from her.

With her best smile fixed to her face, she opened the door. 'Good evening, and how may I help you?'

She froze as the gun came up and smashed into her face. She felt her front teeth splinter, and tasted blood in her mouth. Black shapes swam in front of her eyes. She felt lightheaded. The pain of her hair being grabbed and pulled snapped her back to the present.

She was punched in the stomach. She doubled over. The pain was overwhelming. She had never been hit in her entire life, never mind hard.

She began to cry as fear overwhelmed her. Where was Weston? Where was her husband?

'What do you want?' she said, through blood and tooth enamel. The pain from her mouth was excruciating, worse than being hit in the stomach. She thought she was going to throw up or pass out. She prayed she would pass out.

Her attacker didn't say anything. She found herself being spun around, her arms forced behind her back. She heard the rip of duct tape, then felt it against her skin as her wrists were bound. A hand reached around and spread across her face.

'What the hell is going . . .'

Aubrey Becker stood in the hallway, a glass of red wine frozen in his hand. He seemed to take in the damage that had already been done to Gretchen. He stepped forward.

'She has nothing to do with this. Leave her alone.'

Gretchen was pushed to the ground hard. The attacker stepped over her, and walked slowly toward Aubrey, who began to back away slowly.

Gretchen kept waiting to hear the crack of a gunshot, but the attacker put away the gun they were holding, reached into their jacket and pulled out a knife. It must have been about eight inches long and was shaped like a hunting knife. At the sight of it, Aubrey Becker's glass slipped from his hand, the red wine splattering over the tiled floor.

The phone. There was a phone on a small side table. If she could only reach it. Slowly, her body racked with pain, she got to her feet. She started toward the phone. The attacker was still bearing down on Aubrey.

She snatched the phone from its base, punched in 911, and put it to her ear, only to hear dead air. A second later, she heard her husband start to scream. It was a wild, high-pitched sound. It went on for a long time. When the screaming stopped, it was her turn.

THIRTY-SIX

OST OF THE DINNER CROWD had cleared out of the diner. Ty picked out a booth, away from the window. He sat with his back to the wall, and a clear view of the entrance. He scanned the menu. He wasn't that hungry, but he knew he had to eat.

The waitress came over. She looked to be in her late teens. He guessed she was probably a college kid. He ordered the cheeseburger with fries, and a cup of coffee.

'That everything?' she asked him.

'That's it. Thanks.'

He handed over his menu. Two campus cops walked in. They stood at the counter, bullshitting with the older waitress and one of the cooks. One was older, with a shaved head and a gut. The other was younger. Both were white. The younger one had checked Ty out as soon as they had walked in. Ty didn't think much of it. When you were a six-foot-four African American who looked like he did, old ladies avoided meeting your eye and cops checked you out. The younger cop glanced back at him.

This time Ty met his gaze, hoping he would say something or come over. These were the cops who had ignored Malik. For all Ty knew, one of them, or both, might already be aware of what had happened to Malik's family. Hell, they could have pulled the trigger.

Cops were a sore subject between Ty and Lock. Lock knew there were bad ones, but he saw the police as fundamentally decent. Growing up where he had, Ty was a little more jaded. He had long ago given up arguing about it. People's experiences were different, and the biggest determinant in the country was skin color, even with a black president in the White House – hell, especially with a black president. You didn't get over hundreds of years of history and shared distrust with a couple of elections.

The younger cop kept staring. Ty started to get up. The waitress brought his coffee and he eased back into his seat. He thanked her. The younger officer had gone back to his conversation. The moment had passed. He called after her, 'Excuse me?'

She walked back to his table with a smile. 'Yes, sir?'

He took in the diner with a wave of his hand. 'Seems kinda quiet.'

'Yeah, I think most of the reporters are down the street.' He must have looked puzzled, because she added, 'There's a bar. McGill's. Your cheeseburger shouldn't be too much longer.'

'Thanks.'

The cops were hitting the door, both carrying doggie bags. The waitress came back with his cheeseburger. As he started to eat, his cell rang. He was hoping it was Malik but the screen flashed Lock's name.

'What's up?' said Ty.

'I'm on the road. Should be with you in about four hours. Can you stay alive and out of jail for that long?'

'In this town? It's fifty–fifty, brother.'

'So what's going on?' Lock asked.

Ty brought him up to speed with what he'd found at the house, what the neighbor had said and how it contradicted the story the cops were putting out. He also told him that he was certain Malik was alive, but didn't go into detail in case the line wasn't completely secure.

Lock listened in silence.

Finally, he said, 'Hey, Ty?'

'What is it?'

'Small towns run by cops are never good news. Be careful, you hear me?'

'I hear you.' Ty killed the call. He turned his attention back to his plate of food, but pushed it away and signaled for the check.

THIRTY-SEVEN

A S TY TOOK THE SHORT walk down the street to McGill's, he saw the two cops from the diner sitting in their patrol car, watching him while making a big show of eating. Ty acted like they weren't there and pushed through the doors of the bar. The waitress had been right. The place was packed solid, the college crowd pushed out by a bunch of reporters and TV producers.

Ty moved toward the bar. People shuffled out of his way, and he had no trouble finding a spot. He waved a twenty-dollar bill in the direction of the two harried staff. 'Bourbon. Double.'

'Real drink, huh?'

Ty turned to see the cute blonde woman he'd spoken to in the diner that morning standing behind him. 'Can I get you something?' he asked her.

'Well, I've been standing here trying to order for the past ten minutes.'

'Sorry, I didn't mean to cut in,' said Ty.

'Don't sweat it. But I'll take a beer. Heineken. Although technically I shouldn't be drinking. Might have to go back in front of the camera if something happens.'

When the bartender came back with his bourbon, Ty added the beer to his order. 'You think it will?'

She looked up at him. She had big brown eyes. Man, she was even cuter up close, he thought. 'Honestly? No. I think this guy is lying dead in his car somewhere and that's all she wrote.'

Ty felt a twinge of anger at the way she'd said it. He had to remind himself that misery and human suffering were her job. They were often his job too. The only thing that differed was that this time people close to his heart were involved. To find Malik he had to park whatever feelings he had.

'And you think that because?'

'Isn't that usually how these things go down?' she said.

The barman came back with their drinks. Ty told him to keep the change, and handed the reporter her beer. 'So, you're guessing?' he said.

'Thanks.' She took a sip of beer, closing her eyes while she savored it. 'Educated guess. I must have covered half a dozen of these deals by now. Guy goes crazy, kills his wife and kids. They usually put a gun in their own mouth. Too scared to face the music, I guess. And come on! Retired ball player? Those types are usually the worst.'

Ty looked at her. If she'd been a guy, then right about now she'd have been flying halfway across the bar from a punch. Instead he took a sip of bourbon. 'You're wrong,' he said. 'He loved his family.'

She shrugged. 'Hey, you asked my opinion. Who are you with anyway?'

'With?' asked Ty. She had obviously taken him for a reporter. He looked around the crowded bar. 'I'm not with anyone.'

'So what are you doing here?'

He took another sip of bourbon. He was going to have to make it last. He planned on driving back out to the Shaw house later to try again to find Malik, and he didn't want to give the local cops an easy DUI collar.

He looked at the woman standing with him. 'I don't even know your name.'

'Kelly,' she said, putting out her hand for him to shake.

'I'm Ty. Short for Tyrone. Listen, do you want to take a ride with me?'

She raised her eyebrows, then her glass. 'Hey, I don't know what one beer gets you where you're from . . .'

Ty smiled despite himself. 'Not like that.'

THIRTY-EIGHT

TY STARTED THE ENGINE AS Kelly scooted into the passenger seat, and shut the door. He buried the gas, and Kelly was thrown back in her seat. She grabbed the dash to steady herself. 'If you kill me and dump me in a ditch, my mom is going to be so pissed at me. I just want you to know that.'

'Noted,' said Ty.

They headed down the main street. Ty hung a left, heading for the Shaw house. He wanted a reporter to see what he had. He figured it was insurance in case the cops got really hinky with him.

'So, private security, huh? What does that involve?'

He glanced over to see the red light of Kelly's digital recorder. 'Turn that thing off or I'm gonna toss it out the window,' he told her.

She made a big show of clicking the off button, and jamming it into the pocket of her jacket. She had turned it back on. He was sure of it.

'Off-off,' he said. 'In fact, take out the batteries and give them to me.'

She sighed, pulled the recorder back out, and dumped the two AAA batteries into his open palm. He hit the button to lower the window and tossed them out.

'Hey!' she protested.

'I'll buy you some more. What were you asking me?'

'What do you do?'

Day to day, Ty didn't give it a lot of thought. He doubted most people did. It was hardly a regular job in the commonly understood sense. But it did have its routines and patterns, especially when he and Lock were involved in a straight-up close-protection gig, like the one they'd been doing in New York. You ran walking drills, you moved people in vehicles using well-grooved embus/debus procedures, and you had a plan for actions on attack. 'Lemme see. We protect people. Only we're not the cops.'

'Like bodyguards?'

Empty streets swept by outside. Everyone tucked up inside watching TV, having a late dinner or putting their kids to bed. Lock hated the word 'bodyguard', but Ty understood it was just a shorthand for most people.

'Kind of like that,' he said.

'Who are you guarding here?' Kelly asked.

'Right now?' said Ty. 'No one. I'm looking for someone.'

'The same person the cops are looking for?'

'That's right,' said Ty, pulling in across the street from the Shaw house. 'You want to get yourself an exclusive?'

She looked nervous. Ty killed the engine and got out. Kelly followed him across the street and down the side of the property.

THIRTY-NINE

TY OPENED THE BACK DOOR that led into the kitchen. He turned. Kelly was standing outside. 'Okay, for a "private security consultant" I met in a bar, you are seriously starting to freak me out.'

'I can drive you back there, if you like. Up to you.'

She hesitated.

'You want this story or not?' he said, stepping into the kitchen.

She walked across to the door. 'I already have the story.'

He went over to the dishwasher and pulled it open. It was empty. Ty felt the hairs on the back of his neck stand up. He looked at Kelly as she came into the room. 'No, you don't.'

Ty closed the dishwasher and walked through into the hallway. 'Malik? Malik, it's me, Ty.'

He was met by silence. 'Malik?'

He could see Kelly standing in the doorway. 'He's here?' she whispered, natural curiosity obviously trumping her fear. Ty raised a hand to quiet her.

He started up the stairs and began to check the bedrooms. They were empty. A closet door was open. Ty was sure it had been closed when he had been here earlier. Moonlight filtered in through the windows. Clothes were strewn on the carpet.

He heard footsteps behind him. Kelly stood in the hallway, her eyes fixed on the bloody wall. 'This where it happened?'

Ty straightened up. 'Yeah, except it didn't go down like the cops are saying. Come here.'

She moved deeper into the room.

'See the blood?' said Ty.

She nodded.

'Cops said it was a shotgun Malik had just bought. Which explains the blood, except there would have been a lot more and it would have been spread out further. Plus they were lined up, and killed here, like ducks in a row.' He glanced over to make sure she was listening. Her eyes were wide. She seemed fixated on the wall. He kept going: 'Cops are telling a different story entirely. Saying how they were killed in their rooms. Not room, rooms. Like Malik went to where they were sleeping and killed them one by one. And that's not even getting into how he wouldn't have hurt his family. Hell, he never even spanked those kids. Not even once. Didn't agree with it.'

Now she was looking at him. 'How do you know? People do weird things all the time.'

'I know because I grew up with him. He was my friend.'

'That's why you're here?' said Kelly.

'That's why I'm here. And it's how I know this story about Malik murdering his own family is bullshit.'

'So if he didn't, then who did?' said Kelly.

'There's a lot more going on. A lot that people don't know.'

'Hang on. I have a call.' She pulled out a cell phone from her bag, and listened. 'Okay,' she said. 'I'll be right there.'

'What's up?' Ty asked her.

Kelly looked around the room. 'Can you give me a ride?'

FORTY

THREE BLUE POLICE SAWHORSES BLOCKED the road that led to the Becker home. Ty lowered the window of the Audi as a young patrol cop ducked his head, rain splashing off his hat. 'Road's closed, sir. You'll have to turn around.'

Kelly leaned over from the passenger seat. 'You can let us through.'

The patrol cop nodded. 'Sorry, didn't see you there. Parking's next to the front entrance. Official statement is in a half-hour.'

'You got some pull, huh?' said Ty, hitting the button to close the window. Two cops dragged the middle sawhorse back and the Audi nudged its way through the gap.

'What do you mean?'

'Well, they weren't going to let us in till they saw you.'

'Everybody falls for a pretty face,' said Kelly.

Ty parked next to a couple of other vehicles. 'Thanks for the ride,' she said. She put her hand on the door, ready to get out. 'I'll see you around.'

'You going to look into what I showed you?' Ty asked her.

'Sure,' she told him. 'I'll talk to some people. See what I can find.'

Ty sat and watched the rain bounce off the road. He wasn't going to wait for the official statement. He already had an idea what the story was going to be. He reversed, turned and drove toward the roadblock.

The cops moved the sawhorse and he drove through. He rang Lock.

'It's me,' he said.

'You found him?' Lock asked.

'Not yet. You see the news?'

'About Becker. Yeah. You think it was Malik?'

Ty hesitated. If Becker had been behind the killing of Malik's family, it was possible that Malik had taken revenge. More than possible.

'I don't know.'

Silence settled between them.

'Okay. Well, I'm almost there. Just about another thirty miles to go. Tyrone?'

'Yeah?'

'Regardless of whether he did or not, we need to find him. And fast.'

'I know.'

FORTY-ONE

THERE WAS A HAIRBRUSH NEXT to the washbasin. Malik picked it up and turned it over in his hand. The bristles were tangled with Kim's long dark hairs. There was some of Katy's too. At bedtime Kim would brush Katy's hair. When she was done Katy would insist on brushing her mom's. Sometimes Malik had watched them as they did it. The closeness they'd had was beautiful. Now it was gone.

Still holding the brush, he put down the lid of the toilet seat and sat on it. If only he'd minded his own business, they would still be here. The kids would be asleep in their rooms, and he would be lying next to his wife.

All he wanted now was to be with them in death as he had been in life. But even that would be denied him. A man who was presumed to have murdered his family sure as hell wasn't going to be laid to rest next to them. Kim's sister would see to that. She and Malik had never gotten on at the best of times. Kim's father had been an attorney, and her mother a doctor. They had died in a car accident three years ago. Kim had graduated *magna cum laude* from Stanford. Marrying a ball player, even one who had made it to the NBA, had not been what her parents had had in mind for their elder daughter. They had made that clear to both Malik and Kim. Things had thawed a little between him and Kim's family once Landon was born, but only a little.

As a child going to church, he had learned about Purgatory, a state short of hell but filled with torment. And now he was trapped alive in it. Death offered no release, and living, going on, was hellish. His grief was still too raw, too overwhelming, to offer the comfort of revenge. Revenge required some kind of life force, and Malik didn't have that within him.

He stood up and carefully placed the hairbrush back beside the basin. He walked out into the bedroom. He heard a car prowling in the street outside. He froze as headlights swept the room, then ducked down, and crawled on his hands and knees to the window. Looking out, he saw a campus-police patrol car roll past. It stopped at the end of the road. One of the cops got out. Even from this distance, Malik knew from the waddle that it was Tromso. The cop hefted a shotgun as he made his way back toward the house. In his other hand he was carrying a plastic container. It was too dark for Malik to make out what it was.

Seeing him shifted something inside Malik. He crawled to the bedroom door, out into the hallway and got to his feet. He headed down the stairs.

Malik froze in the downstairs hallway as a shadow fell over him. Tromso was at the front door. He jiggled it. Malik backed into the kitchen as Tromso threw himself against the front door.

It held, and he heard Tromso groan as he bounced off it. He could hear the cop moaning about his shoulder. It was the first thing that had cheered Malik in a long time. He crossed to the knife block, and pulled a hefty Sabatier blade from the wood. Tromso might have a gun, but if he could get close enough to him, he was sure that he had more than enough body strength to overpower an out-of-shape donut-gorger.

Malik turned back to the door. From nowhere a hand clamped over his mouth. Another hand reached down and bent back his wrist. The pain shot up his arm and the knife dropped from his grasp.

'You're in enough trouble already without stabbing up some cop,' said Ty.

Tromso must have given up on the door. There was the sound of a window being broken.

Malik felt Ty drop his hand. He turned to see his friend. They looked at each other for a second.

'Ty, I didn't . . .'

Ty put up a hand to silence him. 'I know. Let's get out of here.'

Malik stood where he was. He could hear more glass dropping to the floor.

'What's he doing here?' he whispered.

Ty's hand clamped on his shoulder and he started to drag Malik backwards. A cone of light splashed across the hallway, presumably from Tromso's torch. 'Anyone there?' shouted the cop.

Malik was torn between fear and his desire to confront Tromso. Ty didn't seem to be suffering from any such confusion. He grabbed Malik by the collar and hustled him hard toward the open door.

They made it out before the light from Tromso's torch flitted across the kitchen. Ty pulled the door to. Malik watched as Tromso walked into the kitchen, put down the container and unscrewed the top.

Even with the door closed, Malik could smell gasoline. He started back toward the door but Ty pulled him away. There was the scuff of shoes on concrete from the side of the house.

Ty hissed, 'We have to go, brother.'

Malik could see Ty's hand on the butt of a handgun. He didn't doubt that his friend was more than capable of killing both cops if it came to it. And that was what they would have to do if they waited around for a few more seconds. If it had been Malik's decision to make, he would have taken them out. But Ty was only there because of him. Malik's life was already in tatters. He couldn't ask Ty to kill two cops to satisfy his curiosity or to stop whatever was about to happen.

Together, Malik and Ty stepped back into the darkness of the yard as the younger cop appeared around the corner. Malik watched as he walked to the back door. He opened it and shouted to Tromso, 'Hey, boss, it was open the whole time.'

He didn't hear Tromso's reply, but he did catch the sloshing sound of gasoline hitting the kitchen floor that Kim always kept spotless. He turned to Ty. 'Go. Leave me here.'

'I can't do that.'

'But they're destroying the evidence,' Malik protested.

Tromso had retreated deeper into the house. Malik imagined him spraying the living room with gas. In a few minutes he would drop a match, or turn the stove on, and everything Malik had to remind him of his family, all the family photographs, Katy's stuffed toys, the first basketball he'd bought Landon, Kim's wedding dress would be gone. His throat tightened and he started to choke.

'You don't want to be here to see this,' said Ty.

Slowly, Malik turned away, and together they disappeared into the woods at the back of the house. They were almost at Ty's car when Malik heard the roar, and looked back to see the orange glow in the distance as his home was engulfed by flames.

Ty pulled his cell phone out of his pocket. 'I got him,' he said.

FORTY-TWO

TY POPPED THE TRUNK, TOOK out a gym bag and threw it to Malik. 'Here. New clothes. Put them on.' He had a lot to say to him, and a lot to tell, but now wasn't the time. A couple of blocks over, they could see the flash of lights from a fire truck as it wailed its way toward the blazing house.

Malik caught the bag and held it to his chest, the flames from the distant fire flickering in his eyes.

Ty watched as he opened the bag and dug through the clothes. 'I had to guess your size.'

'Ty?'

'What is it?'

'Thanks, man.'

Ty shrugged it off. 'Ain't nothing.'

'You get caught helping me it will be.'

Ty gripped Malik's shoulder with his right hand. 'Look at me. We're not going to get caught.'

Malik nodded. He scooted round in the passenger seat, and began to strip off his clothes, dank and fetid from his days on the run. Ty held them at arm's length before jamming them into the bag. Malik pulled on a pair of black denim jeans and a grey sweatshirt. He switched his shoes for a brand new pair of sneakers.

Ty jammed the muddy pair into the bag, zipped it up and threw it onto the back seat. He walked round to the driver's seat, got in, threw the car into drive and took off.

A little later, Ty pulled over to the side of the road. He killed the lights and switched off the engine. He and Malik sat in silence. The rain had slowed to a steady drumbeat.

Malik's chin sank onto his chest. He closed his eyes and started to sob. His whole body shook with the force. Ty didn't say anything. There was nothing to say. The man had lost his family and his home. Even if they could prove his innocence, and bring whoever had killed Kim and the kids to justice, his friend's old life was over.

A car swept past them, its headlights flashing across their faces for the briefest of seconds. 'I'm sorry this happened to you,' Ty said eventually. The words were inadequate, but they were better said than left unspoken.

Malik didn't reply. His head was buried in his hands. He was still weeping.

'Malik?'

He rubbed at his face. Ty dug into his glove compartment, found a pack of tissues and handed them to him. There was a knock on the driver's window. Malik started at the sound. Ty opened the door to reveal Lock standing there.

'This is the guy I work with,' he said to Malik. 'He's going to take you to the safe-house.'

Lock leaned into the car. 'Two black guys in a car around here is asking for trouble. And I'm going to need you to sit in back.'

Malik nodded. He opened the passenger door and shifted to the back seat of the Audi.

'How is he?' Lock asked Ty.

'Too early to say.'

'That good, huh?' said Lock.

'That good,' Ty repeated.

FORTY-THREE

ELEANOR HENSHALL STOOD AT THE end of the street in her slippers and robe, the Shaws' dog next to her on a leash as a truck from the Harrisburg Fire Department doused the last burning embers of the house. The fire must have taken hold quickly: by the time she had been woken by the dog's barking, it was already fully ablaze, the roof gone, the windows blown out from the pressure of the heat.

She had rushed outside with the dog. The fire department had arrived seconds later, but by then it was already too late to do much except secure the properties on either side. She had stood and watched as the flames tightened their grip, and thick, acrid smoke billowed from the upstairs windows.

A police officer from the college had come over and asked if she had seen anyone. She told him she hadn't. She was suffering from a bad cold, had taken some Nyquil and gone to bed early.

The dog barked at the flames, straining at his leash. She wondered if the poor animal thought the family were still inside, if he understood the terrible tragedy that had befallen his owners. She reached down and scratched his head. He looked back at her with soft brown eyes, and she found herself tearing up.

'Ma'am?'

One of the firefighters was walking toward her. He tilted back his helmet and she could see the soot and grime covering his face. 'Ma'am, are you okay? It's pretty cold out here.'

'My house is that one there,' she said, pointing it out. 'Are you sure it'll be safe?'

'It's fine.'

'Do you know how it started?' she asked him.

'Kind of early to say, but we did smell gasoline."

FORTY-FOUR

T HE CAB PULLED UP TWO blocks short of the hotel entrance. Ty got out. He scanned the empty street as the cab took off. A patrol car was parked directly opposite the hotel, its headlights turned off, two cops sitting in front. Malik was safe with Lock and he felt as if a huge weight had been lifted from him. There was still a long way to go, but he had achieved a major part of his mission.

Ty crossed the street so that he was on the same side as the hotel entrance. He kept walking. He could feel the cops' eyes on him as he took every step. As he reached the hotel entrance, he heard the patrol-car doors open, the two cops get out and the doors close again. The glass door into the hotel was locked. Ty tapped at the glass. He shielded his eyes and peered through as the night porter hauled himself up and started toward the door.

Behind him, Ty could hear the cops coming. He didn't turn. He wasn't going to resist, but he wasn't about to make this easy for them either. The night porter peered at him. Ty held up his room key and waved it at him.

The door was buzzed open, and Ty stepped into the warm reception area. The night porter was about to lock the door again when he saw the cops. He held the door open for them. Now Ty turned round.

135

The first thing he noticed was that neither cop was in uniform. Even so, he recognized Tromso from the description Malik had given him – overweight, out of shape, full of his own importance. He recognized the second cop too.

Officer Kelly Svenson stepped forward, opened her wallet and flashed her creds.

'Thought you were a reporter, Kelly?' Ty said to her.

She unhooked a pair of cuffs from a utility belt. 'No, you assumed I was, and I chose not to correct you. Now turn around, please, Mr Johnson. Hands behind your back. I'm arresting you for aiding an offender, pursuant to Minnesota statute six zero nine point four nine five subdivision one, as well as subdivision three of the same statute, obstructing an investigation.'

Ty did as she asked, moving slowly. 'You been rehearsing that in front of a mirror, Officer?' He could see from the look on Tromso's face that he was itching to use his night stick. Ty wasn't about to give him any excuses.

He felt cold metal against his wrists and heard the click of the cuffs as they closed on him. Female hands moved round to his holster, plucking out his SIG.

Meanwhile, the night porter was doing a bad impersonation of someone showing no interest in the proceedings. He had retreated behind the reception desk but kept looking up every few seconds.

Tromso moved in front of Ty and Ty got a better look at him. Three chins and a ratty excuse for a mustache that would have shamed a seventies porn flick. As soon as Ty looked at him, he backed off. It didn't make Ty feel good: it made him nervous.

Ty twisted his head round to look at Kelly. 'Y'know, you, me, a pair of handcuffs. Hey. Do you want to continue this up in my room?'

Kelly did not look amused.

'I got cable,' he said to her. 'Did I mention that?'

'Did I mention that you're under arrest?'

'You're kind of killing the mood here, girl.' Ty glanced at Tromso. 'You ain't helping either.'

'Where's Malik Shaw?' said Tromso.

Ty made a show of looking around. 'Don't see him. Do you?'

Tromso poked a finger into Ty's shoulder. He had to stretch up to do it. Ty's eyes narrowed. He wasn't going to show his hand that he'd seen Tromso pour gasoline all over a crime scene, but he wasn't going to take the cop's shit either.

'Do that again and see what happens,' Ty told him.

'Tough guy, huh?' Tromso sneered.

Ty didn't reply. Tromso would face his moment of reckoning, along with anyone else who'd been involved. Ty would see to that.

Kelly pulled at the cuffs. 'Okay, let's go.'

He let her turn him around. She and Tromso perp-walked him out to the patrol car. He settled himself as the door closed. Ty was wondering if the fate they feared for Malik awaited him at the end of his ride.

FORTY-FIVE

RYAN LOCK TAPPED AT THE earpiece nestled inside his left ear. A thin black cord ran from it to a multi-channel scanner mounted on the dashboard. Lock slowed down and flicked on the turn signal, zipping down the highway exit and doubling back on a surface road.

Malik's head popped up in back. 'What's going on? Why are we leaving the highway?'

Lock glanced at him in the rear-view mirror. 'State patrol have a roadblock set up on I-Eleven.'

Malik grabbed the back of the front seats and sat up. 'I appreciate you doing this for me.

'You're welcome,' said Lock, taking a sharp left turn. 'How you holding up?'

There was a pause. 'I'm still here.'

Lock wondered how any man would be able to come through what Malik had experienced. Then he remembered that he had – or, at least, close. A little over two years ago, Lock's fiancée, Carrie, had been killed while fleeing two men who had abducted her. She had run into the road on a rainy evening in Topanga Canyon, just outside Los Angeles, and been hit by a car. She was killed instantly. Ty had been driving, with Lock in the passenger seat next to him. They had been out in the storm trying to find her when it happened.

'That's good,' said Lock. He knew that right now all Malik could do was exist from moment to moment. That in itself was an achievement. Lock's nightmare had been enough, but to lose two children at the same time as the woman you loved? It was horror beyond imagination.

Lock snuck another glance at Malik in the rear-view mirror. 'When'd you last sleep?'

'Don't know. Last night. I mean, not tonight, the one before that.'

Lock didn't say anything.

Malik went on, 'Every time I close my eyes . . .' His voice fell away. He cleared his throat. 'It's not good – y'know what I'm saying?'

Lock did know. 'I have some Ambien on me. I figured you might need it. It'll knock you out for a few hours.'

'Thanks, but I'm okay for now. Maybe later.'

A moment of silence passed between them. Lock considered telling Malik about Carrie, and what had happened to him, but decided against it. It was way too early for it to do any good. After she had died, Lock had endured an endless procession of people who had shared their own experiences of losing a loved one. He had listened patiently out of respect. But someone else's loss was just that – theirs.

After a few more minutes, Lock said, 'You want to tell me what's been going on?'

'I can try. Where do you want me to start?'

'At the beginning. When did you first suspect that there was something going on with Becker?'

'I didn't even know it was him at first,' said Malik.

There was a crackle of static in Lock's ear, and more chatter. The chatter picked up pace: he caught a mention of an Audi. In his rear-view mirror, he saw the headlights of a car behind them. Its speed was matched to the even sixty Lock was doing. The speed limit on this road, which ran broadly parallel to the interstate, was fifty-five. Doing fifty-five made cops suspicious, like you had something to hide, so he usually drove a little over.

He narrowed his eyes, trying to make out its shape, see if it had a roll bar, but the vehicle's headlights were too bright.

Lock put up his hand. 'Hold that thought. We have company. Stay down until I tell you otherwise.'

The road ahead was wide open. Lock slowed and pulled over, giving the car behind a chance to pass. It edged up behind him a little, but made no move to go around them. The radio chatter moved up a notch. A second later he saw flashing lights behind him. He eased off the gas pedal, and hit his turn signal to indicate he was pulling over to the side of the road.

He waited for the police cruiser to pull in behind him. He kept the Audi in drive, the engine running, and watched his mirrors.

The police cruiser stopped about twenty-five feet behind him. The driver's door opened, and a lone patrol officer stood behind it, his service weapon drawn as he started to bark instructions.

'Driver, turn off the engine.'

The cop sounded young and nervous. Lock tuned in more intently to the chatter in his ear. Other units were on the way, but their ETA was about seven minutes away. Decision-making became a little harder. A lot would depend on how the young patrol officer reacted. The situation was further complicated by the fact that Lock had no plans to shoot an innocent cop. If it came down to it, and his only option was to kill someone doing their job, then he and Malik would both have to take their chances in custody, leaving Ty on the outside to figure out what the hell was going on.

'Turn off your engine.'

Lock raised his hands, but made no move to turn off the engine. It was still in drive, the only thing preventing it from moving his right foot on the brake pedal.

Now the cop had a decision to make. It was likely that he would have a dash cam fitted. That meant he was going to be unwilling to take a shot at a driver with his arms raised in plain sight. If he was bright, he would hold his position and wait for the cavalry. But Lock could already tell from the rising anger in his voice, as the young officer barked at him for a third time to switch off the engine, that he wasn't going to wait. He didn't want to be sitting here like a dummy when his colleagues arrived, even though that was the smart thing to do.

Lock kept watching in the rear-view as the cop shuffled around the lip of the open driver's door, and started to move toward the back of the Audi. Lock kept his arms nice and high and still.

His service weapon punched out in front of him, the young patrol officer moved down the side of the Audi. He was too jumpy to notice the Malik-shaped bundle in back although, to be fair to him, all the windows in the Audi, apart from the windshield, were tinted.

The cop was next to Lock's door now. The gun was pointed straight at Lock's head.

'Are you deaf? Turn off the engine.'

Slowly, Lock moved his neck so that he was looking straight at the cop. 'Didn't want to lower my hands with a gun pointed at me,' he said. 'I have a sidearm. Now why don't we just sit here until you have some back-up?'

'Okay,' the cop barked. 'Get out of the car.'

The cop kept his right hand raised, the gun still up, as his left hand opened the driver's door. Lock watched his hands, and waited. The cop was watching Lock's hands too, making sure they didn't move and that he didn't go for his gun. Another few seconds passed. Lock lowered his arms fractionally so that his elbows were almost resting on the steering-wheel.

'What are you doing?' the cop said, eyes like saucers.

'Thought you'd want my gun,' Lock said innocently.

'Just don't move, okay?'

'Okay,' said Lock, his arms freezing in place.

The cop moved the door another fraction. When the solid edge was between the barrel of the gun and Lock's head, Lock jabbed down hard on the gas pedal, turning the wheel down to his left with his elbow. The Audi shot forward and to the side. The back end of the car slammed into the cop's hip.

The officer fired but he was already going down as he pulled the trigger and the shot went high. Lock put his hands on the wheel and pulled out onto the road. In his side mirror he could see the cop rolling on his side, his hand clutching his hip. Lock killed his headlights, and stayed off the brakes as he drove.

He probably had between thirty seconds and a minute before the cop made it back to his unit and got on the radio. Lock reached a four-way stop. He hung a right back toward the interstate.

FORTY-SIX

T HEY PULLED UP NEXT TO a single-story red-brick building at the edge of the college campus. Kelly was in the front passenger seat, Tromso driving. Ty was sitting in back.

Kelly got out and slammed the door. She didn't say a word to either Tromso or Ty. Ty was waiting for her to walk round and let him out, but she kept walking. She opened a door leading into the campus security building and disappeared.

Tromso reversed the patrol car out of the space he had just pulled into and drove away. Ty knew better than to say anything. This was not a good development, but the last thing he was going to do was show fear to an asshole like Tromso.

Tromso drove them back through the campus. It was still dark. There was no one about to see them. They pulled out onto a street called Buffalo Drive. Ty stared out of the window. Tromso kept flicking glances at him from the front. The fat cop shifted in his seat as Ty continued to ignore him.

They drove past a strip mall at the edge of town. Still Ty didn't say anything.

Finally, the silence got the better of Tromso. 'Want to know where we're going, tough guy?'

Ty finally looked at him. 'Not really. Why?'

Tromso tried to shrug it off. 'Figured you'd want to know.'

'Let me guess. Somewhere quiet with no witnesses?' said Ty.

Tromso's piggy eyes flicked back to him. 'You're good.'

'I know,' said Ty.

'You could save me a lot of trouble and just tell me where your buddy is?'

'I could,' said Ty. 'But I'm not going to. And, by the way, it takes a lot more to scare me than some fat fuck of a mall cop.'

They were out in the boonies now. Trees folded in on the patrol car from both sides. A truck hauling lumber roared past. Ty stared out of the window. There was a glimpse of light through the trees. Sunrise couldn't be too far away.

Ty had to remind himself not to get complacent. The idea of someone like Tromso ending his life, where others had failed, struck him as comical but that didn't mean it couldn't happen.

They pulled off the blacktop road. Tromso stopped the patrol car, opened a gate with a sign that read 'Private Property' and a couple of buckshot-riddled tin cans tied to the post, and drove through. He stopped, and got back out to close the gate. Ty watched him impassively from the back seat. He didn't doubt that Tromso was capable of taking him out. Hell, the guy had brazenly torched the scene of a multiple homicide. But Tromso wanted Malik before he killed Ty, and there was no way that was going to happen. A year in Gitmo wouldn't make Ty dime out a friend so, however this went, Tromso was not going to be a happy bunny.

The track sloped upwards. It was narrow. Branches whipped against the patrol car as it climbed. The road curved right in a wide loop, then flattened out. Ahead was a log cabin with a covered porch.

Tromso parked in front of the cabin and got out. He disappeared inside and closed the door. A few seconds later, he was back.

He opened Ty's door. 'Get out,' he said.

Ty was already fairly sure he hadn't been brought out here – into the woods where no one could hear you scream – for a measured discussion.

They could have had that back at the station with coffee and a nice warm interrogation room. So, given that he was almost certainly about to take a beating, he had made up his mind not to make things easy for Tromso.

As Tromso reached in to grab him, Ty allowed himself to lean back in the seat and aim a boot square at the cop. It hit Tromso in the chest, sending him windmilling away, arms flailing. He landed on his backside.

Ty's heel must have caught Tromso flush in the solar plexus because he struggled to catch his breath. It took him a full minute, by Ty's estimation, to lever himself back to his feet. His face was bright red, and his eyes seemed to have receded even further into his head. His right hand fell to his belt and, for a split second, Ty wondered if he hadn't miscalculated. Maybe Tromso was just stupid and angry enough to shoot him, after all.

Then he saw Tromso's hand reach around and pluck out the Taser from its pouch on his belt. Ty was still lying flat, the soles of his boots pointed out toward the cop. Tromso walked round to the other side, opened the door and fired the Taser. Ty did his best to get out of the way, but with his hands cuffed behind his back, he couldn't move fast enough.

The Taser's two wire barbs embedded in the side of his neck about two inches above his shoulder. His body jolted as the first pulse of electricity hit him. His back arched, and his muscles tightened. The air around him seemed to press in against him and for a second he thought he might pass out.

The pain kept coming. He was having trouble breathing. He tried to speak but his mouth wouldn't open. His teeth were grinding – he could hear them, though that was all he could hear.

Finally, the shock wave fell away. Tromso grabbed the back of Ty's shirt, and hauled him out. His head struck the edge of the car door, as the cop pulled him onto the cold, damp ground.

There was another spike of pain as Tromso hit the Taser again. Ty's body rose, his back arching once more, his limbs going rigid as the current flowed through him. He opened his mouth, gasping for air as the pain kept coming.

He felt a brief agonizing bite as Tromso reached down and ripped the two Taser spikes from his neck. He lay there for a moment before Tromso hauled him to his feet. His legs felt weak. His head pounded. But there was relief that the sharp spikes of pain from the Taser had stopped.

Tromso grabbed the cuffs, yanked them down hard to take control of him, and pushed him toward the cabin. Ty stumbled across the open ground and through the door.

Inside, it was dark and cold. There was an old wood-burning stove in one corner, a table with a chipped Formica top and three chairs standing opposite. Yellowing newspapers were spread randomly on the floor. There was a single kitchen counter with a sink and a draining-board.

Tromso pushed him toward the table and sat him in one of the chairs. The cop's face was still flushed, and he was making a wheezing sound. Ty was out of breath. Being Tasered would do that to you.

Tromso's gasps from hauling him out of the back of the car made Ty feel better. There was an outside chance that the cop might be able to Taser information out of him, but he sure as hell wasn't going to be able to beat it out of him. He'd tire before that happened. Of course, at some point the tables would turn and Ty would really lay down a beating on the fat man.

The cop took a moment to catch his breath. 'You're telling me where he is one way or another.'

Ty stared at him. If it hadn't have been for what he'd done to Malik, and now to Ty, he would have felt sorry for him. Pain was not a great method for extracting information. America had learned that the hard way. Sure, if you tortured a person they would cough something, but rarely would it be actionable. More often than not they would give you what you wanted to hear. Tromso had another problem, too. Ty didn't know exactly where Lock was taking Malik. For operational reasons, Lock had given Ty the general area but nothing as specific as an address. All in, it was going to make for a long day.

There was the crunch of tires outside as a vehicle rolled up the driveway toward the cabin. Ty studied Tromso's reaction. That would tell him whether it was good news or not. Tromso looked nervily toward the door, but didn't panic. 'Last chance to tell me where he is.' He walked across to the door and grabbed the handle. Ty remained silent. 'Have it your way then,' said Tromso, and disappeared outside.

Ty tried to crane his neck to see who had arrived, but it was no use. The door was shut. He moved his hands and tried to slam the cuffs against the back of the chair. Sometimes, if you got real lucky, you could bump handcuffs open.

This wasn't one of those times. He tried twice more, but all he got out of it was sore wrists where the inner edge of the cuffs cut into them.

He could hear Tromso talking to someone outside. It sounded like one other person, an adult male, who answered in a voice so soft that Ty couldn't make out what was said.

'Yeah, he ain't going to give him up easy,' Tromso was telling the other man.

Thirty seconds of conversation told Ty that Tromso was the junior partner in all of this. The words were tumbling from his mouth in an excited jumble. The other man was giving him yes-no answers, his voice low and controlled.

The conversation stopped. Ty kept waiting for the door to open. It didn't. Seconds passed. Then minutes. Ty tried his trick of bumping the cuffs against the back of the chair again. It didn't work this time either. He was stuck.

Finally, he heard two sets of footsteps. The door opened. Tromso walked in, his face set, a soft brown leather bag in his hand. It had a snap clasp. It looked like an old-school doctor's bag, the kind that featured in movies when the local doc arrived to deliver a baby. He set it down on the table. Ty was waiting for him to start calling for hot water and towels. He didn't say anything. He turned and left, pushing past the man framed in the doorway as quickly as he could.

This man was large and lean. He was dressed in black boots and black work overalls. His face was obscured by a black ski mask. He ignored Ty, walked across to the leather bag, opened the clasp and, with gloved hands, took out a series of knives and scalpels, laying them carefully on the counter.

FORTY-SEVEN

A S A GENERAL RULE, SOMEONE wearing a mask in the commission of a crime is a good sign. A mask means that the person wants to conceal their identity. Which usually means that, unless something goes wrong, they plan on leaving their victim or victims behind alive. Messed up. Traumatized. Perhaps changed forever. But breathing.

Right now, though, as the man in the mask walked toward him, a long boning knife in hand, Ty wasn't finding a lot of comfort in any of that. The man stopped in front of him, and hunkered down so that they were eye to eye. He stared at Ty with sparkling blue eyes. They crinkled at the edges as he smiled.

'You will tell me where he is,' the man said.

He didn't have a Minnesota accent, that was for sure. The local accent was pretty distinctive, more Canadian than American. This was someone who hailed from the east coast. New Hampshire, maybe. Not Boston, maybe further north, a little more out in the sticks.

Ty thought about telling him he was correct. Given enough pain, he might well tell him where Malik was. But he didn't know. That wasn't going to convince this guy. He looked way too cool for the truth to have any effect. Ty decided on another tack.

'How much they paying you?' he asked him. 'Or is this personal?' He waited a second, searching the man's eyes for the slightest flicker of a reaction. 'You one of them? Is that it? You like little boys too?'

The man's pupils grew smaller. The man's lips curled up at the edges in a hollow approximation of a smile. It was too late, though. Ty already knew he had got to him. Not that it was going to save him from the world of pain that was heading his way.

The man put the knife down on the floor, and began to roll up the right leg of Ty's jeans. His hand grasped the back of Ty's calf. He started feeling around, a butcher in search of a joint or a hamstring.

A shout from outside. 'Hey!' It sounded like Tromso.

The man picked up his knife, and walked to the door as Tromso called again, a nervous catch in his throat. Ty watched him open the door, the knife still in his hand. He had barely cleared the doorframe when there was the crack of a single shot. The man was blown back into the cabin by the force of the bullet's impact as it smashed into his face, catching him two inches above the bridge of his nose.

The man's arms flailed, and he staggered backwards. His hands found only air, and he went down, falling backwards, an orange-sized hole blown out of the front of his skull.

Outside, Tromso was screaming at whoever the hell had just taken out his buddy that he was police. Like that was going to make a difference, thought Ty. Tromso fired his handgun a couple of times. The sniper didn't reply. He waited.

Ty shook his head, willing himself to sharpen up as a fresh burst of adrenalin hit his system. He used his feet to shuffle the chair forward. He pushed himself up, his hands and forearms raking against the back of the chair. Half standing, half squatting, he made it to his feet, the chair slipping out from under him.

His hands were still cuffed behind his back but he was on his feet. Tromso fired another couple of shots. A car engine started up outside.

Ty duck-walked toward the open door. Trying to keep his balance was next to impossible without his arms free to steady himself, but he made it.

The butcher in the mask was stone-cold dead. From the hole in his head, it had been a high-caliber round. At least a .44. Maybe something heftier.

He heard wheels spin. He made it to the door as Tromso took off in the patrol car, taking the keys to the cuffs with him and leaving Ty alone with the sniper.

FORTY-EIGHT

TY HUNKERED DOWN IN THE doorway. A quick calculation told him that the sniper was almost certainly in a wooded area of densely planted birch trees about three hundred yards to the left of the cabin. He scanned the area, but couldn't see jack.

Tromso's patrol car had rolled almost out of sight. He could see the trunk bumping up and down as it sped away.

There was the sound of another shot. The brake-lights of the patrol car flared and pulsed. The car stopped. It was too far away for Ty to see what had happened to Tromso, and he sure as hell wasn't about to go look-see. Whoever was in the woods had been clinical. Two shots, and likely two dead. This wasn't some weekend warrior.

Still handcuffed, Ty duck-walked back toward the dead man. He turned so that his back was to the man's corpse and, peering through his knees for a visual, slowly peeled back the charred remnants of the mask. Blood and grey blancmange slopped out, oozing onto the cabin floor. The man's eyes were dark blood-filled orbs.

Ty shuffled back around so that he could get a better look. With so much facial damage it was hard to estimate his age, but he was in good shape, and couldn't have been much over mid-thirties. He had blond, collar-length hair, the ends of which had been tucked under the bottom of the black wool mask.

Twisting around, and leaning back, Ty managed to get his fingertips into the man's pocket and pull out a wallet. He let it drop open onto the floor, shimmied back round, and took a look at the clear plastic partition where the guy had a New York State driver's license. New York, New Hampshire, Ty had been close. The name didn't mean anything to him. He filed it away for later. If there was going to be a later.

Back outside it was quiet. The patrol car hadn't moved. No one had emerged from the woods to check their kill.

He waited for another thirty minutes before breaking from the cabin. He walked down the track. He could have run, but the truth was that if the sniper was still there and wanted to take him out, there wasn't much he could do about it.

Tromso was slumped at the wheel of the patrol car, his chin resting on the steering-wheel, eyes open with surprise. With difficulty, Ty managed to haul open the door, and find the keys to the handcuffs.

He spent another twenty minutes trying to open them. With his hands behind his back, it was impossible. He would have had to be double-jointed at the very least. He dropped the key a half-dozen times before he picked it up for a final time, and began to stagger down the track toward the road.

The hairs on the back of his neck bristled as he walked. He could feel eyes on him. He looked around, scanning the trees that crowded in on the track from either side. He didn't see anyone, but they were there.

He kept moving, resigned to the fact that at any second he might hear another crack, and his life would end.

FORTY-NINE

T HE AUDI SPED PAST A wooden sign that read 'Wisconsin Welcomes You'. Inside the car, Lock glanced behind him to see Malik curled up in the back, his eyes closed.

'You sleeping?' Lock asked him.

'Not really. Just couldn't keep my eyes open. Wish I could.'

'Well,' said Lock, 'the good news is we're out of Minnesota. Won't stop you being arrested, but at least it'll be the Wisconsin cops taking you in, so less chance of an accident.'

Malik sat up. 'Hey, Ryan, thanks for doing this. You were taking a risk.'

Lock shrugged. 'If we got caught, I was planning on telling them I'd picked you up hitchhiking, didn't know anything about what had gone down back there. Aiding and abetting is a hard charge to make stick. Prosecutors tend to lose interest once they have the person they really want.'

'Well, thanks anyway. Hey, you mind if I sit up front?'

'Go right ahead. You want me to pull over?'

'No, I'm good.' Malik levered himself through the gap between the front seats, and slumped next to Lock. 'Tell me this isn't happening,' he said.

'You mind if I ask you a couple of things, Malik?'

Malik looked out of the window as a mini-van drove past with a picture-postcard family: mom, dad, and two kids. 'Sure,' he said.

'Ty spoke to your neighbor about the night it happened. She said she was pretty sure she saw you hightailing it out of there.' As he said it, Lock watched Malik out of the corner of his eye.

Malik looked straight at Lock. 'She did see me.'

'So what happened?'

'Does it matter?'

Lock took his time answering. 'Matters if you want us to find the people responsible.'

Malik closed his eyes. 'I do.'

'So?'

Lock had noticed a grey Ford Explorer hanging behind them. It had been there since they had crossed the state line. There were two men in the front, both white, both wearing sunglasses, and both sporting close-crop semi-military haircuts. The Explorer was about two hundred yards behind now, far enough back to remain anonymous (or so the occupants thought), but close enough to maintain a visual on the Audi. Now they seemed to be closing up a little, cutting the distance between the two vehicles. He kept throwing hard glances at it. He wanted them to know he was onto them. That way he could force their next play.

Malik sighed. 'The night it happened, I got a call from Eve Barnes saying that her home was being watched. She was terrified. I could hear it in her voice. She'd been about as calm as could be expected up until then. I couldn't leave her to deal with it alone. Not after I'd tried to push her into pursuing it.'

'She was the mother of the boy you found at the stadium?' Lock said.

'Yes. Anyway, she didn't want to call the cops, for obvious reasons, so I agreed to go over there.' Malik trailed off for a moment. 'Kim was pissed.'

Behind them, the Explorer had tucked in behind a truck. They had, by Lock's estimation, about three miles to the next exit. If the Explorer stayed where it was, he planned on pulling off there and seeing if it followed.

'Anyway,' said Malik, oblivious to what was going on behind them, 'when I got there, they were both gone. Eve and Jack. I tried calling her cell, but it was dead. I drove around for a while, asked some of her neighbors. They hadn't seen anything. I didn't know what to do next, so I headed home to talk to Kim. When I got there . . . it was already too late.'

Lock's heart sank as he listened to Malik. Whoever it was, and it was likely that more than one person had been involved, they had played him well. Chances were that they'd been with Eve Barnes when she'd made the call. Once Malik had got to her place, or someone had seen him leave his house, they'd made their move. Still, even with everything that Lock knew about what had been happening, killing someone's family seemed beyond extreme. Unless, of course, they'd wanted to set him up. With the local cops in their pocket, Malik being shot and killed during capture would have tied things up nicely.

'So you fled?' Lock prompted, realizing when he checked his mirrors again that he had lost sight of the Explorer. It must have tucked in really tight behind the truck, which gave him an idea.

'I didn't want to leave them.' Tears ran down Malik's face as he spoke. 'But I knew if the cops showed up it was over for me. And that meant that whoever did it was going to get away. So I got out of there as fast as I could.'

'You did the right thing,' said Lock. 'Now, you have that seatbelt on nice and tight?'

'Yeah,' said Malik. 'Why?'

'I have to check the brakes on this thing,' said Lock, throwing an arm across Malik's chest and tapping the accelerator to get some distance between the rear of their car and the grille of the truck. Two seconds later, he took his foot off the gas pedal and stomped on the brake. He could feel the tap against the sole of his right foot as the Audi's anti-lock system kicked in.

He and Malik were thrown forward with a jolt. Lock watched the truck driver panic, and stomp down hard on his brakes as he tried to avoid rear-ending the Audi. With only a few feet to spare, Lock accelerated and flipped back out into the passing lane, out of the way of the truck.

His eyes were fixed on his mirror as chaos unfolded behind him. The driver of the Explorer had the same idea. He spun his wheel to try to move around the truck. It was a good idea, but an SUV wasn't the right tool for the job. Lock knew from experience that, to pull off that kind of move, you needed a low center of gravity, four-wheel drive or not.

The Explorer started to wobble. The driver's face tightened with panic. The passenger had thrown his hands on the dash as he white-knuckled it. He had what looked to be a Glock 9mm in his right hand. The way he was holding it, and the angle at which it was pointing, there was every chance he would drop one into his buddy's chest before they crashed.

Amateurs, thought Lock, as the truck's wheels started to seize and the rig's tires began to lose grip on the blacktop. The driver over-corrected. It spun out into the other lane. Lock accelerated harder to make sure the truck didn't clip the back of his Audi, and send him into a spin.

The Explorer was trapped on the outside. Sandwiched between the truck and a crash barrier that ran down the middle of the road, the driver didn't seem to know whether he should stick or double down, try to squeeze past, or hit the brakes and let the truck slide past him.

In the end, he did neither. As the truck inched its way toward him, the driver of the Explorer tried to move out of the way. He had a problem. There was nowhere to go. By the time he realized it, the side of the truck was already scraping his vehicle. There was a grinding of metal on metal.

Lock was safely clear by now. All he could do was watch the chaos behind him. The road had been empty behind the truck and the Explorer for a good distance. He had made sure of that. The truck driver would likely walk away. The occupants of the Explorer might not be so fortunate. He took his arm from Malik's chest.

Finally, they came to a halt. Now Lock pulled over and got out. He looked back down the highway. The truck driver clambered out of his cab, shaken but apparently unharmed.

There was no movement from inside the Explorer. Lock got back into his car, and pulled out onto a clear freeway. He switched the volume up on the scanner. There was already chatter of a traffic incident, but no mention of a police or other official unit being involved.

Whoever the two men tailing them had been, he doubted they were cops. He took a moment to check on his passenger. 'You okay?' he asked Malik.

'Guess my heart's still working,' he said.

'Good,' said Lock. That was a start.

FIFTY

TY WAS ALREADY FINDING IT tough to be a black man in this part of Minnesota. But being a black man in Minnesota with his hands cuffed behind his back, and having to persuade a complete stranger to unlock them, was a whole other level of difficulty. Thankfully, there was, if not American Express, cold, hard cash.

He had made it down to the road, and started walking. The gloom had cleared to reveal a sparkling bright day that was at odds with everything else. At any minute he expected the wail of police sirens, but they hadn't come. In fact it had taken a full fifteen minutes' walking along the quiet country road before he had seen a vehicle, and a further twenty before someone had stopped.

The man who pulled up next to him in a broken-down station wagon, with two hunting dogs in the back, grinned at him through yellowed smoker's teeth from the driver's seat. 'Let me guess, you slipped in the shower, and those cuffs just fell round your wrists and snapped into place?'

'How'd you guess?' said Ty.

'Happens more than you might think round here.' The man nodded behind him. 'Springs Falls? Am I right?'

'You lost me.'

'You're some actor, I'll give you that, young man. Spring Falls Correctional Facility is back there. That's where you've come from.'

Ty looked at him. 'You're not going to believe me if I tell you the truth, so let me save us both some time. I have the key. I have money. You get these things off, you can have the money and we never saw each other.'

The man didn't answer straight away. That was more of an answer than if he had said something. 'I dunno. What you do? I mean, if you robbed a bank, and I let you get away then I guess I could live with myself. But if you're some kind of a pervert or something . . .'

'Then I'm hardly going to tell you, am I? But no, I'm not a pervert.'

The man flattened a ragged mustache with his hand. 'How much we talking? There's money and then there's money.'

Ty knew he had the guy. But at any moment a fleet of cop cars could descend on them. He didn't have time for a prolonged negotiation. 'I have a thousand dollars in cash on me. You can have it all. Full and final offer. You say no, I keep walking.'

The man's eyes narrowed. 'Where's the key, and where's the cash?'

'Both here in my back pocket.'

The man got out of his vehicle. He dipped a hand toward the front pocket of Ty's jeans. 'Sure you're not some kind of a pervert?' he asked.

'Even if I was, I doubt you'd be my type.'

The man fished out the key and Ty's wallet. He took a step back and started to look through the wallet. He took out the cash. 'You got cards here too. Bank of America. Visa. How does a guy who busted out of jail have all this?'.

The man grabbed the handle of the driver's door. He started to open it. Ty took three long strides as he started to climb into the vehicle. He kicked out, catching the guy's ankle with his foot and tripping him. He went down. Ty managed to stay on his feet. He stood over him.

'Don't hit me!'

'Let's try this again, shall we?'

Ty sat down hard on his chest, his back to the man's face. 'Now,' said Ty, wiggling his hands. 'Get that key, and take these off, before I lay my whole weight down and start cracking ribs.'

'I can't breathe,' the man protested.

'Better work fast, then, huh?' said Ty.

'I could have a heart attack.'

'Hey, we all gotta go sometime,' said Ty, feeling less than charitable.

There was a scrambling and scuffling as the man tried to find the key to the cuffs. A few seconds later, Ty felt them pop. He grabbed the driver's door, and hauled himself back to his feet. He rubbed at his wrists. Tromso had made sure the cuffs were on good and tight. He checked out the road in both directions. It was still quiet. No one had passed but the odds were it wouldn't stay that way for too much longer. He put out a hand and helped the man up.

'You could have killed me.' He stood there and rubbed at his chest. He was winded but unharmed.

Ty stared at him. 'We had an agreement. You broke it. By rights, I should kick your ass.'

The man flapped at him as Ty put his hand out. 'My money?'

The guy grumbled. Another look from Ty settled him down. He pulled out the roll and Ty took back his cash. He peeled off two hundred and handed it back.

FIFTY-ONE

THE STATION WAGON PULLED UP at the bottom of the track that led to the cabin. Ty took the keys, the man's cell phone, and got out. The older guy was still rubbing his chest and grumbling about being ripped off.

Ty ducked his head back into the car. 'Wait here and don't speak to anyone. That's another two hundred. If anyone does show, honk the horn.'

The other jerked his head up the track. 'What's up there anyway?'

'Better you don't know,' Ty told him.

Ty left him to it and hiked up the track, staying close to the tree line. He was gambling on the sniper having cleared out. If he was still about, and decided to take a shot at him, there would be little he could do about it. But he wanted to take a look at the scene before the cops finally tracked down Tromso.

It was a short hike. Tromso's patrol car was still where it had been, the fat cop slumped over the wheel. Ty took a quick walk around, trying to estimate the angle and direction the shots had come from. He retrieved his own weapon from inside the patrol car, but left Tromso's service gun with the body.

He walked back to the cabin, keeping an eye on the ridge. Everything was quiet. What made the place perfect for a little quiet torture made it work equally well as a location to kill a cop. Ty took a couple of pictures of the blond guy and his ID with his cell phone. He didn't have a signal here but as soon as he did he'd pass them on to Lock via encrypted email so he could run some checks.

From the size of the hole in the front of his face, the single shot that had taken him out was consistent with the rounds that had been fired at the patrol car. Ty peered back up the ridge at the angles: it didn't look like the sniper had moved much, if at all. He, or they if he had a spotter, had scoped out his spot, set up, then picked off his targets with cool efficiency. If he'd stuck around, he could easily have killed Ty. So either he'd split after he'd finished Tromso, or Ty wasn't on his agenda.

Ty left the cabin, and started toward the ridge. The trees, mostly silver birch with some spruce, were nicely spaced, and though there was a slope, it was easy ground to cover. He followed a line from the cabin door, tacking on a diagonal. The trees thinned nearer the top and the slope became more severe. Ty slowed, looking for signs of disturbance.

He found it about twenty yards further on. A glint of reflected light caught his eye. He bent to take a closer look. It was a brass shell casing. He picked it up, and laid it in the palm of his hand as, below, he heard a car horn sound a long single blast.

FIFTY-TWO

T Y WATCHED AS TWO PATROL cars pulled in behind the station wagon. One had campus-police markings, the other was from the county sheriff's department. Kelly Svenson got out of the campus patrol car on her own, and walked round to talk to the guy, who took about half a second to dime him out. Ty could see him patting his hand to his chest, and otherwise miming the ordeal he'd been through. No doubt any bribery or deception on his part wasn't going to feature in his version of events.

A city cop in plain clothes joined her. He was a tall white guy, whom Ty recognized from outside the Becker residence. They stepped off to one side. Going by their body language, they seemed to be debating who would go on up the track to see what had happened to Tromso. They walked back to their vehicles. The state cop took the lead while Kelly hung back.

Ty decided that he wasn't about to stick around. He already knew how the story had ended for Tromso. Kelly had been happy enough to see her partner disappear Ty from custody. He wasn't going to trust her a second time. And certainly not with a dead cop in the mix.

FIFTY-THREE

LOCK PULLED INTO THE PARKING lot of Walmart. He parked well away from the front entrance. He left Malik in the car, his head resting against the window, a sweatshirt cushioning him from the glass and obscuring his face. Inside, Lock bought Malik everything he'd need for the next week, including clothes and food, stuff that didn't require a refrigerator and wouldn't spoil, like protein bars. He also picked up three cases of water, a pre-paid cell phone, toothbrush, toothpaste, shampoo and soap.

He wheeled his cart out of the store, and loaded the supplies into the back of the Audi. He pulled out of the parking lot, and headed a half-mile down the road to a motel he had scoped out on TripAdvisor. It had the worst reviews in the greater Madison area, which made it perfect for his purpose, as long as Malik didn't mind roaches.

At the motel, he parked at the back, got out and walked to the manager's office. A woman in her late fifties, who must have applied her makeup in the dark, greeted him cheerily enough. He kept the conversation to a minimum, paid in cash for a week, and explained that he would clean his own room.

'No hookers. No drugs,' she said, licking her finger and thumbing through the roll of bills he had just handed her.

Lock agreed politely to the terms, took the room key and headed back outside. As he walked to the car, he saw the empty passenger seat.

He scanned the area. Malik was nowhere to be seen. Then he noticed him by a Dumpster. He was standing there, hands in his pockets, staring out at the road.

Lock went over to him. 'You do know you're supposed to be hiding out, right?'

Malik turned, as if he had only just noticed him. 'Sorry.'

'Listen, Malik, we're both taking a risk in helping you. Not that I'm complaining. But you have to hold up your end. And, right now, your end is staying out of sight. If you're having second thoughts, if you don't think you can stay put, I need to know. I can organize an attorney, and they can speak to the authorities. You'd still be taking a risk handing yourself over, but it would be better than getting picked up by whoever happens to find you first.'

Malik looked at Lock, and for the first time Lock got a glimpse of the man he had been before his family was slaughtered in their home. 'It won't happen again. I promise.'

A half-hour later, with Malik set up in his room, Lock peeled back out of the motel parking lot. Malik had been sleeping when Lock had left the room, the 'Do Not Disturb' sign swinging gently from the handle. He headed for the highway, moving north, back toward Harrisburg, hoping for some answers.

PART TWO

PART TWO

FIFTY-FOUR

J ACK?' HE SAID QUIETLY.

The boy stared at him from under a fringe of brown hair. He got up. Jack's mother tried to grab her son's hand but he brushed her away.

Jack followed him out of the room. Jack understood. They were brothers. Bound not by blood but something much stronger: bound by pain and torment and, more than anything, their controlling emotion. Bound by rage.

'If you touch him . . .' Eve shouted after him.

'You know I'd never do that, right?' he said to Jack. It was important Jack knew that. Vital.

Jack shrugged, like he didn't care one way or the other. 'I know,' he said. 'You're not like them. You're like me.'

'Was like you,' he corrected the boy. 'Not anymore. That's the good news, Jack. It's important you know that all this changes. You don't have to be stuck feeling the same way.'

Jack followed him outside into the sunshine. He closed his eyes and felt the warmth on his face. He took pleasure in the simple things. Sunshine. Fresh air. The smell of the pine trees. The pretty college town laid out beneath them, the people in it oblivious of what lay ahead.

'You have any news about the coach?' Jack asked.

Jack asking questions was a good sign. A very good sign. He was making progress. He had started to see the larger picture.

'He's safe, as far as I know,' he told the boy.

Jack said, 'That's good. I'm glad. He tried to help me.'

'Yes,' he said. 'He did. And look at the thanks he got. That's what we're dealing with here, Jack. An honest man tries to tell the truth, and look what they do to him. That's why they have to be punished.'

FIFTY-FIVE

L OCK PULLED UP IN A silver Chevy Blazer. A second later Ty emerged through the woods at the side of the road. He opened the passenger door and climbed in.

'What's with the new ride?' he asked Lock.

'Rental. Thought I'd let the Audi cool off. We had a little static on the trip down there.'

'How's he holding up?' Ty asked.

Lock didn't know how to answer that one. As he knew too well, when someone had experienced what Malik had, there was no way of measuring how they were holding up. Your head could be clear one moment and the next you could have a gun in your mouth with your finger on the trigger. You were in the middle of the storm and there was no way of knowing how long it would last.

'He's safe,' Lock said. 'Had to change the safe-house last minute so I put him in a fleabag motel outside Madison. As long as he stays put, he should be fine. If he's picked up it'll be by the cops in Madison, the feebs or state. Either way it's better than being pinched here. I told him that if he's arrested, he's to lawyer up immediately and explain the situation he was facing in Minnesota so that at least the cops there are aware of what's going down here.'

'If we can figure out what actually is going down because, right now, I have no idea,' said Ty.

Ty had already taken Lock through his abduction from the police station by Tromso, Kelly's involvement as she, at very least, had turned a blind eye to Tromso taking him, and the events at the cabin.

'Okay,' said Lock. 'So we know Tromso was involved in the cover-up, if not the abuse itself.'

'I wouldn't rule it out either,' said Ty. 'That first night when he rolled up at the stadium after Malik called it in, he must have had an idea it was Becker.'

Now they were on Wolf Road, the stadium over to their right, rising out of the open ground. Lock headed back toward the main college campus. 'We don't know that for sure. Worst thing we can do right now is rush to conclusions.'

They kept driving until they reached the edge of the campus. Knots of students walked to class, backpacks slung over their shoulders or cellphones in hand. They seemed subdued, but maybe not much more so than usual. Lock pulled over and parked.

'What we doing here?' Ty asked.

'Malik told me about the chancellor, Laird, that he was someone else who was keen on getting him to stay quiet. He was using a new contract as bait. Different bait, but the intent was the same. Thought I might talk to him.'

Lock pulled on the parking brake and started to get out. 'I want you to check out the Becker residence. Should be clear by now. They only have the homicide investigation, according to Salas. They're not running anything about Becker's previous activities. Do some snooping. Phone bills, computers, anything you can find.'

FIFTY-SIX

THE CHANCELLOR'S OFFICE WAS SITUATED in a red-brick building housing mainly administration offices that faced a grassy quadrangle in the middle of the campus. On the other side was the main college library. In the middle of the quadrangle a grey statue was mounted on a granite plinth. Students were scattered around on the grass. A couple of jocks threw a football to each other, shooting glances at a gaggle of sorority girls setting up a booth for some charity fundraiser.

Lock walked past them toward the red-brick building. He jogged up the steps, and went inside. As he checked a building directory, a middle-aged security guard wandered over.

'Can I help you?' he asked Lock.

'Chancellor's office? I'm kind of in a hurry. Supposed to be meeting him five minutes ago. Couldn't get parked.'

'Fourth floor. Elevator's kind of slow. Stairs might be quicker.'

'Thanks.'

Lock pushed through a set of double doors into a stairwell. He climbed the stairs, and exited through another set of double doors on the fourth floor. He walked down a corridor, following the signs for the chancellor and vice-chancellor's offices. He pushed through a heavy wooden door with a brass handle into a small waiting area. A secretary was performing the usual gatekeeper function. He leaned close to her, keeping his voice low. 'I'm from Celltech Security. Could you let the chancellor know I need a moment of his time? It's urgent. If you emphasize I'm from Celltech, I'm sure he'll see me.'

Lock had barely had a chance to scan the first mahogany-framed graduating-class picture on the wall before the secretary was putting down her phone. 'You can go straight in,' she told him.

Laird was pacing by the window as Lock walked in. He closed the door gently behind him as Laird turned. Lock registered Laird's lack of recognition. 'Given that your head of security, chief of campus police, or whatever title he had, has just been killed, you might want to do something about your personal security.'

'Who did you say you were from?' Laird asked.

'That's what I'm talking about.' Lock walked around the desk to the window that faced out over the quadrangle. 'Chancellor, it might be an idea if you kept your blinds closed. At least for the next few days.'

Laird looked round as Lock closed them, shutting out the sunlight, leaving them both in the gloom. 'I don't follow. Why would I—'

'Tromso was killed from a distance by a sniper,' said Lock.

Laird began to reach for his phone. Lock grabbed his wrist. 'I'm here to help you, Chancellor. If you're not already beyond help. Now, look at me.'

Laird did. Lock let go of his wrist. 'If I wanted to harm you, it would already have happened. Now, what do you know about who killed Tromso?'

'Shaw?' said Laird. 'You think it was Shaw?'

Lock walked across to the credenza and flicked on a lamp. He wanted to get a good look at Laird's face. He sat down opposite Laird. 'No, it wasn't Shaw. Whoever did this was a professional. A pro sniper, not a pro baller. Almost certainly someone with military experience. You have any idea who that might be?'

'This has all gotten completely out of hand,' Laird said.

'Y'think?' said Lock, unable to keep the sarcasm out of his voice.

Laird slumped forward at his desk. His head was in his hands. 'You don't understand the pressure I've been under. If this got out . . .'

His fingernails digging into the palms of his hands to stop himself exploding, Lock studied the curious specimen of humanity sitting across from him. What he really wanted to do was throw Laird and his five-hundred-dollar suit through the window. '"If this got out" – what?' he said. 'Your college's reputation would be dragged through the mud? You'd lose money? You'd be fired? Listen to me, Chancellor, we're beyond all that now. A man's family has been killed because he was trying to tell the truth. And you'd already tried to pay him off. Was it you, Chancellor? Did you ask Tromso to go kill the Shaw family? How deep are you in?'

Either the shock on Laird's face was genuine or he was one hell of an actor. 'Don't be ridiculous. You think a man in my position would countenance something like that? I offered Coach Shaw that deal to prevent any . . .' He trailed off.

The idea of throwing Laird out of the window was starting to gain fresh appeal to Lock. Not that Laird knew it, but he was lucky it was him he was dealing with and not Ty. Ty would have killed him by now. There was no doubt in Lock's mind about that.

Lock bent over so that he was in Laird's face. 'To prevent any what?'

Laird swallowed hard. 'When I was made aware of Aubrey Becker's activities, I banned him from campus and handed over the investigation to the relevant authorities. I did what I was required to do.'

'Required', thought Lock. A nice neat word. The kind of word an attorney would use. Of course, what it meant in reality was that Laird had done the bare minimum to get the whole mess off his neat mahogany desk.

'And I'm sure they'll give you a chocolate medal. Now, I'm going ask you again. To prevent what?'

Laird looked at Lock. Their eyes met. There was a little steel in Laird's expression now. 'Aubrey was the governor's brother. A scandal like this . . . the stakes were high. I was trying to protect Coach Shaw. It's hardly my fault that he couldn't be persuaded.'

Lock snapped. He grabbed Laird by the throat, and began to squeeze, increasing the pressure slowly, making sure he had the man's full attention. 'Listen to me, you sanctimonious paper-pushing asshole, you are going to tell me everything you know about this. You understand? And if you don't, then this college is going to have one more dead body when I walk out of here.'

FIFTY-SEVEN

TY PULLED UP TO THE Becker house. The gates were closed, and he doubted there was anyone inside to open them. He got out and checked the mailbox. It was full. He separated the real mail from the junk, jammed the junk back in, and tossed the real mail onto the passenger seat. He got back into the car and drove down the road a few hundred yards. He nudged off road, and left the Chevy Blazer hidden from passing traffic by a stand of trees.

He hiked his way to the house. The drapes were still closed from the night of the murders. The front door was locked. He walked round to the back of the property, smashed a glass panel in an external door and let himself in. The alarm had been switched off.

Ty took off his shoes and walked through the house. There was still dried blood in the front hallway where Gretchen and Aubrey Becker had met their end. In the dining room, their final meal lay on the plates. Green mold had already started to form on a basket of bread in the middle of the table. This crime scene didn't trouble him, or give rise to any strong emotions, not in the way that seeing Malik's house had.

He walked back into the hall, and climbed the staircase, with its family portraits of the Becker clan. It didn't look like a child molester's house, but Ty wasn't exactly sure what would. Guys like Becker hid in plain sight. The higher their profile, the less likely it was that people would assume they had anything to hide.

The real puzzle for Ty was Becker's wife, Gretchen. She must have known on some level that the interest her husband took in young boys was abnormal. Even if she hadn't witnessed anything directly, surely she would have had her suspicions. Maybe that was where Becker's money came in. For her to turn in her husband she would have stood to lose a lot, assuming the inevitable civil suits from victims, as well as her status in the community.

At the top of the stairs, Ty stopped and listened. Satisfied that he was on his own, he moved into the master bedroom. He checked through closets and drawers, taking his time, trying to ensure he didn't miss anything. He wasn't surprised that Becker didn't have a gun safe, or a firearm of any description. It spoke of the man's arrogance that he didn't appear to have worried about his own safety.

He moved methodically through the rooms. The master bedroom had a large en-suite. Apart from a prescription bottle of Viagra, which made Ty shudder, there was nothing of interest. It was the same for the three guest bedrooms. He left Aubrey Becker's study until last.

It was almost as large as the master bedroom. The walls were wood-paneled, and the carpet, a red and green plaid pattern, looked as if it had been bought in a country-club closing down sale. There was a green leather chesterfield next to the window, and a large desk surrounded by bookshelves. Apart from the usual leather-bound classics, there was one shelf devoted to photography, and another of books about sailing. The ass end of Minnesota struck Ty as a strange place to settle for a man interested in boats, but there were lakes, he guessed.

On the desk was a large computer screen. Ty would have laid good money that if there was anything incriminating about Becker it was here. He followed the cable running from the monitor to the tower. As he bent, he saw wires trailing where the hard drive had been ripped out. A couple of the screws from where the casing had been removed were lying on the carpet. Becker could have done it himself when things had begun to go south, or it might have been removed by a third party later on. There was no way of knowing.

Ty went back to the books. On one of the lower shelves he noticed a high school yearbook. It dated back to the 1960s. He pulled it out and flicked through, finding a suitably pompous looking teenage Aubrey Becker dressed in a suit and tie. He didn't look all that different from the more recent pictures of him and his wife in silver frames on the desk. The guy looked like he'd born and died middle-aged.

Ty put the yearbook back on the shelf, and worked his way through the rest of the titles, hoping to turn up other personal stuff. He was out of luck. The yearbook was as personal an item as there was in Becker's study. The hard drive was a likely treasure trove, but that had either been destroyed or spirited away to save the Becker dynasty any further embarrassment.

FIFTY-EIGHT

THE ESTEEMED CHANCELLOR'S OFFICE REEKED of the vomit he'd deposited in the trash can under his desk after Lock had cut off his air supply for long enough to get his attention. The blinds were still closed. Laird was half slumped over his desk. He didn't look any better for having got it all off his chest. Neither had Lock learned much more than he and Ty already either knew or suspected.

Laird had been at the college for a little under six years. He'd transferred from an institution in Indiana where he had driven some serious growth in student numbers and alumni contributions via an ambitious football program. The college at Harrisburg had signed him on to perform the same magic here. Leading the appointments committee had been none other than Aubrey Becker.

'It makes it more than a little awkward when you start to suspect that the man to whom you owe your job is less than savory,' he'd told Lock.

There had been nothing specific connecting Aubrey Becker to anything criminal. Becker used the campus as his own private fiefdom, and was often seen with teenage boys. The story was that, as he and Gretchen couldn't have children, this was his way of compensating for a fatherly instinct. Not everyone bought it, including Laird, but there had only been rumors. If complaints had been made, they had not reached Laird's desk.

Lock wasn't sure he believed that part. But he did know that a man like Laird was hardly going to start screaming, 'Child molester!' and pointing the finger at a man like Becker without something more than suspicious behavior and rumors.

It was only when Malik had raised the alarm, then wouldn't let it go that he'd taken action. He'd kicked it down to Tromso to investigate and banned Becker from the campus in the interim. That had led to the threat of legal action from Becker's attorneys in Minneapolis. 'But I held firm,' he said to Lock.

'Yeah, you're a regular hero,' Lock told him. 'So what else?'

'There was no else. It was being investigated.'

Lock had to fight the sneer from his voice. 'By Tromso? Why didn't you contact someone in Minneapolis?'

It was Laird's turn to smirk. 'Are you forgetting the part about Aubrey's brother being governor? What good would it have done? I was hoping that by banning him from campus it would scare him enough to stop him doing whatever he was doing.'

'By which you mean raping kids.'

That wiped the smug grin from Laird's face. 'I didn't have the details.'

'So why not go out of state? Call the FBI.'

Laird spread his hands out of the desk. 'Even if I had, they would have had to wait while the ongoing investigation came to some sort of conclusion. Tromso told me that if he did find evidence he would hand it to a special prosecutor.'

'And you believed him?' said Lock. 'You know he burned the Shaw home to the ground, right?'

Laird blanched. 'No, I most certainly did not.'

'My partner watched him go in with a can of gasoline. Getting rid of the evidence.'

'You think Tromso killed them? That's preposterous.'

Lock stared hard at Laird. 'He lied about everything connected to the crime scene in his report. Must have realized it wasn't going to stand up.

We have pictures to prove that his version of what went down was pure fantasy.'

Lock could see the cogs turning in Laird's mind. Every logical pathway led to how he could extricate himself and limit the damage to the college. 'Then if he did that, and he's dead, and so is Aubrey Becker . . .'

'You're in the clear? That what you're thinking, Chancellor?'

As Lock stood up, Laird flinched. He really was a pitiful sight, thought Lock. A man who thought only in terms of public perceptions and balance sheets. A man who didn't care about the damage that might have been done to those left behind, or the pain of Becker's victims, not to mention how he'd placed Malik Shaw's family in danger, and pretty much signed their death warrant, by not doing the right thing. Even though Lock knew none of that would stand up in a court of law – Laird had dotted his *i*s and crossed his *t*s – it was still how any decent person would see it.

'Not me,' said Laird. 'The institution.'

The intercom on Laird's desk buzzed. 'May I?' he asked Lock.

Lock nodded for him to go ahead. 'Just don't say anything silly,' he said, his hand falling to the butt of his SIG Sauer to emphasize just what a bad idea it would be.

'Yes,' said Laird.

'Officer Svenson is on her way up to see you.'

Lock knew a cue to get the hell out of Dodge when he heard one. 'I wouldn't be so sure that this is over. Malik Shaw didn't kill Tromso and the other person they found.'

'How can you possibly know that?' said Laird.

'Because I was with him,' said Lock. He stopped at the door, and nodded toward the windows. 'I'd keep your blinds closed, and your eyes open, Chancellor. I've a feeling this thing still has a ways to go.'

FIFTY-NINE

T HE ATTIC WAS DARK AND dusty. Head bowed, Ty crawled through the clutter, using a flashlight he'd found in the kitchen. After he'd got through searching the office, he'd tried to think of where else someone like Aubrey Becker would hide something he didn't want the world to see.

Not that Ty knew if there was anything. But while he was there, he figured he might as well go over every inch of the property. There was something else that had lodged in his mind. A story Lock had told him about his time in the British Royal Military Police in Germany. It had been an investigation into a serial predator similar to Becker, and the evidence that had sent the man to jail had been carefully stored in his attic. It made sense. It was a place that a casual visitor was hardly likely to stumble into. Plus the house had no basement so that left this as a storage area.

Ty worked his way methodically through the piles of boxes. Most of it seemed to be soft furnishings, drapes and pillows that he figured had been placed there by Gretchen Becker. At the bottom of one stack, he came across some old files. Maybe this was it. He pulled the box out, took off the lid and began to go through the papers but nothing leaped out at him.

At the very bottom he found a pile of old magazines. Gay porn, and some old naturist stuff from the 1960s, the kind that had families. He didn't dwell on it. He took a quick look at the covers and threw them back into the box. Knowing what he did about Becker's appetites, it made his skin crawl.

He wasn't going to find anything there that would tell him something they didn't already know. He climbed back down the attic ladder and stood in the hallway. He checked back through the rooms. He grabbed the yearbook from Becker's office and took one final look. The young Becker stared back at him, no hint of what he was to become. Ty closed it again, but took it with him. Downstairs he combed through a papers caddy in the kitchen, retrieving some itemized cellular phone bills for both Aubrey and Gretchen. Lock could give them to Salas and see what he came up with.

Finally, and with a feeling that he'd missed something – something important – Ty walked back out of the Becker home and got into the Chevy Blazer. At the end of the long driveway, he turned back toward Harrisburg.

SIXTY

TY PULLED OVER TO THE curb opposite the diner. Lock opened the front passenger door and got in.

'What did Laird say?' Ty asked him.

'Apart from giving me the I-was-just-doing-my-job line? Not a whole lot. He did the minimum. Turned it over to the cops, and banned Becker from campus. He didn't have anything to do with what happened to Kim and the kids. Not directly, anyway. You? Anything turn up at the house?'

'Hard drive for Becker's computer is gone. Found some dirty magazines in the attic.' Ty opened the glove compartment and pulled out the bills he'd filched. 'Got some phone records that were lying around. Maybe you can get Salas to run them.'

Lock leafed through them. 'This is good. This bill here for Aubrey Becker must have just come in. I'll ask Salas to get us everything after the last call on here as well. By the way, that female cop was on her way in to see Laird when I was leaving.'

'She see you?' Ty asked.

'No. I took the stairs. But Laird probably told her about my visit. Wonder where she fits into all this. You said she saw Tromso driving you away?'

'Yeah,' said Ty, his expression sour. He was still annoyed with himself for having been taken in so easily by her. 'Sat and watched it happen.'

'Maybe she was scared of him. Didn't want to intervene,' Lock theorized.

'Or she was in on it?' said Ty.

'Or that.' Lock drummed his fingers on the dash. 'We're missing something here. Hey, can I see your cell phone?'

Ty dug into his pocket and handed it to him. Lock hit the picture icon and started swiping through. 'We should check in with Malik,' he said.

SIXTY-ONE

MALIK SNATCHED UP THE PHONE on the first ring. The food and supplies Lock had left with him were still on the floor, still packed. He was wearing the same clothes. He hadn't showered. He'd barely moved from the bed where he was lying now, staring at the ceiling, afraid to close his eyes. The darkness brought horror. He planned on staying awake until exhaustion overtook him and he had no other choice than to plunge back into the abyss.

'Yes,' he said, his voice ragged and broken, the voice of a stranger.

'It's Ryan. You staying put? Any problems?'

Malik was grateful that Lock hadn't asked how he was or if he was okay. 'I'm here. There's not been any problems.'

'Good. In a moment I'm going to send you through a couple of pictures. They're not very pleasant but I want to know if you recognize the person in them.'

Malik sat up. 'Okay. Who is it?'

'Someone Ty had a run in with. Don't worry, he's safe here. The other guy not so much. Take a look, see if it jogs anything, and I'll call you back in a couple of minutes.'

Lock hung up, and Malik waited. A few moments later the phone chimed twice. Malik opened the pictures. Lock had been right: they were gruesome. Before what had happened, they would have upset him. Not anymore.

He waited for Lock to call back. Again, Malik answered immediately.

'I don't know his name,' said Malik, 'but I know who he is.'

SIXTY-TWO

THEY SAT SIDE BY SIDE cross-legged on the floor of the forest. Through a gap in the pine trees, they could see Harrisburg laid out beneath them. It was getting darker, and as the sun shrank from the town, the cold was bitter. A wind picked up from the east, rattling its way through the trees and making the boy shiver. He took the scope and handed it to Jack.

'Here,' he told the boy. 'Now, press your eyes up against it. Yeah, that's right, close your left eye. Try not to squint, though.'

Jack was so focused, so concentrated, but he could also see the wariness in the boy's eyes. That wouldn't go away. It would stay with him. He knew that because he had it too. The only comfort was that it could serve someone well if they knew how to channel it. Wariness, suspicion, a high level of alertness, whatever you wanted to call it, had kept him alive where others hadn't been so fortunate. He hoped in time that Jack would come to understand that along with all the pain there were also blessings.

'Okay, tell me what you can see,' he said to the boy.

'Hey, I can see the stadium,' Jack said. He lowered the scope from his eye. 'Could you hit the stadium from here with your gun?'

'Lemme see . . . I probably could, but it's a little too far to have any accuracy. You'd want to be closer in.'

Jack frowned, apparently a little disappointed by the answer. 'I don't think my mom wants to be here,' he said.

'I know. But it won't be for much longer. I promise you.'

Jack grabbed a piece of wood from the forest floor, and began to dig it into the ground. His brow furrowed. 'What was it like for you? Y'know, with Becker and . . .?'

That Jack couldn't bring himself to say the other name didn't surprise him. They had both left scars, but the man whom Jack couldn't name had made sure that the wounds he left were physical as well as psychological.

He took a breath. He had known that this question, and more like it, had been coming since he had shared with Jack what had happened to him, the experiences they had in common. He had decided that he owed it to Jack to be honest. And he felt the boy would understand. Victims did, though he tried not to see himself as a victim so much as a survivor. And now as an avenger whose enemy was silence. So, talking about it was good.

'At first,' he said, 'it was nice. All the attention. All the things he would buy me. Getting taken to the college games. I felt . . . special. You know what I mean, right?'

Jack nodded.

'He didn't do anything at first. He'd give me a hug, or there was one time when he was driving me back from the fair and he had to pull over the car because I was feeling sick from all the candy I'd eaten. Anyway, I was throwing up, and he was rubbing my back, telling me to get it all out. And even when I couldn't throw up anymore, and wanted to get back into the car and go home, he kept rubbing. Stuff like that.'

Jack was staring off into the distance. He knew the look. 'Same with me,' said Jack. 'The first time was in the car. I had shorts on . . . And what about, you know, the other one?'

He wasn't ready to talk about that yet, even if Jack was. 'Rougher, huh? No presents. He just took what he wanted.'

Jack shivered.

'But it's all over now, Jack.'

The boy looked up at him. 'So what are we doing here? I mean, if it's all over.'

He got to his feet, grabbed the rifle and the scope and started back toward the house. Jack got up and chased after him. 'Why?'

He turned back to the boy. 'You see all those people down there? They knew. Or if they didn't know, they knew someone who knew someone who did. That's why this happened. That's why we're here now. You and me. Because those people need to pay for what they did.'

'We can't punish all of them,' said Jack.

Up near the house, he could see a car approaching. Its headlights flickered through gaps in the trees. 'Sure we can,' he told the boy.

SIXTY-THREE

ALAS'S NAME FLASHED UP ON Lock's phone. He hit the answer
button. 'What you got?'

'Weston Reeves. Forty-seven years of age. White male born in
New Hampshire. Resident in Minnesota for the past twenty-five years.
Worked in a variety of roles for Aubrey Becker. Security, fixer and general
gopher. I'm still working on him but, yeah, Mr Shaw remembered
correctly.'

'He work for any of the rest of the family?' Lock asked. Across the
street, Ty was getting them coffee and something to eat while Lock kept an
eye out for any other members of the college or town police department.

'You mean like the governor? Not as far as I can tell,' Salas told him.
'Talking to people, I get the impression that the rest of the family had been
distancing themselves from Aubrey over the past couple of years.'

'They knew?' said Lock, watching Ty walk out of the diner and start to
cross the street.

'Impossible to say. But I'd imagine that if there were rumors flying
around they would have picked up on them.'

Ty opened the passenger door of the Chevy and handed Lock a coffee.
'And were there rumors?' Lock asked Salas. He covered the phone and said
to Ty: 'Blond dude who wanted to carve you up was working for Becker.'

192

'Yeah,' said Salas. 'Going back a long time. Couple of out-of-court settlements too. Big ones. Soon as complaints were made the Becker family sent the lawyers in with a check book and an iron-clad non-disclosure agreement. Guess they didn't want it out that there was a pay day for anyone whose kid had crossed Aubrey's path.'

'Any law-enforcement investigations?'

'One. About five years ago. Kid who lived in Murray County and had come up to Harrisburg for a summer camp at the college. Went home, told Mom and Dad that Aubrey Becker had made an inappropriate approach toward him, and this time someone took it seriously.'

'Another pay-off?' Lock asked.

'Maybe. It went away in any case. But here's the twist. The sheriff who was looking into it, six months later he's run off the road one night. Survives the crash but while he's trying to pull his head out of the windshield someone puts three shots into him. No way of saying for sure if it's connected or not, but it did kind of leap out at me.'

The implication was obvious to Lock. Someone connected to the Becker family had been worried enough that they'd resorted to killing a county sheriff in order to save Aubrey Becker. 'Anything else?' Lock said to Salas.

'That's it for now, but like I said, I'll keep digging. Got a feeling I'll find plenty more too. Kind of have me a feeling that our governor ain't gonna be running for president.'

'Think you might be right,' said Lock. Salas ended the call. Lock peeled back the plastic lid on the coffee mug and took a sip. 'You catch that?' he asked Ty.

'Enough, yeah. So who do we think took out this Reeves cat and Tromso?'

'Don't know,' said Lock. 'But sure looks like someone tying up loose ends. Becker's dead, and apart from a bunch of families who've already been paid off, who is there left to throw the family skeleton out of the closet? Tromso, for sure, and this guy Reeves. They go, they pin it on Malik, and that's your ending neatly wrapped up with a bow on top for anyone who looks into it.'

'So why leave me?' Ty asked.

Lock shrugged. 'Any number of reasons. Ran out of ammo. Couldn't get a shot off. Or, more likely, didn't think you were important enough to warrant a bullet.'

Ty dug into a brown-paper bag and grabbed a tuna sandwich. He handed one to Lock. 'Don't buy it. Dude was a pro. If he'd wanted to kill me, he would have. I had my hands cuffed, couldn't move that fast. It wouldn't have been a problem.'

'So,' said Lock, 'he decided not to. Like I said, he probably had you down as some random guy who'd got on the wrong side of Tromso and Reeves.'

A college police cruiser was heading down the main drag toward them. Ty noticed it first. He put his sandwich on the dash, and his hand fell to the butt of his SIG. He and Lock watched it roll past.

'Guess we can speculate all we want. But that's not gonna tell us anything. Let's go check out Mr Reeves's place. See if we can't find something there,' said Lock, putting the Chevy Blazer into drive, and pulling away from the curb before the police cruiser had a chance to take another pass at them.

SIXTY-FOUR

WESTON REEVES HAD LIVED IN a three-bedroom steel-sided rambler that sat on a corner lot on a quiet street in Wolf Falls, a small town about eight miles north-east of Harrisburg. Lock parked the Chevy in the empty driveway. He and Ty got out. The house next door and the one opposite were both dark. The street was empty.

Both men stood back from the house and took a look. They could tell a lot about someone from the outside of their house. Weston Reeves's home was no exception.

For a start, all the blinds were drawn, although it was likely he had left this place for the last time when the sun was up. A metal grille gate covered the front door, which sported a heavy-duty lock. A dummy alarm box was mounted high above the front door, and two security cameras at the front. The cameras covered the driveway and the front door. All the security seemed over-the-top for the location. Security of that kind was usually reserved for high-crime neighborhoods, or a property with something valuable inside, and Reeves hadn't struck them as the kind of guy who had money. His boss, yes, Weston not so much.

The dummy alarm was another tell. Real alarms had a habit of going off without warning, which in turn attracted attention either from private security, law enforcement or neighbors. Fine, if you were home. Less so, if you weren't and someone gained access to the property when you had something to hide. Either that or you were too cheap to pay for a real system, but the other security features told Lock and Ty it wasn't that.

Ty walked to the back of the property. Lock stayed out front, keeping watch for twitching curtains or concerned neighbors.

A minute later, there was the sound of bolts being thrown back, and the front door opened. Ty's face looked grim. 'House is pretty regular, but I found a cellar.'

Lock stared at him. 'The kid?'

Ty shook his head. That had been his first thought. It had likely been in both their minds since they'd got the name and realised the connection between Reeves and Becker. It had turned his stomach. He wanted to find Jack Barnes, and his mom, but he sure as hell didn't want to find either or both of them here.

Ty stepped out of the way to let Lock in, and closed the door behind them.

The front hallway opened up into a living room. The walls were painted a sickly lime green. There was thick red carpet in every room, apart from the kitchen and bathrooms. The living room was dominated by a huge old projection TV. The place was neat and tidy but everything about the decor was dated to the point of retro.

Next to the TV a stack of game consoles was neatly arranged in a metal rack with some kind of switching device that fed into the television. Reeves must have owned every games console going, from the very latest PlayStation to three or four that were no longer manufactured and hadn't been for at least a decade.

On the wall, shelves were filled with computer games and comic books. Ty could barely suppress a shudder as his eyes scanned them. He wondered how many kids like Jack Barnes had been in that room, drawn in by all the junk, not for a second suspecting its real purpose.

In the kitchen, Lock began opening cupboards full of soda, potato chips and candy bars. 'Jesus,' Lock said, his features tight. 'This guy was textbook.'

In another cupboard there were pouches of protein and other supplements. Ty opened the refrigerator. The salad crisper was full of fresh produce going bad. A couple of packs of lean chicken breasts were stacked on the shelf above. Weston Reeves may have enticed his victims with the kind of garbage that kids craved but he ate clean.

They continued their walk-through, giving themselves time to acclimatize and prepare for whatever lay beneath them, hidden away in the darkness of the cellar. The first bedroom they came to had been converted to an exercise room. Apart from a treadmill, essential for Minnesota winters, the equipment was mostly weights. A mirrored wardrobe ran the length of one wall. Ty pulled it open to reveal more weights and exercise gear. A gun safe was bolted into one corner.

The next bedroom looked like a guest room. It had a double bed, and some cheap pine furniture. Pin-up girls and posters of wrestling stars tacked to the walls hinted at the possible nature of the guests. The third and final bedroom was the master, complete with a small en-suite shower room. Another gun safe stood next to the bed, and had been left open. Apart from a box of shells, it was empty.

'Lot of guns for one man,' said Ty.

'Lot of people out there who might want to hurt him if they knew what he was,' Lock said. Then he squared his shoulders. 'So, where's this cellar?'

'Through here,' said Ty, heading out of the master bedroom, and ducking into the main bathroom.

SIXGTY-FIVE

THE TRAPDOOR DOWN TO THE cellar was hidden in a corner, covered with a square of yellow linoleum. Reeves had tacked a bath mat over the top. Ty had found it by stepping on the mat while crossing to the window and noticing the hollow echo.

He levered it open and, together, he and Lock stared down into the darkness. A narrow wooden ladder led into the gloom.

'Flip a coin?' Lock asked him.

Ty took Lock's Maglite. 'No, I got this.'

Lock drew his SIG to cover Ty as he started down the ladder. It was a tight squeeze but the drop was only around seven feet. He landed on a dirty wooden floor. He swept the torch around the cellar. He had already taken a good look around it when he had first discovered it. Now he took his time, his initial shock replaced by a deep, more disturbing horror that pinched at his flesh.

He walked to the wall nearest to him, the one just behind the ladder. He took out a Gerber multi-tool, and dug into it with the tip of the knife. The blade pushed through green acoustic foam to two layers of sheetrock that had a single layer of neoprene rubber sandwiched between them. Reeves, and perhaps Becker too, if he'd used the place, had spent a lot of time, and gone to great expense, ensuring that the cellar was soundproofed. The rest of the room told Ty why that had been important.

Taking out his cell phone, Ty pivoted around, capturing the room on video. As he filmed, he gave the address.

The good news, if a discovery like this could be seen as good, was that there was no sign of Jack Barnes. And the traces of blood on the walls didn't look fresh.

SIXTY-SIX

TY GRABBED LOCK'S HAND AS he breached the lip of the trapdoor. Lock pulled him up. It was a surreal experience to be standing in the small, mundane bathroom, with hell on earth a few feet beneath them.

'You okay?' Lock asked.

Ty thought about it. He had seen plenty of horror in his life, starting out in Long Beach, moving on through his time in the marines, when he had served in Iraq, and on through a few joint nightmares with Lock, but this was beyond anything that had gone before. There was no other word for it than evil. What he had felt while he was standing in the cellar was something that passed any comprehension. He looked at Lock. 'Not really, no.'

'Good,' Lock said. 'I'd be worried if you were.'

Ty looked at his friend. 'You figure he killed any of these kids?'

Lock let out a deep sigh that signaled he might have been pondering the same question. 'Maybe.'

'The boy that's missing?' Ty asked him.

Lock started out of the bathroom. Ty followed. They walked down the corridor. 'He and Becker were getting desperate. Chances are it was this guy who killed Kim and the kids.'

'That's what I was thinking. Him and Becker might have been into this stuff together, but I don't see Becker having the *cojones* to do that to Malik.'

They moved back into the living room. Now that he had seen the cellar, the house itself had changed. The huge television and the rack of video games seemed even more sinister. Ty walked over to the shelves and ran a finger across the spines of the plastic cases.

On the bottom shelf were a half-dozen books he hadn't noticed before. He hunkered down to take a closer look. His hand found the tallest. He pulled it out from the shelf and his heart rate bumped up an extra notch. He opened it and frantically leafed through the pages.

Lock was standing behind him. 'Ty? What is it?'

'When I was leaving the Becker house, I had a feeling like I'd missed something. Like it was right in front of me but I wasn't seeing it.'

Ty held up the book, the same high school yearbook as the one he had found on Aubrey Becker's shelves. He jabbed a long finger at the group picture of Becker's class. 'Look there,' he said to Lock.

Lock and Ty stared at the husky-looking blond kid standing behind Aubrey Becker in the class photograph from his high school yearbook. Although he was a teenager, there was no mistaking Weston Reeves staring back at them.

SIXTY-SEVEN

A LLAN LAIRD TIDIED THE PAPERS on his desk ready for the morning. He crossed to the small closet, opened it, grabbed his raincoat from the hanger, put it on and grabbed his briefcase. His secretary had left hours ago, along with the rest of the administrative team. The only people in the building were the cleaning and security staff.

Laird was looking forward to getting home to his wife, having one of his favorite Scottish single-malt whiskies, a long soak in a hot bath and dinner. Today had been hard. The press were still in a frenzy, and he'd spent most of the day fielding calls from concerned alumni, and the parents of current students who were worried about their kids' safety.

Recent events had set back the college, and his work, a decade, at least. It was going to take a long time for people to get over what had happened here. But, as chancellor, he comforted himself with the fact that, eventually, they would. Time would pass. People would forget.

The elevator opened and he got in. It was empty, and took him straight to the lobby. He wished the security guard on Reception a good evening, and walked outside. He skirted the building to the car park.

Fumbling in his overcoat pocket, he found the clicker for his car and hit the button twenty yards from it. The lights flashed, the car beeped. He opened the driver's door, threw his briefcase onto the passenger seat and got in. He started the engine, and began to reverse out of his spot.

That was when he saw someone sitting in the back seat. The man smiled at him. 'Drive normally,' he said, raising a handgun and pressing the end of the barrel against Laird's face.

'If you want money, look, here,' said Laird, fumbling for his money clip. 'I have four hundred dollars.'

There was something familiar about the man with the gun. Laird was sure their paths had crossed before. Or maybe he just had one of those faces that were bland to the point of familiarity.

'You can't buy me, Chancellor. Now, drive.'

'Where?' Laird asked him.

'Home.'

Laird didn't follow. 'My home? Why? This is all the cash I have. If you want more you're out of luck.'

'I already told you,' the man said, irritated. 'I don't want your money.'

Laird decided that it was probably best if he played along. Then it hit him. Of course. This wasn't about money. It had to be something to do with Becker or Reeves, that whole mess. But he didn't want to ask in case it set the man off. It was better to remain silent.

He finished backing out of his parking spot, then headed out of the car park and onto the road. He didn't say anything. He kept his moves slow and deliberate. The man seemed jumpy, and he had a gun. Laird wasn't going to risk antagonizing him.

The biting wind howling its way down from Canada had taken people off the streets. Laird drove in silence. He could feel the presence of the gun behind him. His heart was beating faster but he was surprised at how little real terror he felt. Perhaps he was too exhausted to be scared. The last week or so had brought so many horrors that his life had taken on a surreal quality. Allan Laird had never known anyone who had been murdered before. Now he seemed to be surrounded by them, with the chance that he might be next.

'Looking forward to seeing your daughter, Chancellor?'

The question snapped him back to the present. He whipped round to look at his abductor in the back seat, and almost went head on into a car coming the other way as he drifted over the white line in the middle of the road.

He had a daughter, but she was twenty-one and at college out of state. 'What are you talking about? My daughter's in Rhode Island.'

'Keep your eyes on the road,' the man said. 'She was. But she's on her way home. In fact, she should be getting there about now. She was worried about the heart attack you had this morning.'

Laird was getting angry. 'What are you talking about?'

'She got a message about it this morning from a cardiologist at Mercy. She spent today rushing home to be with you and your wife.'

'This is ridiculous. Why are you dragging my family into it?'

'Into what?' the man asked. He seemed to be enjoying Laird's discomfort. Laird reminded himself not to lose his temper. He had to stay calm.

Laird's cell rang. He dipped into his pocket. 'Home' flashed up on the screen. Before he could say anything, the man reached over and grabbed it from him. Laird started shouting, 'Call the police. Linda, honey, get out of there. Now.'

The man held the phone up. 'Sorry, Allan. Too late. I already hung up. Don't worry, though, you'll be seeing them soon enough.'

'Why? Why me? Why my family?' Laird shouted. 'I haven't done anything.'

'I think you just answered your own question,' said the man.

Gun or not, Laird wasn't going to deliver this lunatic into the heart of his family to torture and brutalize them. If the sicko wanted to kill him, that was different. But he wasn't going down without a fight.

Allan Laird had never considered himself brave. His life had been dedicated to smoothing things over and avoiding conflict. This time, though, there was no way round it.

In his head, he said a quiet goodbye to his wife and daughter, and the world itself. When he was done, he threw himself forward, out of the immediate line of fire of the gun, and yanked down hard on the steering-wheel. As the car began to lose its grip on the road, he took his foot off the gas and stood on the brake pedal.

SIXTY-EIGHT

A S THE WEIGHT SHIFTED TO the front of the car it started to
fishtail. Despite himself, Laird panicked and yanked down hard
on the steering-wheel, trying to bring the car back under control.
The kidnapper was thrown back into his seat as the car continued to veer
violently across the road.

Laird looked up to see a set of headlights coming toward him. From the
position of the lights relative to the road surface, it was something big.
Laird took his foot off the brake as the car began to slow.

The man in the back seat launched himself forward. The gun caught the
side of Laird's head, smashing into his cheekbone. He yelled with pain as
the lights grew brighter, and he made out the squat shape of the huge rig
bearing down on them, its air horn blasting a warning. Jamming his foot
back on the gas, Laird set a diagonal course across the roadway.

The sudden acceleration sent the kidnapper back into his seat for a
second time. The front of the big rig clipped the rear of Laird's sedan,
which spun round as it continued to hurtle off the road. The passenger side
slammed into a metal stop sign, folding the pole over as easily as if it had
been a lollipop stick.

The impact triggered the airbags, front and rear. Both Laird and the
kidnapper were pressed back, their arms out by their sides. The kidnapper

rocked back and forth, desperately trying to free himself and get an angle to shoot Laird.

Steam rose from the hood of the sedan. The smell of leaking gasoline perfumed the air. Allan Laird sat trapped in the front seat, closed his eyes and waited to die.

Lock was driving them back into town when he saw the car that had smashed into the stop sign. The front half was up on the sidewalk, the rear still on the road, hanging over the edge of the curb. A big rig truck was stopped about a quarter of a block further down the road, the driver pacing back and forth on his cell phone as he called in the accident.

Next to him, Ty's hand fell instinctively to his weapon. Lock pulled up fifty yards short of the crash and both men bailed. As they started toward the crashed vehicle, the rear passenger door popped open and a man clambered out. He was white, about five eleven, slim, dressed in dark clothing, and apparently in no mood to stick around. He took a quick look at the truck driver on his cell, the people gathering on their porches, as well as Lock and Ty, and took off.

Without thinking, Ty started after him. He had no idea who the man was, or why he was fleeing the accident, but something told him it was off. Innocent people weren't in the habit of running, unless they had good reason.

As Ty set off in pursuit, Lock ran toward the car. He checked the back for other passengers, then moved to the front. There was a late middle-aged white guy in a suit in the front. He was bleeding from a cut on the side of his head and looked dazed.

Lock wrenched open the door. It was only then that he recognized Laird, the college chancellor.

The stench of gasoline pouring from the car's tank was overpowering. Lock grabbed his Gerber and used the blade to slash at the already deflating airbag.

'Can you move?' he asked Laird.

Laird nodded, the neck movement more encouraging than the weak 'Yes, I think so.' Lock reached down and shoved the seat back to give him more room, used the knife to cut the seatbelt and helped him out of the car. He was banged up, and pale with shock, but he was mobile.

With Lock's help, Laird hobbled gingerly away from the car. 'My family. I have to contact them. My cell phone's in the car.'

He started back toward the vehicle but Lock stepped in front of him. 'Not a good idea.' He grabbed his own phone. 'Here, tell me the number.'

Laird got it together just enough to remember his wife's. Lock punched it in and handed his cell off to Laird. The cut on his face was pretty nasty, but other than that he seemed to be in pretty decent shape for what he'd just been through. Lock stepped away and left him to the call. He turned around to see Ty emerge from between two houses and jog over to him. 'I lost him. You figure out what was going on?'

'Not yet,' said Lock. 'But I think the chancellor here might finally be ready to do the right thing.'

SIXTY-NINE

S TANDING IN ALLAN LAIRD'S HOME office, Lock punched in the number for the home of the FBI's head of staff in Minneapolis and handed the phone to the chancellor. Laird's hands were still shaking as he took it and said quietly, 'I'm very sorry to disturb you at such a late hour, but it's important.' Through a gap in the door, Lock could see Ty standing with Laird's wife and daughter. The drapes were drawn, and he was keeping them clear of any windows. The house and garden had already been searched and, despite Lock's distrust of them, the local police were on the way to provide additional security.

Lock stepped out of the office and walked over to Ty. 'How's everyone doing?'

'Shaken up.'

Headlights swept across the front of the house. Lock went to the window, and took a peek. 'College security.'

He watched as the female cop who had tricked Ty climbed out of a cruiser and walked toward the front door. 'Your buddy's here,' he told him. Lock had known him long enough to recognize Ty's game face. It was the usual precursor to someone having their day ruined by the six-foot-four marine. 'Let's hear what she has to say first.'

Ty didn't appear convinced. 'She watched Tromso drive off with me. You trying to tell me she didn't know what he had planned?'

'No,' said Lock. 'I'm saying that we already got enough to deal with here. If she was helping Tromso, that's for the FBI to deal with. Not us.'

The doorbell chimed. 'I'll get it,' Lock said.

He walked into the hallway, and unlocked the front door. 'Mr Lock?' she said, putting out her hand. 'I'm Officer Svenson. I'm acting chief since Officer Tromso was killed.'

She didn't look like a cop so much as like a young woman playing a cop in a TV show. It was nothing to do with her gender. Lock believed that in most instances women made for better law-enforcement personnel than men. They generally had better communication and negotiation skills and were less likely to escalate a situation unnecessarily for reasons of ego or machismo.

But there was something about the woman standing in front of him that didn't fit with the uniform. Cops had a look to them when they were on duty. Lock could usually pick one out anywhere. They carried themselves differently from civilians. They looked at you differently. Even when they were off-duty, they gave off an aura of situational awareness not found in the general population. It had been said that it was the same for criminals: a thief could pick out another thief from a hundred yards.

Lock shook her hand. 'Yeah, I think my partner wants to speak to you about what happened with that.'

'I'm sure he does. I'd appreciate the opportunity to clarify it for him.'

Lock glanced beyond her. 'Do you have any other personnel available?'

She looked away. 'We're rather short-staffed right now.'

That wasn't what Lock had seen. If anything he had been pretty taken aback by just how many cops they had for a campus that, barring recent events, was very low crime.

'I've placed a number of personnel on leave pending further investigation.' When Lock didn't react, she added, 'Personnel recruited by Officer Tromso.'

Lock didn't say anything. If she was trying to present herself as some kind of new broom, ready to sweep out the corruption of a previous regime, he wasn't buying it. Ty had been very clear about her having gone along with what had happened. If she knew what had been going on, she could have turned whistleblower long before now.

'You think I was involved in all this, Mr Lock, don't you?' She said it with a smile, as if she knew something that would make him seem foolish when it came out.

'I know only what my partner told me. And I'd believe him over anyone else in this world, so try not to take it personally.'

'Don't worry. I won't. May I come in?'

Lock opened the door and she walked past him. 'Is the chancellor speaking to the feebs?'

'In his office,' said Lock.

'Good,' she said. 'It's about time. If only he'd done it before now all this could have been avoided.'

'If you say so,' Lock told her.

Laird walked into the living room. His wife went to him and placed a comforting hand on his shoulder. Lock had a vomit-inducing feeling that Laird was going to come out of this a hero, even though nothing could have been further from the truth.

Ty hard-stared Svenson from across the room. Lock had a sneaky feeling that part of the reason Ty was so angry was that he'd been fooled by a pretty woman. Most men would have steered clear of him, but not Svenson.

She walked straight over to him. 'Mr Johnson, I owe you an apology.'

Ty scowled at her. 'You think?'

'I can understand your anger. I'd feel the same if it was me.'

From what Lock could see, Ty wasn't about to be taken in again. He grabbed his partner's arm before things got ugly. 'I need to talk to you.' He pulled Ty into a corner of the room. 'What do you want to do about Malik?' he asked.

'What you mean?'

'Well,' said Lock, 'he can't stay hidden for ever. The FBI are going to drag it all out into the open, whether people round here want them to or not. We have enough evidence between the pictures you took at the house and everything else we know about Becker, Tromso and that other lunatic to put him in the clear. Seems like now would be a good time for him to hand himself over.'

Ty weighed it up. Finally, he said, 'You're right. Let's call him.'

Lock handed Ty his cell. 'Here, you do it.'

Ty took the phone and stepped off into a corner as Svenson walked back over.

'You get a look at the guy who fled the car?' she asked Lock.

'Not really, no. White. Five eleven, six feet. Average build. Dark hair. Early thirties. That's about it.'

'Not a lot to go on,' she said.

'Did you know what was going on?'

Svenson met his gaze. 'Knowing and proving are two different things.'

Ty headed back to them. He grabbed Lock and steered him into the hallway, out of earshot of everyone else. 'He's not picking up.'

'It's late. He's probably asleep.'

'That's what I thought,' said Ty. 'But I called the motel manager. He said that the person in that room left this afternoon. I made him go check. Malik's gone.'

SEVENTY

THE ALLEY THAT RAN BEHIND the fast-food restaurant was empty, apart from a few rats foraging for scraps. A cell phone trilled inside one of the restaurant's three Dumpsters. The display flashed the word 'Lock' on the screen.

Finally, the ringing stopped as it defaulted to voicemail. A few minutes later another call came in. Still no one answered.

SEVENTY-ONE

I T WAS A LITTLE AFTER five in the morning. Ty paced back and forth from the door of Lock's hotel room to the window. Lock sat at the desk with a laptop. He ran through the pictures from Ty's cell, making sure he had everything. He had also laid out a time line that documented every event since Ty had received the first phone call from Malik while they were in Manhattan. Finally he had spoken, at length, with an attorney, to ensure that there would be no blowback from his and Ty's full and frank disclosure.

In two hours, at precisely seven a.m., Lock was due to start his interview with the assistant special agent in charge for the FBI's Minneapolis-based VCAC program. VCAC stood for Violent Crimes against Children. The special agent in charge, a twenty-year Bureau vet called Dennis Lee, had already told Laird that he was pulling as many bodies as he could to Harrisburg, leaving only a skeleton staff in Minneapolis. He had requested additional resources from Quantico. He had also requested that Detective Johanssen and anyone else working at state level step off the case after they had handed over all files to the feebs.

Ty stopped for a moment at the window. Down below on what passed for Harrisburg's main drag, the lights of the diner had just flipped on. He recognized the young waitress whom he'd stood up for days earlier. She was standing with the short-order cook and a Somali bus boy, all three sipping coffee, bracing themselves for the day ahead. It was about to get busier. Sheer human misery was good for business, thought Ty. We feasted on it.

The wind was picking up again. It whipped down the street, picking up a missing-person flier with Jack Barnes's picture on it, throwing it up into the air before it came to rest under a car.

Lock looked up from his computer. 'Okay, that's everything.' He stood up and reached out a fist. He and Ty bumped. 'Keep me updated. Okay?'

'You got it,' said Ty.

Ty took a deep breath and walked to the door. Now that Lock had everything, he was leaving, heading to Wisconsin, to find Malik and bring him back. Assuming his friend was still alive.

Downstairs, he walked past a night porter, the man's chin resting on his chest as he dozed. Prominently displayed on the reception desk was the same picture of Jack Barnes, this one laminated. Something in the boy's eyes chilled Ty to the bone. It was a veiled weariness that no child should have.

Out back, Ty climbed into the silver Chevy Blazer, gunned the engine and pulled out of the tightly packed parking lot. His route out of town took him past the stadium and along Wolf Road.

He thought about Malik, and how he and his friend must have looked when they were Jack's age. Even though they had grown up in a place far poorer and more dangerous than Harrisburg, neither of them had spoken of their childhood with anything other than affection. They had had at least one loving parent and lived among a tight-knit community that looked out for each other. And they had had their friendship. When the world seemed organized against you that meant something. That kind of connection ran deep. No matter what had happened over the past week, Ty wasn't about to give up on his friend. He would find him, and he would help him find peace.

SEVENTY-TWO

THE FBI'S SPECIAL AGENT IN charge of the Minneapolis office, Dennis Lee, was an Asian American in his late forties, with an easy smile and a compact former-bodybuilder's physique. He eyed Lock from across a borrowed conference room that linked to Chancellor Laird's office. Laird, finally as good as his word, had gone all in, offering Agent Lee and his team a free run of the entire campus.

Lock had already given Lee and the other person in room, the FBI's legal counsel/media advisor, a woman in her thirties named Becky Coulson, a full run-down of what he knew. He had also handed over the pictures Ty had taken of the Shaw house before Tromso had torched it. Lee and Coulson must already have seen Tromso's initial homicide book because the first thing Lee had done was make a call to ensure that nothing was going to happen to the bodies of Kim, Landon and Katy Shaw until he said so. It was a first glimpse of good news. The delay meant that if Ty could find Malik, he would be able to attend the funerals. Given the story that was out there, Kim's family had been pushing for a quick funeral with Malik, as prime suspect, excluded.

In addition, Special Agent in Charge Lee had also offered to help Ty in locating Malik. Becky Coulson had already drafted, and released, a statement to the media that spoke of new developments, and saying that

216

while Malik Shaw remained someone they wished to speak to as a matter of urgency, he was no longer being sought as a suspect.

As starts went, it was a good one.

'Not your first time helping the Bureau, Mr Lock,' Agent Lee said, filling a fresh cup of coffee from an urn near the window.

'Kind of unavoidable, given my job,' said Lock. It was true. Lock and Ty were usually called upon to provide protection and consultancy services in high-stakes and often high-profile situations. That brought them into contact with United States law-enforcement agencies at every level, including federal. They had been involved in a number of instances when their path had intersected with that of the FBI, sometimes with a good deal of friction, and at others more smoothly.

'You remember Levon Hill?' Becky Coulson asked him, her hand sweeping back a tangled mane of coppery red hair from thick black-rimmed glasses.

'I do,' said Lock. 'Bright guy.'

Levon Hill was a profiler used by the FBI. He had been called in while Lock and Ty were protecting an adult-film star called Raven Lane from a murderous stalker terrorizing Los Angeles.

'You think we have a serial killer involved here?' Lock asked.

'Not really, no,' said Agent Lee. 'But it doesn't hurt to have another pair of eyes on things.'

That was true, thought Lock. It was very easy in an ongoing investigation to lose sight of the obvious. His eyes wandered to the far wall, where the standard photo-montage of victims and anyone connected to the case was plastered, with black lines drawn between them to suggest connection, either familial or circumstantial.

The pictures of the homicide victims were easy to spot. Not only did they have a red outline running around the edge, but the shots were taken from the crime scene. There were seven in total. The Shaw family accounted for a three-photograph cluster, Aubrey and Gretchen Becker added two, and were arranged alongside Weston Reeves, Aubrey Becker's old school buddy and partner in perversion. Off to one side, an arrow linked Weston Reeves to the college's former chief of police, Keith Tromso.

A series of arrows sped off from Becker and Reeves to a half-dozen other pictures of boys and young men. They included Jack Barnes, and ranged up from him to a couple of young men who looked to be in their late twenties.

Lock nodded in the direction of this cluster. 'Victims?' he asked Agent Lee.

Lee glanced across at Becky. As counsel, she would have a say in what they shared with Lock and what they chose to withhold. Despite whatever recommendation Levon or anyone else in the Bureau had given him, he was still an outsider. Although, given the conduct of the college's police department, he was likely to be more trusted than most people around here.

'Jack Barnes you know about. The others have contacted us in relation to either Becker or Weston. So, yes, victims,' said Becky. 'From what we can gather, this is only a very small sample of the number we expect to find.'

One of the pictures of an earnest-looking young man in his late teens had a red frame. 'This one,' said Lock, getting up and tapping a finger against the photograph. 'He was murdered?'

'Suicide,' said Agent Lee. 'The father contacted us. The young man had a history of mental-health problems. He took his life a few days ago. He mentioned Becker in the suicide note he left.'

'He mention Weston?' Lock asked. 'Or anyone else?'

Becky shook her head. 'Just Becker, although there was a reference to "them".'

'Levon's going to be here later today. But while we're waiting, you've given us what you know, how about telling Becky and me what you think's going on?'

'Malik said that Jack referred to more than one person. Of course, that was before any of us knew about Weston Reeves. So, from what the victims have told you so far, was Reeves actively involved in the abuse too? Or was he just the muscle?'

'Both,' said Becky.

Lock walked to the window and looked out over the campus. Kids were still going to class with backpacks slung over their shoulders. Life was continuing.

'I think this had been going on for a while,' said Lock. 'Because of Becker's money and connections, no one had the balls to blow the whistle. Until Malik saw what he did. When buying him off with a new and improved contract didn't work out, someone, most likely Reeves, either alone or working with someone else, went nuclear. They killed the Shaw family, and tried to frame Malik for it. They got wind that Malik had called in people from outside and panicked. Now everyone's ass was on the line. They used Tromso to cover it up by torching the crime scene and destroying the forensics. We on the same page so far?'

'Pretty much,' said Lee.

Lock held out his hands, palms open and facing up. 'Except we have a couple of loose ends. Jack Barnes and his mom are missing. They could already be dead. Taken out as part of the cover-up. But that would still fit. The real head-scratcher, though, is whoever jacked up Chancellor Laird.'

'Third perp,' said Agent Lee. 'They don't want to be caught so they kill Becker and Reeves. Laird is just one piece of the puzzle. They're taking a scorched-earth approach. Likely they're the person or persons who killed Shaw's wife and kids.'

'Except,' said Lock, 'none of your victims mentions anyone apart from Becker and Reeves. That's weird.'

'Some of the victims have mentioned Reeves wearing a mask during the abuse. Perhaps it wasn't him the whole time. Maybe it was this third person.'

Lock glanced back to the wall. 'That would make sense,' he said. 'So we have another perp still out there.'

There was a knock at the door. Lee got up to answer it. He opened the door to Kelly Svenson. She was in blue campus-police uniform. A Glock 9mm hung on her hip. She looked at Lock, then away. She was off, he thought. Way off.

'Just wanted to make sure you had everything you needed,' she said to the two FBI personnel, pointedly ignoring Lock.

'Yeah, thanks, we're good,' said Agent Lee.

'Okay, well, let me know if that changes,' she said, and exited.

Lock gave it a moment, his eyes never leaving the door. 'You know she watched Tromso take my partner out in the woods, right?'

Becky tapped her pen on the desk. 'We asked her about that. She said she had no idea what Tromso was planning.'

'And you believe her?' Lock said.

'You think she's in on it?' Agent Lee said. 'She joined the department here less than a year ago. It's more likely she was worried about crossing her boss than an active accomplice.'

Lock knew that Lee had a point. She might not have known what Tromso had planned. And even if she had, would she, as a new member of the department, try to stop him? Sadly, in the real world, people like Malik Shaw were the exception, not the rule. It took a lot for a member of an organization like a small police department to blow the whistle. When confronted by corruption many people closed their eyes, especially when those who hadn't were killed for their trouble.

'What's her background?' Lock asked. 'I mean you've looked into it, right?'

'Still looking,' said Becky. 'But so far it checks out.'

'She told us that she knew Tromso wasn't right about five minutes after she walked into the job,' said Lee. 'But she didn't have evidence until recently, and by then things were moving at such a pace that she wasn't sure what to do. I thought the same thing you do, Lock, but her background is clean as a whistle. She's worked in law enforcement for ten years and no one has a bad word to say about her. She's a straight arrow.'

Lock wasn't convinced.

SEVENTY-THREE

A S LOCK WALKED OUT OF the main administration building, Kelly
Svenson pushed off the rear of the police cruiser she was leaning
against while talking to one of her officers. 'Mr Lock?'

Lock kept walking. He wanted to check in with Ty, and then he planned
on helping out with the search for Eve and Jack Barnes. He was also
planning a detour back to the home of Weston Reeves to canvass some of
the neighbors, and see if he couldn't get anything on the mysterious third
man, who was still on the loose.

'Mr Lock?' she called after him. Finally, he stopped and turned. 'I'd like
to talk to you. If I may.'

'Oh, we'll talk, all right. Once this is all done I plan on having a good,
long talk with you. I'm sure Tyrone will too, seeing as how you sat back and
watched Tromso drive him off into the wilds to meet Tromso's buddy
Reeves.'

Her face hardened. 'You don't know what you're talking about. It wasn't
what it looked like. Not at all.'

'So what was it, then?' Lock asked her.

She folded her arms. 'You wouldn't believe me anyway so what does it
matter?'

Lock stepped toward her. 'What is this? Junior high? You sat there and watched as your asshole boss took my partner out to the boonies to be tortured by some grade-A wack-job, who liked kids and torture, preferably mixed together. Listen, do me a favor, keep out of my way. You interfere with what I'm doing here, or Ty when he gets back, and that rinky-dink badge won't save you.'

Something flickered in her eyes. It was there, and then it was gone, but Lock had seen it. It wasn't a look a cop gave someone: there was more to it. It was a look that spoke of hidden anger.

'Just stay within the bounds of the law, Mr Lock, and we'll be fine.'

Lock smirked at her. 'You too.'

'I've asked the chancellor to organize a vigil at the stadium. Y'know, for the victims, the Shaw family and the others. The kids. It'll be on Friday night. Hope you can make it.'

She was waiting for some kind of reaction. He wasn't sure what she wanted him to say. That a vigil made it all okay? That she was a good person for suggesting it? That everyone holding hands and singing 'Kumbaya' would mean the students could go back to class and the college back to making money?

Lock remembered Penn State's footballers taking a knee while they prayed for Jerry Sandusky's victims. It had struck him as hollow and self-serving, a public-relations exercise. He had wanted to throw up. By themselves, public shows of contrition meant little unless the regret was sincere. It was like tossing a fifty into the plate at church when everyone else had nickels. It told the world a lot about you, but perhaps not in the manner you had intended.

When he didn't say anything, Officer Svenson walked back to her patrol car without another word.

He walked on across campus. Flakes of snow started to fall. They were tentative at first, almost apologetic. Up above, the sun was struggling to break through watery white-grey clouds. On the horizon there were darker clouds.

SEVENTY-FOUR

T Y STOOD IN THE MIDDLE of the empty motel room. The TV was still on, the jovial game-show host navigating his way between two corn-fed Midwestern families as they tried to guess a hundred people's answers to a question about things you could lick. The host faked outrage at a series of thinly veiled double-entendres as the audience laughed along.

The motel-room bed was still made. The pre-paid cell phone that Lock had given Malik sat on a chipped night-stand that was bolted to the wall. Next to the phone was a Jim Beam bottle. It was empty. Ty picked up the pre-paid cell and put it into his pocket.

He walked into the small bathroom. The supplies that Lock had left Malik were neatly stacked next to the shower. The toilet and sink were pebble-dashed with vomit. Malik was not a drinker. The most Ty had ever seen him consume was a glass of wine with dinner, and that was only if the kids weren't present. Both of them had seen too many people in their old neighborhood being dragged under by alcohol and narcotics. They were an escape from real life, not a solution. At the same time, could anyone blame Malik for seeking oblivion after what had happened? Ty couldn't.

There was no sign of a struggle. No lamps had been knocked over. There was no blood. No broken mirrors or scattered clothing.

Malik had been taken by something more frightening to Ty than a kidnapper or the cops. His friend had been lost to despair.

Ty walked out of the motel room. The manager was waiting for him.

'He's gone, right?' the manager said. It wasn't a question motivated by concern so much as business. The manager wanted to rent the room, even though Ty knew that Lock had paid him up front for the next week.

'You sure you didn't see him leave?' Ty asked.

'I didn't even see a black guy go in there. It was a white guy rented the room.'

'Where are the liquor stores and bars round here?' Ty asked.

The manager dug his dirty thumbnail at a sticker someone had slapped on the counter. 'Take your pick. There ain't any shortage. Y'know, seeing as this guy was hiding out here, I could have been in a lot of trouble. A small consideration might not be out of the way.'

Ty stared at the guy. 'Say what?'

The manager held up his hands. 'Okay, forget it.'

Ty turned away and walked back to the street, leaving his vehicle in the parking lot. About a half-block down, he saw a flickering neon light advertising domestic beer. He started toward it.

The empty bottle weighed heavily on his mind. He and Malik had escaped not just their old neighborhood, but the pattern of despondency and failure that seemed to be genetically coded into the people they had grown up with.

When he reached the sign, he saw that the bar hadn't opened yet. Ty slipped down a side alley and walked round to the back. A truck was unloading. A middle-aged woman with dark brown hair tied back in a ponytail, wearing a thick plaid shirt and jeans, was counting off boxes of booze. Ty pulled out his cell and slid his finger over the screen, pulling up a picture of Malik. 'Excuse me, ma'am, sorry to take up your time, but have you seen this gentleman over the past twenty-four hours?'

She took a look. 'This the coach from Harrisburg?'

'That's him,' said Ty. 'You see him?'

She took a step back and studied Ty. 'You a cop?'

'A friend who needs to find him.'

'He was in here last night, but he didn't stay. Came in, looked around, had a drink and split.'

'You see which direction he headed?' Ty asked.

'Nope. Once a customer is out that door, my interest kinda wanes.'

'You didn't think to call the cops?'

'Nope. If I had to call the cops on every one of my customers that they wanted to speak to I'd be out of business. It's not exactly the Polo Lounge back there.'

'Can I ask you how he looked? I know it's a strange question.'

She took a clipboard from the truck driver and cast an eye down the delivery manifest. She scratched something out. 'There's only one case of Makers Daniel here, not two.' The driver mumbled an apology. Ty had the sense that not much got past this lady.

'You're his friend?' she asked Ty, tilting her head back and studying him.

'I am.'

'Then I'd say you'd better find him fast.'

SEVENTY-FIVE

J ACK BARNES HUNKERED DOWN AND peered through the hole.

'Do you see it?' the man asked him. 'Look, over there.'

Jack's eyes roamed the woods, but it was difficult to see anything through the tumbling snow. It was cold, even with the thick socks and hiking boots he'd been given. He was tired and hungry and he wanted to go back to his mom.

That was when he saw it, circling a red pine no more than a hundred yards away. It was about the size of a large German shepherd dog with a thick mottled gray-white coat and piercing pale green eyes that held him spellbound. The gray wolf threw its head back and howled. The sound ran all the way through the carpet of snow, through his boots and along his spine. 'I see it,' he whispered.

The man, whom he was starting to think of as a friend, had his rifle with him. Jack was afraid he might want to kill the wolf, but he seemed as transfixed by it as Jack was. Not that Jack trusted him entirely. After all, that was how things had started before. With someone who had pretended to be his friend, only for him to discover that they were his friends for what they could get or, rather, for what Jack would do or allow to be done to him.

'You see, Jack, there are wolves and there's prey. Which would you rather be?'

Jack didn't have to think about it. 'A wolf.'

'Me too, Jack. I started as prey and then I turned myself into a wolf. You can make that journey too.'

The wolf froze. Either it had heard them or it had picked up their scent. It turned its huge head toward them. For a magical second it stared straight at Jack. The eyes of boy and beast met, and Jack felt a sudden, perfect peace. He knew exactly what the man was talking about. It was his choice. He could be prey or he could be a wolf.

The wolf stuck its muzzle into the snow, then took off with long, bounding strides. In a few seconds it had faded into the pine trees.

The man reached down and flipped open the locks of the hard plastic gun case. 'Ready to get some target practice in, Jack?'

'We're not going to shoot the wolf, are we?'

'No, Jack, we're going to kill the sheep.'

SEVENTY-SIX

THE SNOW MADE NAVIGATING THE rough terrain tough. Lock was at the end of a line of local people who had turned out to look for Jack and Eve Barnes. They had been assigned an area of woodland near to the cabin where Tromso had taken Ty. Kelly Svenson was co-ordinating the search as part of a joint college/town police operation, with advice from the FBI, who already had their hands plenty full. Still, there was something about the search that made Lock feel like it was busy work.

The people of Harrisburg, including a large section of the student population, had turned out *en masse*. Beneath the somber mask that the searchers felt duty-bound to wear, like so much makeup, Lock detected a certain giddiness. Finally, Harrisburg could prove that it cared, when all along at least two, and possibly three, serial child molesters had been going about their business under the town's nose.

Lock didn't believe that people here hadn't known about the activities of Becker, Reeves and the third man. In Lock and Ty's job of close protection, Lock knew that most people walked around with their eyes wide shut. They looked but they were too lazy, or distracted, to see, and when they did see, it was often too late. And of those who saw, few chose to make the connections. Of those who did join up the dots, very few then took the next step and confronted what was taking place.

Individuals like Becker and Reeves weren't invisible. They had wives, partners, colleagues, workmates, relatives and neighbors. Since the truth had surfaced, more and more people had revealed to the media that they had seen Becker 'hanging out with young boys' or that they'd heard 'a lot of screaming' one night from Reeves's home. And no one had pursued it. No one apart from Malik Shaw. An outsider.

Lock was at the end of a line of about a dozen people. To his left was a beefy frat-boy type, who looked like he was no stranger to a Big Mac or ten, to his right a blonde coed who was wearing enough makeup for Lock to suspect she had recently run away from a circus. The two kept shooting glances at each other as they inched over the snowy slopes toward the tree line. Love or lust was in the air among the misery. Never one to stand in the way of true romance, Lock tapped the frat boy's elbow. 'Switch with me. I'll take the end.'

He shuffled over as Lock stepped around him. 'Thanks, bro.'

'You're welcome.'

As the two fell into conversation, Lock looked back down the slope. Officer Svenson was waving at a small group of newly arrived townsfolk to join the line.

Lock shook his head. Unless Jack and Eve Barnes were dead, and the woods had been chosen as a burial site, which was possible, there were two chances they would find the boy and his mother here – zero and none. For a start, if Becker and Reeves had used the cabin with the third person involved, after what had happened that location was now dead. A kidnapper wasn't about to hole up anywhere close to it. It was too obvious, and if this person had eluded capture so far, they weren't dumb.

He started back down the slope toward Svenson. Maybe there was something she knew about this location that he didn't.

Lock was about ten yards from her when the first shot rang out. A sharp crack followed by an echo. He looked back up the slope to see the frat boy he had switched places with moments before fall forward. His face was planted in the snow. The coed next to him screamed. Everyone else in the line started looking around, startled and unsure of what had just happened.

229

SEVENTY-SEVEN

A S A SECOND SHOT RANG out, Lock powered back up the slope. In the confusion it was next to impossible to tell where the gunfire was coming from. He threw a glance down the slope to Svenson. She was still standing by her vehicle, rooted to the spot. Lock shouted to her: 'Help me here.'

She seemed to snap out of it. Most of the search party of a dozen people were scrambling down the slope. An elderly man tripped and fell. Lock ran toward him, and helped him back to his feet.

The tree line was about forty yards ahead. The road at the bottom of the slope was about ten times that distance. Lock was close enough now to see that the shot had hit the frat boy in the back. Unless there was another shooter, the gunman was up on a ridge to the left of where they were standing.

The contours of the immediate landscape meant that the slope and the road beneath it were directly exposed and within range. The only cover available was in the woods, yet people were spilling back down the slope where they could be picked off easily.

The elderly man was back on his feet as another shot cracked, missing them by feet. A puff of snow marked the entry point to their right. Lock shouted at people to head for the woods. They were still in shock, overwhelmed and disbelieving.

Lock reached down for his SIG. He fired off a round in the direction of the ridge where he thought the gunman was. At the very least, incoming fire would give the shooter something to think about. It would also draw fire to him rather than to the unarmed civilians, who had slowly begun to change direction and head for the line of pines.

Lock began crawling toward the frat boy, who was still down. The blonde coed was kneeling next to him, asking if he was okay, as the snow around them turned red. The frat boy's eyes were flickering. He was starting to lose consciousness. Lock took off his jacket as the rifle cracked one more time from the ridge. This time, Lock saw the muzzle flash nice and clear. The shot slammed into a man with grey hair, who was helping the stragglers into the woods. It caught him in the right thigh, spinning him off balance. He went down with a yell. Lock handed his jacket to the coed as he sat the kid up, and slashed at his clothing with his Gerber.

'Okay, see the wound,' Lock said to the girl. 'Take my jacket and press it against it as hard as you can. You understand?'

She nodded and jammed it against the entry point. The frat boy yelped in pain. 'And keep him conscious,' added Lock. 'Keep him talking. Make sure his eyes don't close.'

Glancing back over his shoulder, Lock saw a pick-up truck with a serious gun rack pull up. Two townies in hunting gear got out of the cab, each hefting a Bushmaster, the gun that had done so much damage at the school in Newtown. By the way they were carrying the guns, safety off, muzzles pointed out at waist height, fingers on the triggers, something told him that these individuals had not been trained for such a situation.

The sniper must have sensed the same thing because, as the driver of the pick-up stepped off the road and onto the slope, he took a single shot to the head. It smashed into his mouth. His body jerked, as if he'd been plugged into the power grid, and he fell. As his buddy went to his aid, another shot rang out. This one caught him in the shoulder, spinning him round. He duck-walked behind the truck, crying with the pain.

'Lord, give me strength, and save me from amateurs,' Lock muttered, under his breath, looking back up toward the ridge, where it had fallen quiet. Hunkering down, he ran over toward one of the fleeing search party, his eyes never leaving the ridge. He had noticed that one of the searchers had a pair of binoculars. He took them from the man's neck, and ran in a zigzag from the group, drawing fire from the ridge as he moved.

He found a bump in the terrain, and lay belly down, using the contour of the ground to provide him with cover. As he raised the binoculars to his eyes and racked the focus wheel, a muddy, battered SUV pulled in behind the truck. The driver's window slid down, and the business end of a semiautomatic popped out and let off a three-round burst toward the ridge.

Lock used the haphazard and unwelcome covering fire from the ridge to take a peek. He narrowed his eyes to make sure that he really was seeing what he thought he was. Next to the sniper, whose face was covered with a ski mask, was a young boy with a fringe of brown hair that fell over his eyes.

All four doors of the SUV were flung open, and four men in hunting gear, each wielding an assault rifle, began to rake the ridge with gunfire. Lock waved at them, shouting to be heard over the barrage of rounds. 'Hold your fire! There's a kid up there!'

Either they didn't hear him or they were past caring. They moved forward in a line, each taking it in turns to launch a fresh barrage of random gunfire at the ridge.

Lock saw the sniper began to scoot backwards. He tapped the boy, whom Lock was sure was Jack Barnes, on the shoulder as Lock got to his feet, still screaming at the four idiots to stop firing until he had to draw breath.

Lock ran for the ridge, the binoculars dropping from his hand. That was when he saw the boy make an amateur mistake. Rather than staying on his belly, and snaking down the other side of the ridge, with his elbows and knees, he stood up.

The sniper grabbed for him, but it was already too late. At least two of the four vigilantes had noticed the movement, and the figure silhouetted against the sky. They sighted their weapons, finally drawing down on an identifiable target. There were two separate cracks, separated by less than a second.

The shots were followed by a cry, sharp and high, and the boy fell forward. The four vigilantes stopped in their tracks, and Lock saw two of them exchange a high five. It was as much as he could do not to kill them where they stood.

Lock continued his charge toward the ridge. His heart sank as he drew closer. He turned back to the road and waved down Svenson, who had finally slunk out from behind her police cruiser.

On the other side of the ridge, where the road curved round, he heard a truck engine roar to life and a door slam as the sniper took off. He crested the top of the ridge.

The body of Jack Barnes lay in the snow. He was on his front, his head twisted to one side. His eyes were open, the pupils wide with shock. Next to the boy lay a dozen shell casings. There was no one else to be seen. The weapon was gone. In the distance, through the shimmer of the quickening snowstorm, Lock caught the red brake-lights of a truck as it careened down the mountain road back toward Harrisburg.

Sounds came and went. Lock brushed a lock of brown hair from the boy's eyes. 'Jack? Can you hear me?'

His eyes opened. That was good. Lock got in close and listened to the boy's breathing: shallow but steady. The shallowness could be down to shock, the second main danger, after loss of blood, when it came to a gunshot victim.

He scanned the boy's body. He had been hit in the leg – that much was clear from the blood that had soaked through his clothes, turning the snow crimson.

Because of the boy's history, Lock knew he had to be careful about touching him. Any extra anxiety would elevate his heart rate and deepen the shock he was in. At the same time, he had to figure out where he'd been hit.

He spoke quickly, keeping eye contact, trying to discern if the boy was taking in any of what he was saying. 'Jack, listen to me. I'm a trained trauma medic. I've seen a lot of people who've been shot and I haven't let one die on me yet.' That last part was a lie. Lock had seen more than one victim of a gunshot wound die in front of him. But right now the truth didn't matter. 'You understand me? You don't have to talk, you can nod if speaking's too painful.'

'Yeah,' Jack said, his voice high and strained.

'That's great. Okay, so I have to take a closer look to see where you've been hit. In the left leg, correct? It's sore there?'

Jack nodded. 'And the arm,' he said, clenching and unclenching his left hand with a grimace.

'You're doing great, buddy,' Lock told him. 'Now, I'm going to sit you up, see if we can't slow the bleeding a little. If anything else hurts, you tell me. Okay?'

He reached under the boy and helped him sit. Jack winced and grimaced but he made a lot less fuss than most adults. Kids could be like that. Where adults screamed blue murder over a hangnail, some kids approached pain with fortitude.

Lock unzipped the boy's jacket, talking to him the whole time, telling him what he was doing and why. His torso was clear of any trauma. That was about as good as it got in a situation like this. Lock ran his hands over the boy's scalp, and down his neck. Clear. Head wounds from a bullet or fragment were usually pretty damn obvious but it was better to make sure.

He eased off the boy's jacket, ripped out the lining and began to tear it into strips. Down on the road an ambulance had pulled up and two paramedics had decamped. They waded through the snow toward the survivors and got busy doing basic triage, establishing who was a priority. Meanwhile, Lock rolled up the left leg of the boy's pants. He must have been hit side-on because the bullet had gone straight through his calf, luckily missing the bone and, by the look of it, the popliteal artery, damaging only muscle. There was a nice neat exit wound on the other side. As getting shot went, the kid had been lucky.

Lock tied a strip of jacket lining just above the wound, pulled it tight-ish and tied it off. He wanted to staunch the flow of blood without cutting it off entirely and perhaps doing longer-term damage by depriving the lower leg and foot of oxygen. The kid had been through enough without having to face an amputation.

Behind the paramedics, Lock could see Kelly Svenson striding toward him, issuing orders over her radio as she walked. Now that the shooter was gone, she seemed to have snapped into something approaching a professional mode.

The paramedics arrived. One knelt next to Jack. Lock brought them up to speed on the boy's condition, gave him some final words of reassurance, then went to speak to Svenson.

'How is he?' she asked, as the paramedics went to work.

'He'll live.'

'He say anything about the shooter?' she asked Lock.

'I didn't ask.'

Her jaw tightened. 'What do you think this is about?'

Lock stared at her for a moment. 'Hey, you're the cop. You tell me.'

She shrugged. 'Maybe there was someone else involved with Becker and Reeves. Maybe he took the boy and was hiding out round here when the search party turned up. He panicked and started shooting.'

Lock didn't buy it. 'He had a truck. He wasn't cornered. No one had found him. Why not just slip away? Why open fire and pretty much guarantee that you're going to be found?' He paused for a moment. 'You have roadblocks up, right?'

'We do, but there are plenty of off-road trails around here.' She sighed. 'At least we have the boy. I'd better go check on him. Say, Mr Lock, are you going to be sticking around?'

The way she said it suggested to Lock that she was hoping to hear a no. Lock surveyed the carnage of the slope, the blood vivid red against the virgin snow. It was a war zone. And he had a feeling that wasn't about to change any time soon.

'Yeah,' he told Svenson, 'I'll be sticking around. This whole thing has me kind of curious now. Too many people with something to hide for me to leave now.'

SEVENTY-EIGHT

LOCK STOOD SENTRY OUTSIDE THE private intensive-care-unit room where Jack Barnes was being treated. His eyes narrowed as a tall, bearded man loped down the corridor toward him, but then he relaxed and smiled. Levon Hill stuck out his hand and the two men shook.

'Hey, stranger,' said Hill, his southern drawl dragging out the vowels. 'How's the kid?'

'Critical but stable,' Lock told him.

'Dennis Lee told me you were there. You want to tell me what happened?'

A nurse flitted past them. Lock studied her for a second, making sure it was one of the seven medical personnel whom he knew were providing care for Jack Barnes. He had already stopped one reporter in a lab coat going into the boy's room. Unless he knew precisely who they were, no one was getting through the door to Jack's bedside. Especially not with the boy's mother still missing and the gunman still on the loose.

'Not a lot to tell. I was out helping a civilian search for the boy when a gunman started taking people out. Bunch of . . .' Lock searched for the word. In this climate, they could hardly be called rednecks. He chewed over the appropriate terminology for a second more. 'Bunch of assholes showed up, let loose, and the boy was caught in the crossfire.'

'The boy was with the shooter?' Levon asked.

'That's what it looks like.'

'You see him?'

'Not much apart from his back,' said Lock. 'He was wearing a ski-mask. He was maybe six three, two twenty pounds. I'd guess Caucasian, but I couldn't be a hundred per cent. Oh, and he could handle a gun. But we knew that already.'

Levon arched his eyebrows. 'White? Well, that narrows it down.'

Lock laughed. 'Yeah. Ty's buddy the coach and some of the kids on the team are probably the only African Americans round these parts.'

'I wanted to ask you about the coach, and what happened to his family,' said Levon. 'I saw the material Tyrone passed to us from the house.'

'You see what we were saying about it being a set-up?' Lock prompted.

Levon scratched at his beard. 'And not a very good one at that. Tromso had the right idea in torching the place. If it had been me, I would have done—' Levon stopped mid-sentence and Lock followed his gaze down the corridor. Kelly Svenson was heading for them. 'This his replacement?' Levon whispered.

'That's her,' said Lock.

'You think she was in on it?' Levon asked.

'No evidence that she knew, but I'd say there's a good chance. There's something off about her.'

'How so?' said Levon, as Svenson reached them.

'Have you met Levon Hill?' Lock said to her.

'Briefly,' she said, giving Levon a curt nod, then turning her attention back to Lock. 'If you need a break, I can cover the door. I have an officer on the way to take over from you anyway.'

'You want to get a coffee?' Levon asked.

Lock looked from him and back to Svenson. He didn't like the idea of leaving the boy. Not even with a cop. In fact, in this town, especially not with a cop. Still, he could hardly say that, and the small coffee shop was less than a hundred yards away, close enough for Lock to be back within seconds if anything happened. And the machines to which Jack Barnes was hooked up would set off an alarm if his vital signs began to dip.

'I could use some caffeine,' said Lock. 'Thanks.'

As he and Levon walked away, she reached out and touched Lock's elbow. 'Do you have a moment?'

'I'll catch you up,' he told Levon.

Levon walked away, leaving him with Svenson. She cleared her throat. 'Back at the scene,' she said. 'I froze.'

'I saw that,' said Lock.

'I don't know what happened to me,' she said.

Lock didn't say anything. He wasn't sure why she was telling him this. He wasn't her boss. She must have known that he had probably already shared with the feebs what had happened.

'Anyway,' she went on, 'it won't happen again.'

Lock nodded toward the ICU room. 'Make sure it doesn't.'

Levon handed him a cup of coffee and they sat at a small table in the corner. Lock chose the seat with the wall behind it and a view into the corridor. He couldn't quite make out Svenson standing sentry outside the boy's room, but he was close enough to hear any commotion.

Levon spooned sugar into his coffee. 'What she want?'

'Good question,' said Lock. 'When the shooting started, she froze. Guess she feels guilty. So, what do you think is happening here, Levon?'

'Well,' said Levon. He stopped to take a sip from a cup that had to be half sugar and half caffeine. 'Looks to me like we have another predator on the loose.'

'To add to the two that are dead?' said Lock.

'If there were two acting in concert — and we know that was the case — then a third isn't that much of a stretch.'

Lock knew that was the obvious answer. A third person who was so far undiscovered would have all the motive in the world to take Jack Barnes and his mother. 'So why stick around?' he asked. 'Why not kill the boy and his mother or, better yet, just get the hell out of Dodge?'

Levon took another sip of coffee. 'How do guys like Becker get away with what they do? They hide in plain view, right? They become part of the fabric of the community. And if that's the case for mystery guest number three then it's not so easy to up and leave without looking suspicious. The US government has a long reach. Russia might take in some spy or a whistleblower, but a podunk child molester? No country in the world is going to offer asylum to someone like that.'

It made sense. But it still didn't feel right, Lock thought.

Levon said, 'You're right, though. It still doesn't explain why you wouldn't just kill Jack Barnes and his mother.' He gave a little shrug. 'We have to remember, though, that someone like this, under pressure, might not be dealing with things entirely logically.'

'Any news on the mom?' Lock asked.

'Not so far. You ask me, we're lucky we have the kid back.'

That was true, Lock acknowledged. And once he was conscious, he would likely be able to solve the puzzle and bring the killing to an end.

The nurse opened the door and walked out. Kelly Svenson greeted her with a smile, and a pleasant 'How is he?'

'He's come round. I'm just going to get Dr Daniels to take a look.'

'That's great news. Would you mind if I stole a minute with him?'

The nurse folded her arms. 'Yes, I would. Once Dr Daniels has seen him you can talk to him about it. But until then . . .'

Kelly Svenson waited until the nurse had disappeared from sight, checked that no one else was looking, opened the door into the boy's room and slipped inside. Her stomach lurched as she looked at him.

Quickly, she crossed to his bedside. She knelt down next to him, and began to whisper into his ear.

SEVENTY-NINE

T Y'S SEARCH FOR MALIK CONTINUED through every liquor store, dive bar and dope house he could find. When it came to such places, all that had changed from back home in Long Beach was the skin color of the clientele. In two more bars he found people who had seen, or thought they had seen, Malik. One had even called the cops, hoping to cash in on a reward, only to hear that Malik was no longer a suspect. By the time the cops had shown up, Malik had already slipped out the back way.

The news of fresh sightings cheered Ty and gave him the energy he needed to keep looking. If Malik had planned on taking his own life, he would probably have done it by now. Hell, he could have done it back at the motel.

As he walked, he tried to imagine what Malik might be going through. To lose Kim would have been heartrending enough. She and Malik had always been so close. But the kids as well? It was a reality that lay beyond nightmare.

How did someone come back from such a loss? It seemed impossible that anyone could go on after such a tragedy. Yet people did.

Lock had gone on with his life. It hadn't been easy, Ty knew. Lock was a hard man to gauge, not given to even fractional displays of raw emotion.

But Ty knew him well enough to see his partner's pain. It had shown on Lock's face when someone mentioned an impending marriage or one of Carrie's favorite songs came on the radio. A thousand and one reminders lay in wait for the grieving. But Lock had come through it somehow. He had taken one day at a time. He had returned to work and, Ty believed, through it he had found salvation. Their pursuit of a wealthy serial rapist into the drug-war-infested Mexican borderlands had been Lock's moment of redemption. Since then his partner's mood had lifted.

Would it be the same for Malik? Ty could only pray that it would.

The afternoon was drawing to a close as Ty started the long walk back toward the motel. As he walked, he checked back in at some of the places he had already visited. There had been no fresh sightings.

A local patrol car drove past. Ty flagged them down and spoke to the two officers. They assured him that they were on the look-out for Malik. Better yet, they told him that no fresh bodies had been retrieved from the nearby rivers or lakes, and no John Does were pending identification in any of the local hospitals.

Ty grabbed a sandwich and a cup of coffee from a convenience store. He ate the sandwich outside, his eyes scanning the street, praying for a glimpse of his friend. As night fell, his prayers went unanswered.

EIGHTY

H IS LEGS DANGLING OVER THE side of the bridge, Malik stared
down at the oil-slicked ripples of the water twenty feet below. He
reached out his right hand, his fingers closing around the neck of
an empty bottle of Jim Beam. Somehow he had convinced himself that if he
could let go of the bottle, and allow it to drop, he himself could do the
same.

Rather than terrifying, the thought of falling, to be swallowed by the
dark water, seemed comforting. He did not fear whatever lay beyond this
life. Either he would see his family again or oblivion would end the ache in
his heart. He closed his eyes. He could feel the glass neck of the bottle cool
against the tips of his fingers as he closed his eyes and let it go. He kept his
eyes closed, and listened for the sound of bottle hitting the surface, but the
noise was drowned by a car engine.

A calmness settled over him. He had let go. He was beyond arguing with
himself. The questions in his mind about what he should do were falling
away to an echo. He had thought about seeking revenge, but against whom?
Ty had told him that Tromso was dead. Laird was culpable, but he'd had
nothing to do with the murders. In any case, more killing, more death,
wouldn't return what he had lost. There was already enough grief and loss
to go round.

And what about Malik's own guilt? Hadn't Kim pleaded with him to walk away, once his attempts to draw attention to what was happening had been shunned? He had put his sense of justice above his own family, and for what? The world wasn't a fair place. Every day of his childhood had taught him that. For all that was great about America, not everyone was dealt the same hand. The system was in place to keep people where they were. His beating the odds didn't change that but it had made him forget how things worked. Playing ball had given him status. People listened to him. He had forgotten, though, that they only wanted to hear him talk about certain things, and those things revolved around the game.

He should have left it alone after he had spoken to Laird. He should have accepted the deal and tried to figure out his next move, instead of throwing it back in the chancellor's face. What had he thought would happen? The rich and powerful didn't get that way by refusing to defend themselves. Coach or not, to the likes of the Becker family and those around them he was still an uppity nigger from California who didn't know his place.

He had to take his share of the blame for what had happened. Not that it mattered anymore. Not that anything mattered. He opened his eyes and looked down into the void, into the deep nothingness, and let the calm surround him.

No, Malik told himself. This way was better. A gentle lean forward until gravity took hold, a short drop into the water, and it would be over. No more pain. No more regrets. Only sleep.

From nowhere, Malik felt a hand fall onto his shoulder. He knew who it was before they spoke. He recognized the steel grip of the man's fingers from their childhood.

'You forget you can't swim, brother?'

'That's what I was counting on,' Malik said, his voice cracked from the booze and days of silence in which he had spoken only to ask for the next drink.

'Mind if I sit down?' Ty said, his fingers still tight on Malik's shoulder. 'My feet are pretty beat up from walking to Hell and back looking for you.'

Malik said nothing as Ty sat next to him. 'I get it,' Ty said finally. 'I can't say I wouldn't want to jump either, if I was you. But if you're gonna do it, then do it sober.'

Malik didn't want to turn his head to look at his friend. He was scared to. He knew he wouldn't be able to hold back the surge of tears, or the fresh waves of grief he could feel rolling toward him. A nod was about all he could manage without falling apart.

'Plus,' Ty went on, 'that river down there is probably only about five feet deep. More than likely, you'd break your neck, and I ain't pushing your sorry ass round in a wheelchair until we're both ready for the old folks' home. So, come on now, let's go get some coffee, get you sobered up. There'll be other bridges.'

Ty stood and helped Malik back to his feet. Together, the two men climbed back onto the roadway and headed into town.

Much later, Malik would wonder how many times Ty had saved him, and how he could repay him. He'd come to the conclusion that he couldn't, but that hardly mattered. True friendship, brotherhood, didn't demand a ledger, or a running total of favors asked and granted. That was the point. That was what made it brotherhood.

EIGHTY-ONE

H ARRISBURG WAS QUIET. THE FEW people who were out were driving, not that the weather allowed for much else. Drivers barely idled at the town's few stop lights, throwing nervous glances as they waited to get moving again. At the local mall, folks parked close to the entrance, leaving the vast expanse of the parking lot empty. When they exited their cars, they did so deliberately, everything they needed already in hand. They speed-walked toward the doors where the Walmart greeter had been replaced by two armed guards.

Levon Hill watched it all from the passenger seat of Lock's newly hired vehicle. Lock was supposedly driving him back to his hotel, but they had agreed a detour to some of the key points of the investigation to see if anything suggested itself to either of them. Lock knew that Levon might have insights into the psychology of killers that he didn't. And he figured that maybe if he followed the trail of events from start to finish his subconscious would offer something that would bring this to an end.

Their first stop was the Shaw home. A chain-link fence had been placed around what was left of it. Lock stopped the car and they got out. He took Levon through what he knew of that first phone call to Malik Shaw, and the subsequent events that had led to the house being torched. This time, Lock decided not to bother the elderly woman who lived next door, but he could hear the Shaws' dog barking at their presence inside her house.

When they had seen everything they could, which wasn't much, they headed for the stadium. It was quiet and the parking lot was empty, just like it had been the evening Malik Shaw had found Jack Barnes. Tomorrow it would be packed. Not for a game. The PR team Laird had hired to do crisis management had made sure of that. No, tomorrow the stadium would be hosting a gathering of the college and town community. It was being billed as a memorial for the victims, more of whom were coming forward with every hour, many of them contacting the FBI team from out of state and even overseas. Becker, Reeves and whoever else was out there had been nothing if not committed and prolific.

Lock stood with Levon at half court. 'What is it with sports and this kind of stuff?' he asked, as his gaze swept around the bleachers, breaking down every detail of the layout, his question hovering somewhere between incidental and rhetorical.

Levon shrugged. 'Kids love sport. They love kids.'

Lock squared his shoulders as a shudder ran up his spine. 'Love?' he asked.

'You know what I'm saying. Y'know, a lot of pedophiles are victims of abuse.'

'That makes it worse to my way of thinking,' said Lock. 'You'd think they'd know what kind of damage they're doing.'

Levon open-palmed a *mea culpa*. 'I wasn't making excuses. I'm paid to understand why people do the things they do.'

They lapsed back into silence. Lock started to walk toward the door that led to the locker room. Levon followed. When they got there, Levon asked, 'This was where the coach found the boy?'

'Yup,' said Lock. 'Becker had taken off but he'd left the kid behind. My guess was that Weston Reeves was there too, and he drove Becker away.'

Levon slapped a hand against the tiled wall. A drop of water shook itself loose from a leaky shower head and splashed onto the floor. 'So either there was a lot of panic or they were pretty certain that the boy wouldn't name them.'

'Or,' said Lock, 'they knew it wouldn't matter if the kid did tell the cops because the cops, the campus cops at least, were unlikely to do anything about it.'

'Apart from tell Becker to be more careful in future,' Lock added. 'How many folks round here you reckon had suspicions about these guys? I mean, when one of these stories breaks a ton of people crawl out of the woodwork to say they knew something wasn't kosher. So how come they don't say anything?'

Levon pushed off the wall and walked back into the locker area. 'Because it's a pretty big accusation to actually make without proof? Because they fear reprisals?'

Lock joined him, and Levon took a seat on a bench. 'Because we don't like to believe there are monsters like this who walk among us?' he continued. 'If you ignore something, Ryan, then maybe it doesn't exist.' He worked at a knot in his neck with his fingers. 'Now, you throw a bunch of money into that equation. Hell, I'm amazed our friend Coach Shaw went as far as he did. Took some balls.'

'And look where it got him,' said Lock, unable to conceal his bitterness. Even though he only knew Malik through Ty, it didn't matter. It sickened him to think of how the man had received a biblical punishment for having the courage to confront evil.

A cell phone trilled. 'I'd better get this,' said Levon, plucking it from his jacket and going into the corridor.

Lock took out his own cell. He called Ty. It defaulted to voicemail. He left a brief message, asking Ty to call him with an update. A second later Ty's name flashed up on the display. Lock hit the answer icon.

'Ty?'

'I found him.'

Lock felt one of the knots in his stomach begin to unravel. The damage couldn't be undone. It rarely could. But at least one small part of the universe was tilting back toward an uneasy equilibrium. He had been to the place where Malik was. He knew the jagged, pain-ridden landscape. 'How is he?' he asked Ty.

'About as good as I'd expected,' Ty said, 'but he's breathing. I'm driving him back there so he can talk to the feebs. Plus I'm gonna help him make the arrangements.'

Lock felt his own throat tighten a little at the reminder. He remembered helping to arrange Carrie's funeral. If it would serve as any consolation to Malik, he had found it helpful, or at least a useful distraction. He had been forced to make choices when all he had wanted to do was crawl into the ground next to her. Life was a process of choice. Being made to choose between a thousand different details had forced him back into the realm of the living. Refusal to engage hadn't been an option.

Levon walked back into the locker room. His eyes studied the floor, his brow furrowed. Something told Lock that his call hadn't been good news.

'Just be careful,' said Lock, wrapping up the call. 'We still have someone out there with a bad attitude and a decent shot. Malik could be in the firing line.'

'I hope they do try something,' said Ty. 'Later.'

Levon cleared his throat. 'That was Dennis Lee. They've found Eve Barnes.'

EIGHTY-TWO

S NOW TUMBLED FROM THE GREY Minnesota sky as Lock pushed open the front door of Weston Reeves's home with the toe of his boot. Levon Hill was up in the hills above Harrisburg, taking a look at where they had found Eve Barnes's dead body. The news was that she too had been shot in the back of the head, execution-style. Lock pondered the detail, wondering if it somehow tied in with how Malik's family had been killed, as he walked into the living room.

Inside the house was the evidence that Weston Reeves's name had hit the news. The place was a mess. Most of the books and video games had been stripped from the shelves and strewn over the floor. The couch had been upended. The carpet had been stripped back in one corner to expose dirty floorboards. Graffiti was scrawled across the walls in red spray paint. 'Sicko!'; 'Monster!'; 'Burn in Hell'. Lock hoped that the FBI had gathered all the evidence they needed. He knelt down next to a pile of books. The high school yearbook that linked Reeves to Becker was long gone, but there was still some material from the college – yearbooks and a couple of annual reports, some of which dated back twenty years.

He dug out his cell phone and called Dennis Lee. It went to voicemail. He tried the college and was bounced around until he had one of Lee's other agents on the line. He asked the woman a couple of questions about who had taken care of the forensics and evidence-gathering from the Reeves house. A minute later, the agent came back with the answers. Lock thanked her and killed the call. He went back to the material at his feet.

Reeves didn't seem like a compulsive hoarder – in fact, quite the opposite. Lock began to work through what was there. If Reeves had kept something, it struck him that there had to be a reason for it. If the FBI hadn't taken it, there was a reason for that too, and after his brief conversation with them, Lock had an idea why that was. They had out-sourced the task.

Methodically, he began to flip through the pages. After about half an hour, he at least had a picture of how Aubrey Becker had slowly worked his way to near the top of the college's structure. In the early years there were mentions of donations. At first they related solely to Aubrey. Later there were others from the Becker family, including Aubrey's brother, the now governor and, until a week or so ago, presidential hopeful.

The pattern set off alarm bells for Lock. He would have expected it to be inverted. If the Becker family had been close to the institution, wouldn't they have been the initial donors? Not a younger son, who was busy building his business. Their money, the big money, had come in later, once Aubrey was firmly ensconced within the fabric of the college. It suggested to Lock that perhaps they were lending their greater financial muscle to buy silence. It would be next to impossible to prove, but that was what it looked like to him. He had been around enough of the very wealthy to know that there was rarely such a thing as a no-strings-attached charitable gift. Especially not when it came to old money.

Lock kept scanning. As he picked up a college report from 1994, a pamphlet fell out. He almost jammed it back inside. It looked like Reeves had been using it as a bookmark. But something about it caught Lock's eye. He opened the pamphlet and scanned the pictures. His eyes slid over the text, reading the names written under the main picture, taking in the smiling children's faces and connecting each one to a name, starting on the right and working left.

Ten seconds later, the twelve-page faded pamphlet tucked inside his jacket, Ryan Lock ran outside into what was now a blizzard. He raced toward the main road. As he ran, he pulled out his cell phone and called Ty.

EIGHTY-THREE

LLAN LAIRD PALMED TWO BLUE Xanax pills into his mouth as his office door opened and Kelly Svenson showed herself in. He chased down the Xanax with a glass of water. The pills had been his wife's idea. He hated drugs of any kind but rationalized that anti-anxiety medication was more than justified under the circumstances. All he needed to do was hold things together for the next few months, and then he would likely be able to slip into retirement. His legacy was tarnished beyond repair, but that mattered less to him now than it once had. He had come within minutes of being slaughtered by a lunatic: a perspective changer.

He waved a hand at the chair across from him. Kelly Svenson sat down. She looked exhausted. Her skin was pale and she had dark, scaly patches under her eyes. Her hair was tied back in a ponytail and the front of her uniform was stained with a blob of what looked like ketchup. 'We're all set, Chancellor,' she said. 'Nineteen hundred hours at the stadium. The college pastor will speak first. Then you. Then a couple of people from the student body, including the captain of the basketball team, and finally the governor.'

The event she was talking about had been the idea of the PR consultants that Laird had called in to deal with the fallout. The college had already suffered from a hundred or so students looking to transfer out, and applications for the new academic year had come to a grinding halt.

The college was a business, and it needed customers. The scandal and its bloody aftermath had tainted their brand, and now it was time to begin the repair. That was how he saw it. Perhaps if he began the process, history would judge him a little more kindly.

'The governor's coming?' Laird said. He knew there had been an approach, but he was still surprised. It was a bold move, coming to the place where his brother's deviancy had finally been uncovered. Then again, thought Laird, what better way to deal with it than head-on? 'And the candlelight procession?' he asked her.

The student body and faculty marching with candles to the stadium had been Svenson's idea. She had explained to him that this would be more important than anything that was said: it would be the key image and would run on the news. The candles were loaded with all kinds of symbolism. They hinted at contrition and remembrance. They also suggested forgiveness. She said, 'All set. It's going to look amazing.'

Laird managed to smile at this. She might not have been up to much in a shoot-out but in terms of planning the event his new acting chief of security had been outstanding. She was totally on board, far more so than Tromso would ever have been. She got it. She understood, as he did, that what mattered to the great American public was the perception more than the reality. 'How many students?' he asked.

'I'd say the majority,' Svenson said. 'Just like a home game.'

EIGHTY-FOUR

LOCK STRODE INTO THE RECEPTION area, and headed toward the athletic-department offices. The receptionist called after him, 'Sir, you have to sign in first. That area is for authorized personnel only.'

'Don't worry, I'm authorized,' Lock said, pushing through the doors, and coming face to face with a white-faced assistant coach. The coach was staring at the gun on Lock's hip.

'Relax,' Lock told him.

The coach stayed frozen to the spot.

'What's your name, son?' Lock asked him.

'Mike.'

'Okay, Mike. The athletic department here runs a summer camp for troubled kids. Do you keep records of all the children who've attended? I need to go back a ways.'

Mike started to speak. 'That information is—'

Lock cut him off. 'Listen to me really carefully here, Mike.' He met the young coach's eyes, never blinking or breaking his gaze. 'If I have to ask you again, or you try to impede me in any way, you and I are going to have a problem. Now, where are those records?'

'I – I don't really . . . They might be down here.'

Lock followed Mike down the corridor to a storeroom full of old athletic equipment and benches. Along one wall there was a row of olive-green metal filing cabinets.

'There might be some stuff in there about it, but that program stopped running a while ago.'

'When? When did it stop?' Lock asked.

Mike shrugged. 'I don't know. I was here as a student and I think it might have been running then, but not since I've been on staff.'

'And how long has that been?'

Mike tilted his head back, his lips moving like he was counting off dates. 'Maybe three years.'

'Do you know why it was stopped?' said Lock.

The young assistant coach shrugged. 'I know Mr Becker was pretty involved with funding it so I guess that was maybe why.'

'But you didn't hear that back then. I mean, there wasn't any suggestion it was because of anything inappropriate.'

'No, sir. Listen, I know what everyone out there is saying, but I wouldn't have signed up to work here if I'd known what was happening.'

Lock believed him. He imagined that went for the vast majority of people there. They were caught in the crossfire as much as anyone else. Their reputations had been tarnished for something they hadn't done. 'This is important. I need to find the names of the kids who participated. Can you help me get some of this crap out of the way so I can look?'

Soon they had cleared a path to the cabinets. Mike left Lock to it. He started with the cabinet in the furthest corner from the door. There were six cabinets and each had five drawers.

The third cabinet was locked. He left it while he checked the others. They hadn't been locked so if the records were here they would be in the third cabinet. He used his Gerber to force it open. The top drawer was empty. So was the second.

Opening the third drawer, he hit pay dirt. The summer kids' program had been divided by years. As he rifled through the files, looking for 1994, he wondered why someone had locked the cabinet when they could have removed, and then destroyed, the files. He guessed it came down to laziness and complacency. Securing the cabinet would deter a casual search. And even if someone did grow curious and open it, they would most likely have no idea what they were looking at.

He wondered, too, what had happened to cause the program to be closed. Had a concerned parent or guardian contacted the university? Had a different version of Malik Shaw walked in on something? Whatever it was, it must have given someone somewhere a scare.

Like so many cover-ups, thought Lock, this one had deep roots. There was rarely a single moment of discovery when it came to these things. Often there were repeated attempts to bring the truth to light that were ignored or, like this one, simply buried. People were paid off, threatened or ridiculed. The really persistent faced intimidation. But the truth could rarely be denied forever. It had a way of surfacing.

Lock found the printout that listed the names of children who had attended the summer camp in '94. He ran his index finger down it. He already knew what he was looking for: a surname. That surname was Svenson. It had been the name of one of the boys pictured attending the camp in '94. Daniel Svenson, a scrappy-looking little kid with a bad haircut and a gap between his front teeth.

When he had seen the name beneath the picture, he had almost blown straight past it. What had stopped him was the kid's resemblance to Jack Barnes. It was eerie. They were separated by twenty years but they might have been brothers. They had the same bone structure, the same features, and they were about the same height.

But that in and of itself hadn't been very significant. Lock imagined that men like Aubrey Becker and Weston Reeves had their types. No, the resemblance between Daniel and Jack had been fortunate only in as much as it had delayed Lock by a few seconds. Those seconds had been long enough for an alarm to sound in his mind about the boy's surname. Like someone he knew from a different context, then bumped into them in a store, Lock had to think about why the name seemed familiar. Then it had hit him.

Could there be a connection? It was a name that was neither rare nor common. It warranted more investigation, but it could well turn out to be a dead end. Now he had his answer. Like everything else in this mess, there were few coincidences. Everything linked. Everything fitted together.

He kept scanning the file. Midway down the third page, he found what he had been looking for. It was there in black and white, the name Svenson. Typed twice. Not an error of repetition, but for good reason. Two names. One just above the other. Daniel and Kelly Svenson. Next to the names was their date of birth. The dates were the same.

EIGHTY-FIVE

LOCK PULLED DOWN THE EDGE of his jacket to conceal the gun on his hip as he waited to be buzzed into the campus security office. A few seconds later the buzzer sounded, and he hauled open the door.

'Officer Svenson?'

The civilian at the counter dusted some donut sugar from her hands, and picked up the telephone on the desk in front of her. She cupped a hand over pursed lips as she made the enquiry. A moment later she put it down again. 'She's not here.'

'Where is she?'

'I'll need to know who's asking first.'

Lock advanced on the receptionist. 'I don't have time for games, lady. Now where is she? Or do you want to explain to Special Agent in Charge Lee why you're obstructing a federal investigation?'

'She's probably out at the stadium.'

By the time she had finished the sentence Lock was pushing back through the door.

EIGHTY-SIX

THEY HAD ALWAYS BEEN CLOSE. Not all twins were, despite what people believed. Forced into the same clothes, and constant proximity, some twins couldn't stand the sight of each other. But from very early in their lives, Kelly Svenson had felt a strong connection to her brother, Daniel. Part of that might have been down to biology and having shared a womb, but she believed it had to do with their upbringing, not the early years, but what had happened later, when Aubrey Becker appeared in their lives.

Aubrey the charmer. The pillar of the community. The man with the perfect wife, who went to church every Sunday and put so much of his money into good causes.

Kelly had been of no interest to Becker. Girls weren't his type. Weston Reeves had been a little different. He didn't appear to mind whether it was a boy or a girl. Sex, normal sex anyway, didn't interest him. He enjoyed instilling fear and inflicting pain. That was where Reeves got his kicks.

Until the age of nine, the twins' childhood had been regular. Then their father had gotten sick. Cancer. He had felt unwell for six months before their mother had forced him to see a doctor. By then it was too late. He had died three months later, leaving her a widow trying to survive on her income from a part-time job at the local Coborn's supermarket.

Their mom had done her best. Daniel had been closer to their father than Kelly was. He had taken it hardest of all of them. Where once he had been bright and extrovert, now he was dour and withdrawn. He had even lost his interest in sport.

In the late spring after her bereavement, their mom had visited the campus to enquire about a secretarial job in the English Department. She had run into Aubrey Becker somewhere along the line and they had got chatting. She had shared her story and Aubrey had mentioned the summer camp. It must have seemed a Godsend. She didn't have money for someone to mind the kids while she worked over the summer, her family was scattered, most of them living in Florida, and the camp was right there at the college. If she got the job, which Becker made sure she did, she could drop Kelly and her brother off in the morning and collect them in the afternoon. And it was free, thanks to the generosity of Aubrey Becker.

So, in the summer, Daniel and Kelly had started at the camp. They hadn't known much about Aubrey Becker for the first three weeks, other than that he paid for the whole deal. They didn't see him. They saw only the coaches and the other kids. It was all perfectly normal. Better than normal. It was well run and a ton of fun.

Kelly remembered the first time she had met Becker. He had arrived with a large man, whom she later discovered was Weston Reeves. Becker was all smiles. He asked the kids about themselves. He had brought two coolers full of soda and ice cream for them. He stayed around for a half-hour and then he left. She realized later that this had been a reconnaissance trip. He was scoping out potential victims.

It was a week before he came back, again with a glowering Reeves as his driver. Again with sodas and ice cream. This time he stayed a little longer.

And that was how it went. Each visit a little longer. He was making sure the kids and the coaches were comfortable with his presence. After two more weeks he started to do a little coaching of his own, although he passed it off to the other staff as helping the kids who lacked confidence. Again, he was careful never to be alone with any of them.

The summer passed. The camp ended. They didn't see Aubrey Becker again until the late autumn when he appeared at their house. She and Daniel got home from school one afternoon to find him sitting in their living room, in their father's chair, sipping coffee and chatting to their mom. He was extending the summer program to a weekly camp. For boys. Sadly, Kelly wouldn't be able to participate. They didn't have coaches for girls and, with the children being in their teens, well, boys were easily distracted. That had been Aubrey Becker's line.

Most of the boys were from difficult backgrounds or had been in trouble with the law. They had been referred to the program by a young police officer in Harrisburg named Tromso. He had worked for the city before he became head of the college police, and the lines between town and college became even more blurred. The club would run on Friday and Saturday nights. It would use the college facilities. It would be free. Aubrey Becker told their mom that while Daniel didn't fit the profile − he was a model student rather than a delinquent − he might benefit from it because of his athletic talent.

And that was where it had started. On Friday evenings after school, her brother would head to the college to play basketball, touch football, baseball or soccer. At first, there was no change. He seemed happy. He even teased Kelly about being excluded. Something she had resented at the time.

The change in Daniel's mood was gradual. At first she put down his outbursts to the changes they were both going through. Then he started to shut down. They had always been able to talk. But that changed as he spent more time at the college. He started picking on her at dinner. Teasing her. Generally being an asshole. Then, a while after that, he seemed to get really low, like he didn't even have the energy to rile her anymore.

By then he was spending more time with Aubrey Becker and the kids from the program. Weekday activities started to spill over into the weekend. There was a sleepover at the college, in one of the dorms. When he had come home from that, she had gone to pick up his laundry and noticed blood where a young girl might leave blood, but a teenage boy wouldn't. She had asked him about it. He had flown into a rage.

She thought that perhaps he was being bullied by some of the other boys. Some were older. They were rougher, a lot more streetwise. Two weeks after the bloody underwear, he had got into a fight with one of the older kids. At first he wouldn't talk about it. After many hours Daniel told her that the boy had called him a fag, but he wouldn't say any more than that. It was only later that she found out the result of the fight. She had assumed that Daniel had lost. He hadn't. Far from it. The rage he was feeling had been unleashed: Daniel had broken the other boy's nose and three of his ribs. If it hadn't been for Weston Reeves stepping in, one of the other boys told her, Daniel would have killed his tormenter. As the boy lay injured, Daniel had walked over to a weight rack in the gymnasium and grabbed a bar bell. Reeves had shown up and grabbed it just as Daniel was going to bring it down on the other kid's skull.

It took Daniel a long time to tell her what was going on. By the time he did, she knew, even at her age, that the damage had been done. By then Daniel was nearly fifteen, and Aubrey Becker had begun to lose interest him. One day, after another weekend sleepover at the Becker house, he had dropped Daniel off and never called again.

Kelly had tried speaking to a teacher at school about it. The woman, in her fifties, had taken it seriously. She had even gone so far as calling the cops. Tromso had turned up at their home and warned Kelly and Daniel about spreading malicious gossip. They had realized then that Becker was untouchable.

Daniel had joined the army. She had left Harrisburg too, going to college out of state and eventually drifting into law enforcement. She'd thought that being a cop would mean being able to make a difference. She had been right and wrong. You could make a difference, but not in a place like this.

Kelly walked up the stairs that led to Daniel's apartment door. She took out her key, turned it in the lock and walked inside. Daniel was sitting on the couch. The curtains were drawn. The place smelt of rotting garbage and sweat.

She looked at her brother. He didn't move. She went over to him and touched his shoulder. His hand moved up and clasped hers. They didn't need to speak anymore. They had done their talking when they had decided to come back.

Once upon a time she had failed her brother. She had promised him when he had first told her about Becker and Reeves that she would never fail him again. Whatever he needed to do would be okay with her. She had never imagined her promise would bring them to this.

Once she had crossed certain lines, she had known that there was no return. You either upheld the law or you didn't. She had chosen to break it. There was no grieving about that now. What was done was done. There was no going back. Not now.

'It's all set,' she said to Daniel. 'Just like you wanted.'

He nodded. There was a hint of a smile. He had that faraway look he got sometimes when he was happy. She recognized it from when he was little. He'd be sitting outside on a sunny day, playing on the front lawn, and he'd have that same look, like he knew a beautiful secret about the world that no one else did.

'They all stayed silent, sis,' he said. He ran a hand through his hair, sweeping it back from his face. He'd grown it long since he came out of the army.

'I know they did,' she said. She walked to the window. Part of her knew what she was helping him do was wrong. That it would solve nothing. That it would only make matters worse. And yet . . .

The man with the sign had changed things. She and Daniel had seen him in the newspapers. It was during the Penn State scandal. He was an alumnus. When Penn State had decided that someone having used their campus to rape kids was no reason to stop their precious football games, that man had driven to Happy Valley with his sign and held it silently in protest. People – young, old, men and women – had cussed him out and spat at him. Someone had thrown beer over him. Most of the crowd, well, they'd just ignored him and walked in to watch the football game. His sign had read: 'Put abused kids first. Don't be fooled, they all knew.'

Daniel had talked about that man a lot. He'd said that such things would keep going on unless people understood that silence came with a price. As soon as he'd said it, she knew he was right. Silence wasn't neutral. It was an endorsement. So was inaction. If you saw someone drowning in a river and walked by, that didn't make you a casual observer: it made you the asshole who had let them drown.

They would all tag along to the stadium tonight, the college kids and the people of Harrisburg. They would hold hands, sing songs and nothing would change.

Laird wanted a PR exercise. Well, her brother was going to give him a lesson in PR. One that no one here, or in the rest of the world, would ever forget.

EIGHTY-SEVEN

L OCK STOOD FOR A MOMENT in the half-light of the empty
bedroom. The bed was still unmade. Underwear and clothes were
strewn over the floor. The apartment was best described as
utilitarian. There was everything someone would need to live comfortably
but there were no homely touches: no flowers, no plants, no evidence of
any pets.

He tensed a little as he heard the front door open and someone walk in.
He moved quickly to the bedroom door, and peeked through into the
corridor. He pulled his SIG from his holster, and held it by his side.
Quietly, he opened the door and slipped out into the corridor.

Kelly Svenson was in the kitchen. He watched as she took off her jacket
and slung it across the back of a chair. She walked toward the refrigerator.
He raised his gun, and waited until she opened the fridge.

'Take it easy,' he told her.

She twitched. The movement was more shudder than jump.

'Keep your hands in plain sight,' said Lock. 'Raise them up, and turn
around.'

Her face gave nothing away as she stared at him. She raised her hands.
He walked over to where she was standing, his SIG still punched out in
front of him, his finger on the trigger, ready to squeeze off a shot if he had

to. He was hoping she wouldn't do anything stupid. He didn't want to kill her. He didn't want to kill anyone. There had been more than enough killing in Harrisburg.

'Becker send you?' she asked, as he plucked her service weapon from her hip and made it safe.

He had a good idea whom she was referring to, but he would see where her assumption took them. It would be good to get confirmation of what he already suspected. 'Becker's dead,' he said.

She smiled, but it was forced. Her mouth turned up at the corners but her eyes were dead. 'Governor Becker.'

Lock stepped back and lowered his gun. 'I try not to work for politicians. Tends to interfere with getting a good night's sleep. I'm here because of what happened to Malik Shaw's family. My partner grew up with him.'

Nothing from her. In another life she would have made one hell of an actress. She betrayed nothing that she hadn't already decided to show. 'Then,' she said, 'why do you have a problem with me? I wasn't involved in that.'

'You knew about it,' said Lock.

'After the fact. Tromso was a scumbag, along with the rest of them, but even I didn't think he and Reeves would go that far. You know about Reeves, right? I mean, you wouldn't be here otherwise.'

Lock nodded. 'Where's your brother? Where's Daniel? And don't lie to me. I know he's here, just like I know that he's a very dangerous man.'

That finally got a reaction from her. A bitter laugh. 'Dangerous? Y'think? He's what they made him.'

Lock said, 'I'm sorry about that. I truly am. Just like I'm sorry Malik Shaw had to pay the price he did for trying to do what was right.'

'One honest man among thousands, and he was an outsider.'

Lock advanced on her. 'This is over, Kelly. Now, tell me where Daniel is before more innocent people get hurt.'

'So everyone can lawyer up and walk away and my brother can go to prison? No, thanks. I've seen how the law operates around here. There's one rule for the likes of the Becker family and another for everyone else.' She took a step toward him. He moved back. 'He was a kid. Do you want me to tell you what those animals did to him?'

'I think you should tell everyone so that there's less chance it can happen again,' said Lock. 'But first I'm going to need you to tell me how to find that brother of yours.'

'Go to Hell.' She flew at him. Lock didn't raise his weapon. She was unarmed, forty pounds lighter, and five inches shorter. If he couldn't handle her, he'd be as well to retire. He didn't like the idea of hitting a woman much either, but it beat shooting one.

As she got within a foot of him, he pivoted hard and brought up his elbow, striking her hard on the jaw. She tumbled backwards and fell against a wooden chair. He went to pull her up. She kicked out hard, catching his shin. He lost balance for a fraction of a second. It was enough. She half crawled, half ran past him.

Lock went after her. She was headed for the bedroom. He eased back a little, letting her push through the bedroom door. He already knew what she was going for.

He stood in the doorway as she ripped open the bedside cabinet, pulled out a gun and leveled it at him. Lock stared at her. He reached into the pocket of his jacket. He withdrew his hand, and opened his palm to reveal a half-dozen bullets. 'Games are over, Kelly. You're going to tell me where I can find him.'

'And if I don't?'

Lock palmed the bullets from her bedside gun back into his pocket and came out with his cell phone. He held it up so she could see the screen. 'Then I have the FBI on speed dial.'

'And if I help you?' she asked.

Her asking the question was a good sign. But whatever he said now had to be credible. 'You can have a head start getting out of here. Best I can do.'

'And Daniel?'

Lock said nothing.

'Your friend Tyrone would be dead by now if it wasn't for my brother,' said Kelly.

That made sense to Lock. From what Ty had said, Reeves and Tromso had been picked off. But, then, so had a bunch of other people whose only crime was . . . what? Hell, the kid from the frat had been out looking for Jack Barnes. What had he done to deserve being shot?

'Your brother needs help,' said Lock.

'And you think he's going to get that in prison?'

'He's going to hurt more people, Kelly. We both know it.'

EIGHTY-EIGHT

T Y KILLED THE CALL FROM Lock, and spun the wheel of the SUV hard as he pulled a U-turn. Next to him, Malik stirred. Exhaustion had taken him down hours ago.

'We there?' Malik asked. His eyes were flecked with red. He rubbed at his temples. 'My head is killing me.'

Ty plucked a bottle of water from one of the cup holders and tossed it to him. He caught it one-handed. 'Taking a detour,' said Ty. 'You ever hear of a guy called Daniel Svenson?'

Malik shook his head. 'The surname, yeah, place is full of Svensons, but a Daniel Svenson? No.'

'His sister's the cop. Daniel's her brother. He was one of Becker's victims way back when. And we need to find him.'

Malik unscrewed the cap of the water bottle. 'They're going after him?'

'Not exactly,' said Ty.

Twelve minutes later, Ty turned off the small country road they had been driving down for the past mile and onto a dirt track with ditches at either side. They headed for a stand of trees, and drove through an open farm gate. A mutt greeted their arrival, chasing alongside and barking.

Ty scanned the low ranch house ahead. He looked for movement – the twitch of a curtain, a door opening. He was starting to think that maybe he should have dropped Malik off before now and let him hitch-hike back into town, but time wasn't on their side, and he still didn't fully trust Malik not to do something stupid.

He stopped twenty yards short of the front porch and parked their vehicle side-on. He started to get out. 'Give me five minutes. If I'm not back by then, get out of here.' He dug into his pocket. 'Here. Call Ryan when you get a safe distance away. His number's the first on the list.'

'The hell I will,' Malik said, reaching for the door handle. 'I'm coming with you.'

'No, you ain't.'

'Hey,' said Malik, 'from what you've been told, this guy's pissed at people here for looking the other way. Well, I didn't. And look what it cost me. He'll talk to me.'

'And if he won't?' asked Ty.

'I'm not scared of dying,' said Malik. 'You?'

Ty thought about it. 'Hell, yeah.'

Together they exited the vehicle and walked toward the house. Lock had given Ty only the briefest run-down of Daniel's military background. That had been enough. If he was still here, and he wasn't in the mood, they were both likely dead already.

Malik stepped ahead of Ty. His right foot was an inch shy of the bottom step leading up to the porch when Ty grabbed him and pulled him back. Malik stumbled. Ty held up a hand to silence his friend. He bent down and examined the fishing line that been strung across the step. It disappeared into some bushes.

Ty slowly parted the leaves of the undergrowth. He glanced back at Malik. His friend's eyes widened as they checked out the green chunk of metal shaped like a butterfly's wing that was rigged to the fishing line.

'What the hell is that?' Malik asked.

'Something that will most definitely ruin your day,' Ty told him. More specifically, it was a Russian-manufactured anti-personnel mine. The rigging was crude. It would have taken moments for someone who knew what they were doing to disarm it. But it could do one hell of a lot of damage. The butterfly mine also told Ty that Daniel wasn't home, and that there were plenty more nasty surprises where that one had come from. People tended not to land-mine their front porch. Neither did they rig boobytrap windows – as the two small piles of sawdust on the nearest ledge where someone had drilled into the frame tended to suggest. Ty was just grateful that Daniel hadn't mined the driveway. He turned back to their vehicle.

'Let's get out of here,' he said to Malik. 'And watch where you're putting your feet.'

EIGHTY-NINE

F IVE THOUSAND TINY LIGHTS FLICKERED along Wolf Road as the people of Harrisburg walked in silence toward the stadium. Parents pushed babies in strollers, elderly couples walked arm in arm, but mostly the crowd was made up of college students, their youthfully earnest faces lit from underneath by the battery-powered candles they held. Heads down, their breath misting in the freezing night air, Malik's team of college basketball players held pictures of their coach's dead family as they led the athletic department toward the stadium.

At the head of the parade, Allan Laird walked arm in arm with his wife. In his free hand, he carried a wreath. It would be laid in remembrance of those who had died. Behind him came the great and good of the college administration staff, along with the college chaplain and the leaders of the three main churches in Harrisburg.

Beyond the candlelight parade, the town was bathed in darkness. As a mark of respect for the victims, it had been agreed that the street-lights would be turned on at the conclusion of the remembrance ceremony. Until then only a few homes in every street had their lights on.

In the stadium parking lot, a half-dozen satellite trucks were parked up. A couple of reporters gave breathless updates to camera. Institutional corruption, college sport, a presidential hopeful and a mounting body count, not to mention the sleaziest of sexual overtones, had ensured national and international interest. Movie studios and publishers were already circling, ever ready to translate unimaginable human misery into dollars. No detail would prove too debased, no moment too salacious, that they wouldn't pore over it in ghoulish detail.

Daniel Svenson looked down at the people directly beneath him from the metal walkway that ran around the edge of the stadium's roof. He smirked at the crowd's forced solemnity, the furrowed brows and glistening eyes as, one by one, they trickled into the stadium and began to take their seats. In the distance a minor cavalcade sped along Wolf Road – a Town Car sandwiched between two police vehicles. Of course, thought Daniel. Every theatrical production needed its star attraction. And every star insisted on making the most dramatic entrance possible.

The crowd parted as the vehicles pushed slowly to the main entrance. A bodyguard opened the back door of the Town Car and Governor Andrew Becker climbed out, all teeth and tan, his features arranged so that they conveyed just how bad he felt about what had happened. Daniel could imagine him practicing his pained look in front of the mirror, a coterie of advisors suggesting minute facial adjustments.

Daniel shouldered his rifle and studied Becker through the scope as Allan Laird stepped forward to shake the governor's hand. Cameramen jockeyed with the crowd. College kids held up their cell phones to snap a picture. Two people held up great slabs of iPads to do the same. It was as much as Daniel could do not to burst out laughing. He lowered his rifle. He could have killed them both where they stood. No one could have stopped him. But that would have been too easy.

He stepped back from the overhang and took ten steps toward the access door. He dug out a key and opened the padlock he had placed there prior to the security sweep of the stadium.

Slipping inside, he moved swiftly along the narrow metal walkway, and lay down. A hundred and fifty feet below, people were still taking their seats. At the far end of the stadium a photo-montage of the dead was thrown up onto a screen. In front of it was a podium from which the speakers would address the crowd.

Half a dozen cops stood at various points inside the auditorium, thumbs hooked into their belts, their eyes scanning the crowd for Daniel Svenson. Daniel studied each of them in turn. He was glad they were there. They gave people reassurance but, in reality, they might as well have been cardboard cut-outs for all the good they would do when it came time for the real show to start.

NINETY

T HEIR FACES SHADOWED BY HARRISBURG basketball hoodies, Ty
and Malik walked out of the players' entrance tunnel as the crowd
took their seats. Ty hit the answer icon on his cell as Lock's name
flashed on the display.

'We're about to hit start,' said Ty.

'Any problems?' asked Lock.

'All good so far. You?'

'We just got here. Should know in five minutes,' said Lock.

Lock braked slowly as the lumbering Chevy reached the bottom of the
track leading to the cabin where Weston Reeves had almost killed Ty. He
switched off the engine and glanced across at Kelly Svenson, who was next
to him in the passenger seat, her hands cuffed behind her back. 'We'll walk
from here.'

He got out, came round, opened her door and helped her out. Ty had
already brought Lock up to speed on the security measures Daniel Svenson
had put in place at his house. Lock hadn't survived this long to get blown
sky high by a jerry-rigged IED in Minnesota. He pushed Kelly in front of

him, using his left hand to guide her forward. With his right hand he drew his gun.

As they stepped onto the track, Lock let her walk ahead. He waited until she was twenty yards clear, then followed her. He wasn't exactly proud that he was using Kelly as a human mine detector, but the situation was as it was.

It took them five minutes to reach the cabin. He closed in behind her as they got within a hundred yards of it.

'Okay, call for him,' Lock told her.

She stayed silent.

Lock jabbed his gun into the small of her back.

'Daniel?'

A moment passed. Lock jabbed her again, a little harder this time.

'Daniel! It's Kelly. Come on out.'

There was no answer from the cabin. Lock decided to try another tactic. 'Daniel,' he shouted, raising his SIG and pressing it against Kelly's temple. 'I have your sister here, and if you don't come out in the next ten seconds, I'm going to blow her head off.'

NINETY-ONE

A BANK OF TELEVISION CAMERAS, photographers and reporters hunkered down in front of the stage as Minnesota's governor, Andrew Becker, strode purposefully toward the lectern. It took a moment for the crowd to settle as the stadium lights faded until only the stage was lit. They had already been softened by speeches and prayers, and a long, carefully crafted apology from Laird that had danced between contrition and admitting legal liability. But Becker's speech was the big gamble. It had been his brother, Aubrey, who had visited this chaos on Harrisburg, and the stench clung to him. Now he planned to do what any modern career politician would do under the circumstances: make himself out to be the real victim.

The governor's hands clasped the podium as he surveyed the crowd. He cleared his throat. The silence was close to complete. He took out a silk handkerchief from the top pocket of his suit and dabbed his eyes.

'My advisors told me not to come tonight,' he lied. 'But I figured I owed it to everyone here, and the people of this great state who have placed so much trust in me, to be here to honor all of those affected by this horrific—'

He felt something hit his chest. There was a burst of flashes from the photographers. He looked down to see orange paint spattered all over his suit. Confused, he looked around for the source, but the auditorium was dark beyond the podium. He could hear a couple of police radios crackle nearby. The others on the stage looked at each other.

It's only paint, he thought. Someone had obviously thrown a paint pellet at him. He tried to wipe it off the tips of his fingers. It wouldn't budge. He decided to continue. If he skulked away now, that would make the news. It was better to go on.

He held up his hands. 'I understand that people are upset.'

This time he heard the dull thud of the Airsoft gun as another paint pellet sailed through the darkness and hit Chancellor Laird in the same spot, slap-bang on his heart. The governor looked around as Laird's wife darted in front of her husband, fussing over the mess the paintball had made of his suit.

The governor was confused and angry at the interruption. 'Folks, can we remember that this is a memorial service for the victims?'

The same sound echoed through the stadium as another paintball slammed against the chest of one of the trustees who was seated next to the governor's wife. 'Security? Can we have the lights—' said the governor, as the crowd's murmurs grew louder and the paintballs kept coming, the next one slamming into one of the campus cops stationed next to the stage.

The lights came on full blast. People in the crowd squinted. The cops were busy scanning the crowd for the source of the disturbance. The photographers were on their feet, rushing the stage for a better angle of the governor and his paint-spattered suit.

Then, as quickly as they had come on, the lights went out. The entire stadium was plunged into total darkness. A young woman screamed. Murmurs gave way to the sounds of panic. People began to move, heading for the exit but stumbling over each other in the dark.

The only thing visible were the spatters of paint. They glowed with a fierce luminosity, marking out each of the four people who had been hit by the pellets.

A second later there was a loud bang and a blinding light as a flash-bang grenade was tossed into the middle of the crowd. More people screamed and scrambled from their seats. The sound of a single gunshot rang out. The orange paint adorning the governor's suit gave way to blood as a single round slammed into his heart, killing him instantly.

NINETY-TWO

L OCK WATCHED KELLY SVENSON CLOSE her eyes as he began the countdown from five. Daniel had until then to step out of the cabin and give himself up.

'Five.' He allowed a second to pass. His heart was thumping. Kelly took a long, slow breath.

'Four.' Another second elapsed.

Lock moved his finger to the trigger, and counted off three. 'Last chance,' he shouted toward the cabin.

Tears were rolling down Kelly's cheeks. 'Two!' he said.

He started to tighten the trigger. Kelly screwed her eyes tighter still. He could feel her body tense. She bit her lip. Slowly he eased the pressure so that the barrel of the SIG was no longer pressed against her skin.

'One!'

At the last second, he snapped the gun down and to his right, and shot into the ground. The sound echoed back toward them. Kelly was sobbing now.

'He's not here, is he, Kelly?' he said to her.

She shook her head.

He reached up and swiped the tears from her eyes with his thumb. 'Look at me.'

She opened her eyes.

'You would have let me kill you? For what?' said Lock.

Her voice fell to a whisper. 'I made him a promise.'

Lock raised his SIG again. 'Did you pinky-swear when you made it?' he said. 'Listen to me, this shit's real. People are going to die. Playtime is over. I don't have time to reason with you, or tell you how sorry I am that this happened to you and your brother. We're past that, and I'm not going to let more innocent people die because of Aubrey Becker and what he did. So, you're going to stop yanking my chain, and tell me where Daniel is before anyone else gets hurt.'

'And if I don't?'

'Oh,' said Lock, 'you will.'

She stared at him, defiant. 'No, you won't. You wouldn't shoot a woman. Especially not one who's handcuffed.'

'You think?' said Lock, aiming the SIG at Kelly's right foot and pulling the trigger. Kelly shrieked in pain. Nothing in the cabin stirred. She fell backwards. Lock let her. She writhed around on the ground, screaming, barely able to breathe. Lock stood over her, and aimed the gun at her left knee. 'I'm going to keep shooting until either you're dead or you tell me.'

She started to speak only to be stunned back into silence as a series of explosions boomed their way toward them from the valley below. Lock whipped round to see a plume of black smoke rising from the stadium.

NINETY-THREE

A MOTHER CLUTCHING A TODDLER stumbled and fell as people forced their way toward the exits. Together Malik and Ty fought their way through the crowd, picking people up and tossing them out of the way. Malik reached the woman first, and hauled her back to her feet as Ty grabbed the howling little girl she'd been holding. Ahead, a dense mass of bodies was pressed up against a door as more people piled in, adding to the mêlée.

Malik glanced at Tyrone as they found a pocket of space and reunited mother and child. 'Exits have been locked.'

'How do we get them open?' Ty asked.

Malik shrugged in frustration. 'Hell if I know. Everything here's centrally controlled. Lights, doors, everything.'

'Then where's the control?' said Ty, grabbing a young college girl who was about to go under the feet of the panicked crowd.

'Follow me,' Malik said, as another shot rang out, this one tearing a hole in the floor, narrowly missing Chancellor Laird who was crawling on hands and knees across the court, an orange dot in the darkness, marked for death by the paintball gun that Daniel Svenson had used to select his targets.

They eased their way through the crowds, and found a pocket of space near half court. Glancing behind him, Malik could see a couple of men, their bodies pressed against one of the exit doors. They weren't moving. They only remained upright because of the mass of people behind them. They were almost certainly dead.

Ty bent over, hands on his knees, catching his breath as another shot was fired from high above. It caught one of the college cops in the neck, spinning him round as blood spurted from him, soaking the ground next to him. 'What about them?' Ty asked Malik, with a nod toward the dignitaries fleeing the stage as another shot rang out.

Malik's eyes narrowed as his gaze fell on Laird. 'Fuck 'em,' he said. 'We need to get those doors open.'

Malik started toward the locker room, Ty following. Clear of the crowd, they broke into a run as more bullets tore through the stadium and the screams of panic were overlaid with sobbing and pleas for help from those dying in the crush.

High in the gantry, Daniel Svenson steadied his breathing, and searched through his scope for a fresh dash of orange paint. The killing was easy. He was inside. No wind to contend with. Clearly defined targets. It didn't get much better. By his count he had only a couple of cops and Laird left to kill.

As for everyone else's fate, that was up to them. If they kept calm and looked out for each other, they'd be fine. If they behaved like animals, they would die. It was as good a test of human nature as any. They had come here to show that they cared for someone other than themselves. If that was true, they would live. The paint had been his signal to them that they would be spared. Yet they hadn't grasped it. That was on them.

Malik racked his brain for the location of the control panel. He must have passed it a thousand times. He was sure it was next to the locker rooms, but he couldn't see it. He stood in the corridor and scoured the walls. It was grey, about two feet by three, and mounted about five feet from the floor.

'You sure it's here?' Ty asked.

'I think so. I don't know.'

He remembered. A few months back there had been some work done and it had been moved so that it was next to the alarm control.

He ran twenty yards to the office. It was locked. He hefted a foot to kick down the door. It didn't give. Pain shot all the way up his leg.

'In here?' Ty asked.

Malik nodded.

Ty pushed him back, and took a kick at the door. This time it flew open. They pushed their way inside. The elderly caretaker was behind his desk. He'd been bound with duct tape and rope. Malik stepped past him and opened the cabinet that held the control panel. All but two of the switches that controlled the exits were flipped to 'lock', which would only ever happen after midnight when the stadium was closed to the public.

Malik started flipping switches to the open position as Ty ripped the strip of silver duct tape from the caretaker's mouth. The man gasped for air.

Ty turned back to Malik as he flipped the last switch. 'How'd I get up into the gantry?'

'The steps are back here,' said Malik.

Ty followed him through a door at the back of the office and into a narrow corridor. At the far end a set of metal steps snaked their way up into the stadium roof.

NINETY-FOUR

T HE CHEVY LURCHED TO A halt outside the stadium. For a moment Lock stared through the windshield at the chaotic scene that greeted him. People were laid out on the ground, motionless: men, women, young, old. Few of them were moving. Others wandered among the dead, looking for lost relatives or friends, sobbing, with the blank mask of shock people wore when they'd been caught up in something horrific.

Lock glanced back to Kelly Svenson. A makeshift tourniquet, tied tight around her ankle, had staunched much of the bleeding. 'There's your promise to your brother,' Lock said. 'Couple of dead kids in the mix. You must be so proud.'

The color had drained from her face. 'He's only going to harm the people who covered up.'

Lock opened his door and started to get out. 'It ever occur to you that people lie?' He slammed it and left her sitting there. He started toward the building. Close to the main entrance, Dennis Lee was establishing a command post. Levon Hill and the other feebs were with him.

In no mood to wait for directions, Lock skirted them, and ran down the side of the building, pushing past survivors who were stumbling into the freezing night air. He stepped over a dead body splayed half in and half out of an emergency exit, and ducked inside.

NINETY-FIVE

Y'S CELL PHONE VIBRATED IN his position. He read the text from Lock and took a deep breath. He pressed his cell phone's earpiece into his right ear, and tucked the phone into his pocket. He drew his SIG and made sure it was racked, ready to go.

Gun in hand, his feet clattered on the first of the metal steps as he began the climb to the roof space. He checked behind for Malik, relieved that his friend had followed his instruction to go back outside and help the injured. Down below, he could hear shouts as the surviving cops regrouped. With any luck, they wouldn't get in Lock's way.

The shooting from high above the basketball court seemed to have stopped. Ty slowed down, trying to minimize the noise of his feet on the metal treads. He had six steps to go before his head would clear the top of the ladder and he'd be exposed. Five steps from the top, he'd be able to sight and fire. He would have one shot at Daniel Svenson. If he missed, he'd be coming back down the ladder a hell of a lot faster than he'd climbed up it.

Lock opened the door, and stepped into the private box. Four ran the length of the court. Each offered the highest vantage-point of the stadium.

He guessed they were used by the college to entertain trustees, donors and other VIPs. This one was at the far end and gave him a view of the steel gantry built into the roof.

He hunkered down and duck-walked to the window. His eyes adjusted to the darkness. He circled a long conference table, reached the viewing window, got down on his knees and peered out.

Midway along the gantry he could make out the man hunkered down, an assault rifle in his hands, his torso covered with a body armor vest. Lock hit the call button on his cell and waited for Ty to answer.

Ty reached down and tapped the answer icon on his cell phone's screen. He didn't speak. Lock's voice filtered through his earpiece: 'You're clear. He's looking down. He'll be on your left, about twelve down the walkway from your entry point. He's hunkered down, wearing a vest. Looks like it has plates. You'll have to go for a head shot. I could try if I had a rifle but I'm not close enough here.'

Lock stayed on the line as Ty hauled himself up another rung of the ladder. He could feel his heart thumping hard enough to burst clean out of his chest. Adrenalin shot through his body. Ty eased his right boot onto the next tread. Three steps to go, and then it was down to the one-shot deal to end all one-shot deals.

Daniel Svenson shuffled down the walkway a few feet, staring through the scope of his rifle as the last stragglers fled the arena. A fat cop darted from behind a row of seats. Daniel swung the barrel of his rifle round, sighted and squeezed the trigger, catching the cop in the right knee. He went down, screaming like a stuck pig.

A man's voice came from his right.

'I'm not armed. May I come up?'

Daniel lowered the rifle and spun round as a black guy popped his head up. Daniel trained the rifle on him, and flicked the lever to the three-round-burst setting as Malik Shaw hauled himself onto the gangway.

Lock saw Malik as he surfaced from the opposite end of the gangway to Ty. 'What the hell?' he said, forgetting that Ty was still patched in. 'Ty, stay where you are. Svenson's got company up there. Just hold your position for now.'

In that instant, Lock knew that if he told Ty that Malik was up there, he would move fast to take the shot and, with the situation as delicately balanced as it was, fast could get both men killed. If someone else popped their head up from the other end of the walkway, Daniel Svenson would likely assume a trap and open up on Malik without stopping to ask questions.

'Ty, listen, it's a negotiator. I can't get a good look, but it might be Levon. He's come up the ladder at the other end. Svenson's holding his fire so sit tight. You can take the final two rungs, but real slow, real quiet, and don't clear the top until I tell you.'

Malik had figured out a whole long speech while was he climbing up there. Now he was facing down Daniel Svenson's assault rifle, he wasn't so sure.

Daniel had the rifle by his side, but it was still pointed toward Malik. 'What do you want?'

'You know who I am, right?'

Daniel nodded.

'They killed my wife. My son. My little girl. You know that too?'

He gave another nod. 'And now I killed them.'

'That doesn't make me feel any better,' said Malik.

Daniel took a step toward him. 'That's what you came up here to tell me?'

'You sent me that text, right?'

Daniel nodded.

'Then you owe me way more than I owe you. Give yourself up,' Malik told him. 'There's been enough killing.'

'Get out of here,' Daniel said to him.

Malik noticed a large canvas bag lying next to Daniel. The zip was open. From what he could see in the gloom, it didn't look like it was full of cupcakes or a change of clothes. Malik had never seen a grenade, apart from on TV, but he guessed that that was what the green fist-sized metal balls with the spoon handles were.

Daniel took his eyes off Malik for a second as a phalanx of a half-dozen SWAT officers in full body armor and carrying anti-blast shields shuffled into the arena. 'Okay then,' said Daniel. 'Stay for the show.' He reached down to the bag and brought up one of the grenades.

Without thinking, Malik hunkered down, like he was playing defense, and pushed off, launching himself at Daniel. Daniel began to raise his rifle, but Malik was too close. The rifle dropped from his hands.

In the next half-second there was a flash of silver, and Malik took what he thought was a punch to the chest. It was like no punch he'd ever felt. It seemed to empty his lungs instantly, and a searing hot pain exploded in the center of his body, tearing its way down his left arm. He looked down to see the handle of a knife sticking out of his chest. He felt sick. He staggered back as Daniel advanced on him, reaching to his waist and coming up with a handgun. Malik tried to raise his feet to shield himself from the shot.

Everything slowed in front of him. There was a blinding flash. At first he thought it was the blaze of gunfire. Then he realized that the stadium lights had been switched back on.

A black shape rose from the space behind Daniel as his finger began to squeeze the trigger of the gun aimed at Malik. There was a loud clang as the round hit the top of the metal handrail, missing Malik by less than a foot.

Ty was on top of Daniel who was face down on the walkway. Daniel did his best to wriggle out, the gun still in his hand. Ty grabbed for his wrist, but he moved it away just in time.

Ty drew back one of his massive hands, bunching it into a fist, and slamming a punch into the back of Daniel's head. Malik heard the dull crunch of bone as it made contact. Daniel's grip loosened on the gun. Ty managed to prise it from his hand, peeling back his fingers one by one, breaking the first two with a snap before he would let go.

A face loomed over Malik as he lay bleeding. Ty's partner Lock punched out his SIG, aiming at Daniel, as Ty dug a knee into his back. Malik was starting to drift. The lights around him were fading. He closed his eyes. His mouth was dry. He could feel himself letting go. The pain was receding. Kim appeared in front of him. Not as a victim but as the young woman he'd married. He was standing at the front of the church as the doors opened and she appeared on her father's arm. She smiled at Malik as their eyes met.

More than anything, Malik wanted to be back with her. Her and the kids. If he could just allow himself to surrender, he could be. Then he heard a shout, and Kim faded.

'Bomb!' screamed Lock, as he saw the grenade appear in Daniel Svenson's left hand, his fingers working frantically at the pin, easing it out.

Lock dove over Malik and grabbed for it. Daniel's grip was tight. His fingers closed around it. His knuckles were white with the effort.

For all Lock knew the pin was no longer in contact with the rest of the device. Trying to prise the man's fingers from it would risk Daniel losing pressure on the spoon lever that prevented the grenade exploding. There was only one option.

Lock pressed the barrel of his SIG Sauer 229 into the back of Daniel Svenson's head at the approximate point where the bottom of his brain stem met the top of the spinal column. He pulled the trigger, firing a single round.

Daniel's body spasmed. His fingers opened. The grenade rolled from his grasp, the spoon-shaped lever popped out. The fuse delay was four seconds. Lock swatted at the device as fast as he could, pushing it over the edge of the metal gangway to the empty court below.

Malik felt the press of a body landing on top of him. Seconds later there was a deafening bang that popped his ears, and sent fragments of metal slicing through the air around him. When he opened his eyes again, Ty was kneeling next to him. Lock was leaning over the edge of the walkway shouting for a medic.

Malik looked at Ty, who took his hand. 'Stay with me, okay?'

NINETY-SIX

L OCK STOOD IN THE CAR park and watched Ty help two paramedics load Malik Shaw into the back of the ambulance. He was hooked up to a blood bag, but he was still somehow breathing on his own. In itself that was a miracle, given where the knife had penetrated. Lock had tried to persuade Ty to get himself checked over, but the retired marine had treated his suggestion with contempt. He had come here to help his friend, and he wasn't quitting now.

Lock took in the chaos as more and more emergency personnel responded. A helicopter sent from St Paul was touching down in a field next to the stadium. The wind whipped up from its blades rustled the edges of the black plastic body-bags laid out in the car park.

Kelly Svenson sat in the back of a nearby patrol car. Her head was bowed, and she was sobbing. He wondered whether she was crying for her dead brother, the man he had killed, or the innocent people who had come to remember Becker and Reeves's victims and somehow ended up as collateral damage.

Lock doubted it mattered. There was more than enough guilt, blame and misery for this town to last ten generations. His hand had developed a tremor. He had noticed it as he'd climbed back down the ladder. It was slight, barely visible, but it was there, and he hadn't managed to throw it off.

He figured it was an echo of putting a gun to the back of a man's head and pulling the trigger.

To Lock, it had never made sense to describe an individual as evil. Becker could have been said to be evil. But that didn't seem adequate. It was too neat. Evil was more fluid, more amorphous than that. Evil cascaded down. It worked its way outwards, corroding what it touched, taking even the innocent and twisting them back on themselves. That was what had happened with Daniel Svenson, a little boy who had grown into an adult with an uncontainable rage. Lock took no comfort from having ended his life. He had done what he needed to do to save Ty, Malik and himself.

Morality hadn't come into the equation when it had come time for him to pull the trigger. At the end, all that remained were degrees of loss.

Lock holstered his weapon, and walked toward the small knot of FBI agents still gathered at the stadium entrance, Dennis Lee and Levon Hill among them. He was ready to give them his statement.

EPILOGUE

Long Beach, California
Five months later

H IS RIGHT ARM STILL IN a sling, Malik Shaw bounced the basketball three times. Ty stood under the hoop and spread his arms wide. The last splash of sunlight from a perfect California fall day was fading on the horizon.

'This is a dumb-ass idea,' said Ty. 'What did the doc say to you? No strenuous exercise for another three weeks.'

Malik stopped, the ball gripped in his left hand. 'You're just afraid of getting your ass whopped by a guy with one good arm.'

'Yeah, right,' said Ty.

They had both come back to their hometown for a high school reunion that was short on men. Most of their male classmates were either dead, their lives lost to drugs or violence, or in prison. Ty had joked that they would have been better holding the reunion at one of California's many maximum-security correctional facilities.

Malik started toward the basket. Ty stepped in front of him. Malik spun round a full 360 degrees, the quickness of his feet sending Ty sprawling to the ground. Malik stopped, drew back his good arm and sent the ball sailing toward the basket. It swooped through without touching metal. He walked back and reached down. Ty took his hand, and Malik helped him back to his feet. Breathing heavily, the two men stood in silence for a moment, watching the orange sun duck below the skyline as the day drew to a close.

<u>THE END</u>

Other books by Sean Black

The Ryan Lock Series
Lockdown
Deadlock
Gridlock
The Devil's Bounty
Lock & Load

The Byron Tibor Series
Post

For more information about Sean, and his work, you can go to:
www.seanblackbooks.com

CPSIA information can be obtained at www.ICGtesting.com
Printed in the USA
LVOW01s2120100715

445874LV00011B/152/P